This book has great swag. It's like a cool screenplay already

I rarely finish a book any more. I read this in one sitting.

Run—do not walk—to buy this book!

I couldn't put this book down!

Wonderfully developed colorful characters without going overboard with super hero powers.

Great read - humor, action, good stuff! Buy this one!

The Librarian Her Daughter and the Man Who Lost His Head

SAM LEE JACKSON

For Carol always.

And, for Amanda who never quits, for Lance, whose reach will always exceed his grasp. And for all those across the world who won't bend honor or principle, and always ask "Why not?"

ACKNOWLEDGMENTS

As always, my thanks to my editor Ann Hedrick of UC Davis, who keeps my writing from looking like an eighth grade essay. And, of course, to the amazing Mariah Sinclair for the outstanding cover design. And, a huge shout out of appreciation to fiction readers everywhere. If you don't read, you will only live one solitary life.

1

They set the girl on fire.

I swore under my breath.

I broke the glass out of the window with the Israeli Ace 32 assault rifle I had been given, and threw the concussion flash grenades as fast as I could. Which didn't seem very fast. The broken shards of glass, still in the window, hampered my action. The delay gave the two guards inside a split second, and they began firing toward me.

Blackhawk fired through the other window as the flashbangs exploded, and the guards went down. As they fell, something blew through the wall and kicked my foot. I almost went down. I regained my balance and looked at my foot. Half the prosthetic was gone. Damn it. I've had bad luck with that foot. Prosthetics are expensive. The fact that I lost the foot a couple of years ago was the primary reason I was here in the first place. Here was the middle of a jungle somewhere in Guatemala. I had been enjoying a balmy day on my houseboat with Blackhawk, his girl Elena and Detective First Grade Boyce. Boyce had taken a bullet meant for me, and we were enjoying the convalescence. At least I was. Then the Colonel had called, and he had some work he needed us to do.

Back in the day I had belonged to a covert team of specialists, commanded by the Colonel. Ten of us, code named Adam through Jackson. I was Jackson. Blackhawk was number two. Then I stepped on an IED and that screwed the pooch.

And then, I was a civilian bum living on an old scow of a houseboat on Lake Pleasant, north of Phoenix. The disappearance of a young girl got me involved with a couple of bad news drug cartels and I called the Colonel for some intel that only he could dig up. That's when he told me Blackhawk now owned a nightclub in south Phoenix. I enlisted his help with my problem, then I met Boyce who was assigned to the Phoenix P.D. gang-squad. And, I'm sorry to say, that's why she took a bullet meant for me, thus saving my life. The least I could do was wine and dine her on the boat while she recuperated.

The Colonel and most of the team were now out of that old life, but the Colonel had kept most of his old contacts and picked up occasional jobs in the civilian sector. They paid a hell of a lot more than Uncle Sam.

And, a week after I left Boyce sunbathing on the houseboat, I found myself here. Mosquito heaven. With half my foot shot off. Now I was hobbling as fast as I could around the corner to the hutch door. Blackhawk was faster. He had already kicked it open and was inside. Both guards were down, and our package was shackled to a cot in the corner. The unconscious girl was across the room from the package. Her hair and dress were smoldering. There was a rank smell in the room.

The package was a gaunt and hollow-eyed man, who looked to be in his forties. He had been a prisoner for over a month. It didn't look like he had been fed that whole time. Blackhawk and I reached him at the same time, and as Blackhawk took his arm, he began to sob.

"Thank you, thank you," he blubbered.

"Shut the fuck up," Blackhawk said as he pulled him up by his arm so I could get to the blanket underneath.

I yanked it loose and hurried to the corner. There was a bucket with liquid in it, and I couldn't tell if it was water or piss, but it was wet. I dipped the blanket and started putting the girl out. Her eyes fluttered and she began to moan. Luckily, her damage looked mostly superficial, but I didn't know what they had done to her. She had blood and bruises on her face. One eye was a deep saffron and purple. I couldn't tell how old she was, she was so small. Most of the Ixil women natives were small.

She was groaning, and I ripped her smoldering clothes off her, and wrapped her in the vile-smelling blanket. Blackhawk had rifled the pockets of the dead guards and found the keys. He freed the man. He looked at my partial foot.

"You take her, I'll take him," he said.

We heard the sudden report of the high-powered sniper rifle manned by Fabian, then another shot from Echo on the other side of the compound. Two more members of the old team the Colonel had recruited.

3

"We have to go," I said.

I took the girl's body, and slung her over my shoulder in a fireman's carry. I started hobbling out the door. Blackhawk lifted the sobbing man as if he were no more than a package of potato chips.

I touched the button by my ear and loudly said, "Coming out! Have the package, and coming out!"

"Roger that," Echo's voice echoed in my ear.

I followed Blackhawk as he raced across the open compound. I know we both had that little itchy spot in the middle of the back where the cross-hairs would be. No shots came. Our guys had successfully neutralized the bad guys. Despite the half prosthetic, I made good time. A couple of years wrangling the prosthetic makes you dexterous.

Our team had been named Black Mamba. We never knew anyone's real names. They didn't matter. A is Adam. B is Blackhawk. C is Charlie. D is Dakota. There were ten to a team, and I never knew how many teams there were. Specially selected men and women who had survived the toughest training the military had to offer. Seals, Rangers, Delta, whatever.

The dropout rate for Seal training was huge. The ones that couldn't handle it, and it was usually a mental toughness thing, rang the bell. Then they were out. The rest of us morons kept pushing. Too stubborn to quit. Then one day you graduated, and it was the greatest day of your life, and you got drunk. And, then you waited for your orders.

And you waited. And you watched the others called up and pack their shit and leave, and you waited.

Then you receive a strange order. Get on a plane with nothing but the clothes on your back. You followed orders. You got on, and it was a long flight. No one spoke to you. At the other end, there was a car waiting on the tarmac. There was a man in a suit with the car. He drove you to a non-descript industrial building and took you inside. Other men met you. They asked for your wallet. They took your identification. Then they guided you through an impressive array of detectors and stuck you in a plain, drab room. The only furniture in the room was a plain wooden table, and a chair, and a camera high up in the corner. Then a colonel came in. A colonel you had never seen before. He shook your hand, and in his deep baritone, told you that you had been chosen for a special team.

Then the real training began, and you thought the other was bad? Not just physical, but very intense covert skills training. Intense problem solving, technical training and fierce hand-to-hand. They taught how to use ordinary objects to kill people. A toothbrush, a rolled-up magazine. They didn't ask if you would kill people, they just assumed you would.

One time they put me in a dark room with a blindfolded instructor, who had his hands tied behind him. They ordered me to beat the shit out of him. He kicked my ass with just his legs and feet. They taught every form of survival training. Desert, swamp, mountains, ocean, taught it all. There was no set timing on the training. It depended on you. It was how the trainers thought you were doing.

Finally, the end came, and the Colonel explained you

were now ready. Oh, by the way, you had been discharged from the service, and your records had been expunged. You were a civilian. Plausible deniability. If something went wrong you were just a fool in the wrong place at the wrong time. Then he introduced me to my team. One of the first things I learned was that no one in Black Mamba had family. That naive orphaned kid that had joined the service was long gone. Black Mamba was family now.

But now, Echo and Fabian were covering our backs until we reached the hole in the fence we had snipped earlier. Blackhawk went through, and I handed off the girl. The blubberer wasn't functioning well so I had to literally stuff him through the opening. Once through the fence we turned and covered the open compound, where the hutch was going up in flames.

Echo and Fabian came skittering across the open ground, but no bad guys showed their heads. A second later they were through the fence, and we were hot-footing it down the jungle path to the river.

We had come up the river in the dead of the previous night. We had chosen, or rather, the Colonel had chosen, a moonless night. Charlie had lost the draw, and was left behind with the boat. The boat had been equipped with a very powerful electric motor that made no noise. Charlie had used it to push us through the dark river water the last mile. We had silently eased up to a spot a hundred yards down from the path that led to the compound. We went over the side, silent as snakes, into the water. We didn't make a ripple as we silently swam the rest of the way. It was completely dark before we had climbed out of the water and settled into the underbrush. We waited till light.

The target was a journalist. Or, at least, he was down here in the guise of a journalist. He was really a negotiator for a mega-billionaire by the name of Glick. H. Walton Glick owned any number of rightwing rags and cable networks. Glick was all about less government. Which, to him meant no taxes. In fact, he would be happy with no government at all. Except maybe the government he had in his pocket. Mayan rebels had disrupted his plans by kidnapping his man. Bad timing for Glick. It was just as the man was about to make a deal with the country's strongman. A deal worth a billion to Glick. Unfortunately for Glick, real journalists began reporting the man's disappearance. Glick hired the Colonel to get the man out before he opened his mouth. Of course, Glick thought no one knew all this backstory, but Glick didn't know the Colonel.

Charlie had the boat on the bank, and we all piled in. He looked at the girl, then at me.

"What the fuck is that?"

Blackhawk pushed the blubberer into a corner. He turned to Charlie, "Just go." Charlie looked hard at Blackhawk but knew not to push it. He started the motor. Soon we were roaring back up the river to where the MH-47G Chinook was waiting to hoist us up and away.

2

Two days later I was back. I came through the dock gate and looked down the line of moored houseboats to the end. Down to where I called home. Home is Pier C, Slip 32, Pleasant Harbor Marina on Lake Pleasant. The lake is located north of Phoenix. Home was a tired old scow I purchased after I had been laughed at by the realtor. She was amused at the figure I gave her. The amount of money I had saved to buy a place. She had kindly told me about the houseboat. I could afford it. The original name, Tiger Lily, is still on the stern. I get teased about it but I'm too lazy to change it. Now it just seems natural. The gilded lettering is just a little more faded, chipped and worn.

Walking down the dock, the boat looked shuttered and empty. The letter was on the galley counter. It had Boyce's familiar scrawl. After the number of phone calls Boyce didn't answer, I wasn't surprised. That didn't make the feeling in the pit of my stomach any better. I knew what it would say before I opened it.

Boyce didn't like her first name, so she was just Boyce. I

only called her by her first name once. Once was enough. We had spent the last few months together on the boat as she convalesced from the bullet wound. The bullet had been meant for me. The months had been idyllic. Sun and rare good beef, and fine drink, and slowly getting the body back. Swimming and exercise, and lots of sun. But now, I guess, she needed to get back to her life. She was a cop through and through.

I lifted the blackout curtains and opened doors, bow and stern, for a cross breeze. She had left the boat tidy and spotless. It was also stuffy and warm. It was the time of year when the nights had begun to cool, but the highs during the day were still in the 90's. I kicked on the air unit.

I unpacked my small ditty bag, completely stripped down, unhooked my foot and slipped into swim trunks. I took a beer from the locker and drank it. Not for thirst. For therapy. I set the alarm that would warn me if someone stepped aboard, and lay back on the oversized yellow couch. Several hours in the air and several time zones do things to a body and although it was only mid-afternoon Phoenix time, I was soon asleep.

When I awoke, I hit the button on my watch that illuminated the face. The watch was a gift from Blackhawk's girl, Elena. She couldn't stand that I didn't have one, and did not understand that I usually didn't give a rat's ass about what time it was. She was really appalled I didn't have a television on board.

The two glowing hands on the watch told me I had slept for almost twelve hours. It was dark out, with the ghostly dock lights providing the only light. I turned on the soft lights that were in the stove hood. I made coffee and took a frozen bagel out and toasted it. I slapped butter on it, and went to the stern. I sprawled in one of the chaise lounges. The air temperature was perfect. I sipped the coffee. I munched the bagel. I waited for the dawn.

I tried to think of the Chicago Bears and Walter Payton, and how such a great player had led a very short life. I tried to put together an all time, all Bears team. But, try as I might, the thought of Boyce came slowly slipping in. And with it, a slow ache in the gut. I gave up on Walter. As usual, Boyce took over.

I had never felt this before. She was my first. Not first woman, but first woman I had let inside. First one that had gotten by the defenses. And while I was trying to wallow in this exquisite sorrow of memory, this bittersweet sense of loss, I could feel that other thing. I tried to hold on to the delicious sorrow as long as possible, but then the other thing kept coming. At first, a pinprick of discomfort. Like the pea under all the mattresses. It was a tiny sliver of unease that kept peeking out from under the pain. I pushed it back. It returned. I pushed it back. Back it came. Finally I gave up. You win. I eased it out, I turned it over, and studied it. And there it was. It was guilt. I didn't like it. Guilt is self-induced. No one can make you feel guilty unless you are complicit. You do it to yourself. I didn't like it. I tried to think of Boyce. Beautiful Boyce. Boyce topside, sunbathing nude. Boyce's nose covered with zinc sunscreen. Boyce in the galley in a pathetic attempt to cook. Boyce's green eyes appraising me over the top of a book. Boyce fixing appletinis. But the guilt got larger. The guilt started making noise. The guilt started shaking the tree. Hey there, fella. You can't ignore me.

It was relief. Relief. I was relieved to have my place back. I had never lived with another person, one on one, since I was a kid. A small kid. My single life had become a comfortable old shirt I put on each day. And now I had it back. I stood up and shook myself like a dog coming out of the water. I took a shower and fixed a thermos. I grabbed some tackle, and as the first light brushed the sky, I went fishing. I walked over to the adjacent pier where I kept the Grumman Sport Deck, took the green canvas cover off her, and went fishing.

It was the next afternoon before I made a trek into the city to restock the boat with food and drink. I also took the time to drive through my bank's ATM. I needed to, as the banker would say, enhance my cash position. I pulled up, punched in my PIN, which was my birthday, and the amount I wanted. I know it is a security sin to use your birthday as your PIN, but I didn't use the machine enough to remember anything more complicated. The machine spit money back at me and a little piece of paper that had my balance on it. The balance was a lot larger than normal. Thank you, Colonel.

I pulled around to the parking lot and went inside. I withdrew the majority of the money. The clerk was young, round, and pretty. She let me into the safe deposit boxes. I put half the cash in the box to rest with the other cash, the semi-automatic pistol, the box of ammo, and the fake passports and I.Ds. The remainder would go back to the boat. To a special hidey hole. It was indistinguishable from the rest of the hull. I had Blackhawk search for it while I waited at the marina bar with a beer. An hour later he joined me, admitting defeat. If Blackhawk couldn't find it, it couldn't be found. I kept my cut and run money there.

On the way back to the boat, I stopped at a hardware store and picked up some brass cleats. I was slowly but surely replacing every piece of hardware on the old lady. Even older women like a new hairdo. Forty minutes later I pulled into my assigned parking spot midway down the hill, above the marina. I caught a ride with the new kid, Gary, in the golf cart the marina supplied for visitors. The hill was steep, and the marina was a good hundred yards below. I could see someone sitting on my bow. I got closer, and could see it was Eddie.

3

Eddie was one of the few, like me, that lived at the marina. He was old, grizzled and tougher than a Norwegian boot. From his looks, he could be somewhere between seventy and two hundred. He lived on an old barge-style river runner one dock over from me, and did odd jobs around the marina. He could do about anything. A handy guy with tools. He never talked about himself, but over time I learned he was a retired Chicago cop, and a prolific slayer of crappie and stripers. Those were his preferences, and he was good at it. Occasionally I would go out with him. We always brought something back.

He had set off my warning system, which activates a blinking LED light if someone comes aboard. The light is positioned so you have to lean low and look to see it. I stepped aboard and disengaged it. He was sitting on one of the locker boxes I keep rope and life jackets in. He was holding an opened Pabst Blue Ribbon, and had the remainder of the six-pack next to him. He pulled one out of the plastic ring that holds them, and stood and handed me a beer. I set the bag of hardware aside, and took the beer. I popped the tab and saluted him with it. I took a swig.

"Come on inside, out of the sun," I said.

I unlocked the sliding door, and pulled it back. He grabbed the rest of the beer, and followed me inside. I waved at the couch, and he sat down.

"Been gone," he said.

"Yep," I said, pulling the blackout curtains back.

"Girl left a few days back," he said.

"Yep," I said. I slid a haunch up on one of my bar stools that line the counter between the galley and the lounge. Eddie wasn't one to come visit and make small talk. I knew he would get to the point.

"Want a shot of something to go with that?" I asked.

"No, thanks," he said.

He looked around as if he were seeing my place for the first time. He wasn't. I sipped the beer and waited. If he wanted, Eddie could outwait a rock. After a time, he looked at me.

"Got a nephew," he said.

"I didn't know that," I said.

"Sister's kid. Sister Emily was still in diapers when I was growed and gone. She don't like me much. She got religion early. Found Jesus. Lips that touch alcohol won't touch hers. That kind, hard core. Thinks I'm a drunk."

"Jesus drank wine," I said, unnecessarily.

He looked at me. "I drink, but I ain't no drunk."

"I know."

"She had a boy, and when he come of age he looked me

up. Good kid. He's a policeman up in Cottonwood."

"That's not far. Do you get to see him much?"

"Couple, three times a year. Comes down to fish once in a while. Usually around Thanksgiving. He'd bring a bottle of Wild Turkey by and we'd have a bump. He would keep me up on the news of his mom and the others."

"Thanksgiving isn't far away," I said.

"Don't think he'll make it this year."

"Oh?"

"Why I came over. He's in jail."

"He's in his own jail?"

He took a long drink of beer and looked out the port window.

"They say he killed a guy." He looked back to me. "You ever been to Cottonwood?"

"Been through it," I said. "On the back way to Sedona."

He nodded. "High desert," he said. "Nice little place. Verde River goes through it but it don't supply enough water so all around the town they got well sites. City owns most of them, lease some of them. Couple are shut down, not being used. Fella's dog found a body in one of those. High weeds. Been there awhile. Missing his head."

"Missing his head?" I said.

"Never found the head. Identified the body with fingerprints and tattoos. Tattoos are like bar codes now days."

"They say your nephew did it?"

"Yep."

"Why?"

15

He shrugged. "It was a short phone call. I asked why he didn't call a lawyer. Said he didn't have one yet. Said he just couldn't call his ma so he called me."

He looked back out the window, and I could see the pain in his eyes. He was a tough, hard man, and I knew he was here for a favor. Probably the hardest thing a man like him could do. Ask for a favor.

"If he can't afford an attorney, they have to provide him one."

He nodded. "I know," he said softly. "He says he didn't do it. He's like me, he said he didn't do it, he didn't do it."

Now he shifted around, and looked straight on at me.

"Everybody knows how you and your friend, Blackhawk, saved that girl from them drug gangs. I figure a guy like you is about what I'll need to figure out what happened to that fella, and to get my nephew out of jail. I made a couple calls, and found out that private investigators get about $300 a day. I figure it might take thirty days for us to figure out what happened so I'll pay you $9000 to help me figure this out."

I shook my head.

"I know that you know," he continued, "I ain't got that kinda money. But I'll sign a note, and I'll pay it off if it takes five years."

I looked at him. It took an awful lot for him to be sitting there asking this of me, and I knew he meant it. He would pay his debt if it took forever. I also knew that he would not agree to anything that even smelled like charity.

"Private investigators have state licenses, are regulated

and pay taxes," I said. "Let's do this. I'll go up with you, and if I think I can help I'll take a hundred dollars a day."

"Done," he said. "I'm supposed to work the store tomorrow, so one of them kids can have the day off." He worked when needed at the marina store that was attached to the bar. The store sold a lot of things for the tourists and weekend boaters, but it had essentials for those of us that lived here full time. Milk, eggs, bacon and such. Beer, some hard stuff.

"How about the day after tomorrow?"

"Works for me," I said. "Tell me about your nephew."

"Billy's always been a good kid. Played football in high school back in Iowa. Got some size on him. Went into the Marines. Made Military Police and become a sergeant. Got out a while back, and got the hots for a gal and followed her to Arizona. He got on the force last year, the girl moved on, and he stayed."

"You don't know why they think it was him?"

He shook his head.

"Leave early, day after tomorrow?" I said.

He stuck out his leathered old hand and I shook it.

"O dawn thirty," he said.

4

Blackhawk owned a nightclub in south Phoenix he called El Patron. It was a large, stand-alone building surrounded by an asphalt parking lot. It was really three separate bars under one roof. One catered to the country music people, one to the rock people, and the largest, by twice, was where Blackhawk's lady, Elena, and her large salsa band held forth three nights a week. The other two bars did okay, but Elena brought the customers in by droves. Blackhawk lived in an exquisite apartment he had built into the top level. How he paid for it, I never asked. Once he was out of the unit, he was obviously better at accumulating cash than I was.

I had reconnected with Blackhawk when I had contacted the Colonel for some help. It was the first I learned that Blackhawk was also in Phoenix. I had pulled a little teenaged girl out of the lake, and she had disappeared into a mess involving street gangs and drug cartels. Blackhawk came to help me out.

Now when it was necessary for Blackhawk to be running around holding my hand, he left El Patron to Elena and his segundo to run. His segundo was Nacho, real name Ignacio Pumbo.

I parked where I normally did. It was early yet and Elena wouldn't take the stage for a while, so the place was empty. Nacho sat in his usual place, at the corner of the bar, reading the paper. Jimmy was behind the bar at the other end, stocking the lockers. Nacho looked over the top of the newspaper at me. He started laughing.

"Hey, Superboy, I hear you lost another foot!"

Nacho was tall and broad with raven black hair down his back. His massive arms were covered in old gang ink. The tattoos no longer applied. Nacho was what was called a reformed criminal. Did the deed, did the time and didn't want to go back. There was never any trouble at El Patron, or if there was, it didn't last long.

"Bad foot karma," I said. "He upstairs?"

"With Elena. Be sure you knock."

Against the back wall of the large, open saloon was a flight of stairs. They led up to an inside landing that lined three of the four walls. At the top of the stairs, to the right, was a closed door. I went up the stairs and through the door. On the other side was a wide hallway. In the hallway, spaced thirty feet apart, were two doors. I knew that one opened into a spacious waiting room which led to Blackhawk's even more spacious office. The other door was living quarters. I knocked on that door. I waited, then knocked again.

Blackhawk opened the door.

"Why don't you just barge in? Everyone else does."

"I was warned."

I followed him inside. Except for the lack of windows this was a luxury apartment. Blackhawk lived well. The furniture was high grade leather, the paintings on the walls were quality originals, and the recessed lighting could be cued to any mood he liked.

He walked over to the bar and set up two glasses. He filled them with ice, then poured a good dollop of Plymouth Gin in each one. He added a dash of bitters and handed me mine.

I stirred it with my finger, then moved to his ornate couch and sat down. I took a small bite of the drink. It was delicious.

Elena came through the doorway, fussing with her hair. "I'm going to fire that bass player." She stopped when she saw me. Her eyes turned to fire, and I almost winced. She came over to stand in front of me.

"What did you do?" she demanded.

I started to answer. She waved a hand at me.

"Don't! Don't even talk. You make me very angry! That poor girl, she just gets well."

I looked at Blackhawk, and he was smiling, but it was behind Elena and I knew I would get no help from him. Have someone shoot at me and he's my guy, but get Elena pissed and he runs like a scalded dog.

"She left," I managed to get out.

"Of course she left! You act like that, anyone would leave."

"Act like what?"

"Act like whatever you acted like. You did something and you know it."

Now Blackhawk was grinning.

"I liked her," Elena continued.

"So did I. I still like her," I said.

"You like her? You like her? She took a bullet for you. How many girls will do that? No one! I sure as hell wouldn't. I'd have let that little weasel shoot you right in the balls. What, you got another girl now?"

I shook my head, bewildered. "No, no other girl."

"No other girl," she repeated. She was shaking her head in disgust. "How many girls, how many girlfriends have you ever had?"

I started to answer, but she kept going.

"How many in the last two years? Answer that."

I shrugged. "One," I said meekly.

"Yeah, one. And now none." She turned to leave the room. "You are impossible."

As she turned, Blackhawk abruptly stopped grinning. She started out, then swung back, catching Blackhawk as he grinned again.

"You think it's funny? You think, you break a woman's heart it's funny?"

Blackhawk's eyebrows went up, "How did I get into this?"

"You are like him." Her head tilted toward me. "You men. You are all alike!"

She had him there. He didn't know what to say.

"You think you can treat women any way you want? You think you can treat us like we're your pets? Well, I'm not your pussycat!"

She stormed out of the room.

Both of us were a little stunned.

"What the hell was that?" I said.

He was still looking at the doorway. "She liked Boyce, I guess."

"I like Boyce. Boyce isn't gone. We're just not together."

"That's probably worse yet," Blackhawk said. He sat down and took a drink. "It's not just the Latin side of her," he continued. "It's the Latin female side. An unattached male inherently has something wrong with him, otherwise, why is he unattached?"

"Can I change the subject?"

"Please do."

"You remember Eddie? The ex-cop that lives out at the Marina. The one I go fishing with sometimes?"

Blackhawk nodded.

"He has a nephew that lives in Cottonwood. He's a policeman there. Except now, they've got him in jail for murder."

"Got a cop in jail?"

"Eddie says the nephew says he didn't do it. Eddie believes him. Says he's a straight shooter."

"Who got killed?"

"Don't know yet. Eddie says the phone call was brief. He wants me to go up with him to see if we can figure things out. Says the body was found without a head."

"Without a head?" he repeated. "Ever find it?"

"Don't know yet."

He carefully moved a porcelain coaster to the coffee table and set his glass on it. "Don't hear about that often. I know the cartels will do it to scare the shit out of people. And the terrorists do it for the same reasons. Unless you are in Mexico or the Middle East, ain't too many killings where they take the head. Probably a whack job. You really don't know anything yet?"

"Not yet."

"Why you?"

"Eddie knows about us helping that Revera girl. Says he thinks he needs someone like me. Says he wants to pay me."

"Pay you?"

"Yeah. He's a proud guy. He offered $9000."

"He's got $9000?"

"Nope. I told him a hundred a day because I know if I offered free he wouldn't do it."

"You going to take the $100?"

"Nope."

"How does that work?"

"Not even sure I can do anything. If I can, I work the money thing out later. Charity don't fly with old Eddie."

"Want me to come along?"

I shook my head, "I'm in enough trouble with Elena. And I don't know anything yet."

I finished my drink, and stood up and handed him a key.

"If for some reason, I'm up there a while, here's the key to my mailbox. It's always 99 percent junk but the box is small and it irritates the gal that delivers the mail if my mailbox gets too stuffed."

I went to the door, and opened it.

"Good luck," I said.

"With what?"

"Elena," I said.

"Hell, she'll come breezing back in here, give me a big kiss and won't even remember she's mad at me. It's her Latin temperament."

I turned to leave.

"Hey," he said. I turned back.

"If Boyce was still there, she could get the mail," Blackhawk said.

"Funny as a crutch," I said and left.

5

It was still dark. O dawn thirty. Early in the morning. I battened down the Lily and walked down the pier toward the marina. Eddie was already waiting. Without a word he followed me up to the parking area. Normally they have a golf cart shuttle to take people up and down the hill, but the place was deserted this early.

I carried a small canvas bag with a change of clothes. Tee shirts, underwear and a change of socks and jeans. I wore a lined, satin Diamondbacks jacket and an Arizona Cardinal cap. The bag also held a .45 caliber Kahr, a shoulder holster that fit it, and a 357 Taurus model 66. And a box of ammunition for both. Eddie carried a crumpled paper bag under his arm. I popped the trunk and put my bag in. He nonchalantly tossed his bag in. It landed softly on mine. I looked at it, then back to him.

"Underwear and socks," he said. "Figured you'd bring the hardware."

The early morning air was cool. It was too long a drive to put the top down. In the movies it looks cool to have the hero breezing along with the top down, but at 75 miles per hour the wind beat the crap out of you. Traffic was light, and we headed across Carefree Highway to Interstate 17. As we turned north, following the signs to Flagstaff, the first of the early morning commuters were filling the southbound lanes.

I had left the radio on and an NPR announcer was reading the latest news. She was talking about another senseless act of evil a half world away. Another aid worker in Syria had been beheaded by some radical asswipe. Considering the circumstances, I reached to turn it off.

"Leave it on," Eddie said.

The woman's voice described what was becoming a common occurrence. Aid workers trying to ease the suffering of refugees, refugees mostly made up of women and children, being kidnapped by radical sub-humans and held captive. Then the male aid workers were either sold for ransom or executed. The murders were usually on camera. Usually with a beheading. These monsters loved the shock value, knowing that the world media just couldn't resist. If there is a hell, there's a special room for these animals.

The announcer went on to talk about a suicide bombing in Australia, and Eddie reached over and turned it off. We rode in silence for a while.

"If they didn't publicize this stuff, there would be less of it," Eddie finally said. "Two tours in Vietnam and thirty years on the force, you'd think I saw everything. I never saw evil like this. Not a group like this. I always believed that evil was individualistic. Never saw a group of murderers like this."

I didn't have an answer for that. He watched the traffic heading the other way.

He turned slightly to look at me.

"Saw a lot of bad things in Nam, but I don't know, it seemed different."

"War is hell," I said.

"Yeah, it is," he said. "But that was war. The kind we're used to. One country fighting another country. This stuff here, I just don't get. I don't see what these guys get for doing such bad things. Were you ever over there? In the Middle East?"

I drove a while before I answered. I could feel him watching me. Finally, I nodded.

"See combat?"

I nodded again.

"Kill anybody over there?"

I kept driving. Never met a soldier yet that had been in the ugly part of the business that wanted to talk about it. Usually the ones drinking beer and holding forth in the bar were the ones that did the typing, or strung the telephone wire. Maybe worked in the car pool.

I wasn't even technically a soldier. When I lost the foot, no one filed a report.

"Yeah," he said quietly, "None of my business. Got any idea why those assholes are doing that to people?"

"Not a clue," I said.

"Me neither."

We rode in silence for a while. The speed limit in Arizona is 75 miles per hour. You had to pay attention. Especially on the upgrades. That's when one trucker felt he had to go a mile an hour faster than the trucker in front of him. Just as you came zooming up on him, traveling forty miles an hour faster, out he'd come, into the passing lane. You jam the brakes, then wait the hour it seemed to take for the truck to pass and get back into the slow lane.

Eddie said, "The world is becoming such a dangerous place, a guy is lucky to get out alive." I turned my head to look at him.

"W. C. Fields," he said.

I smiled and drove on.

After a while Eddie was watching the stream of lights heading the other way. He said, "Look at all them lemmings heading down the hill. Live up here, work in the city."

I glanced at him. The lights of the passing cars flashed across his face and I could see what he had looked like fifty years ago. "Down the hill?"

"Local term. If you are heading south from up north you are going down the hill."

"Going north toward Flagstaff is heading up the hill?"

"You got it."

"Big hill," I said.

He shrugged.

We rode in silence for a while. Every once in a while I could feel him glancing at me.

Finally he said, "I appreciate you doing this."

"I'll help any way I can, but there is no guarantee."

"Ain't never no guarantee," he said. "Appreciate it just the same."

I think that was the most conversation I'd ever got out of him. We passed through the developer-created town of Anthem. North of it was New River and then Black Canyon City. Twenty years ago these had been havens for the proud misfits and oddballs who couldn't stand the big city. Back then I might have been one of them. Today the mega sprawl of the growing city was already enveloping New River and knocking on Black Canyon City's door.

Despite the sprawl, every time I took an Arizona highway I always marveled at how much of Arizona is wide-open land. After Black Canyon City we climbed a twisting and winding road, dodging RV campers and more semi-truck trailers. We had moved past most of the commuters. Now most of the traffic was commercial. The eastern sky was beginning to lighten when we broke over the top of a wide and spacious mesa. In the new light you could see for miles across golden empty plains and rugged purple mountains. Only the light glinting off of distant power lines showed any sign of civilization.

The drive to Cottonwood takes about an hour and a half from Phoenix, and just as suddenly as we climbed to the top of the world, we dropped straight down into the Verde Valley. At the bottom, we took the Cottonwood exit and pulled into town twenty minutes later. It had barely had time to get to full light.

Eddie was familiar with the town, and gave me directions. We drove to the police station. I don't know what I expected but this wasn't it. It was large and new and had an even newer emergency call center right behind it. It was across the street from a civic center that advertised indoor pools, tennis courts and game rooms. Next door was a modern library. All worthy of a bigger city. So much for me believing this was a backwater burg.

6

It was early, and the parking lot was mostly empty. So was the foyer. There was a policewoman at the far end behind a counter. She was tapping away at a computer. We waited politely. Finally, she finished and looked up.

"Help you?"

"I'm Billy Bragg's uncle," Eddie said. "He called me, said he was in trouble."

She looked at us with new interest.

"Yeah, you could say that." She studied him some more. "I can see the resemblance," she said. She looked at me. "You family too?"

"Family friend," I said.

She looked back at her computer and hit a few keys. Then hit some more. She looked up.

"He's scheduled to enter a plea this morning at eight. Room B12. Second floor. Chief's not in yet. He comes in, I'll tell him you are here. He'll probably want to talk to you."

"What happened?" Eddie asked.

"Sir, I don't know all of it. You will have to talk to Chief

Berry." She looked at the clock on the wall. "It's early. You have time to get some coffee."

We thanked her and left. Eddie knew of an early morning restaurant on Main Street. It was a mom and pop place, and the parking lot was full, which is always a good sign in a small town. I had some scrambled eggs and toast and Eddie drank black coffee. We were back at the station by 7:45. We found room B12 as she had described.

We were among the first ones there, but the room began to slowly fill. It was two-thirds full when the judge finally came in, and we all stood. The bailiff began calling names, and one by one, men came forward and stood in front of him, took the oath, then stood in front of the judge. I heard the same thing over and over. It wasn't my car. It belonged to a friend. How would I know it wasn't registered or insured?

About ten minutes into the session, the back doors opened and two women came in. They looked enough alike to be sisters. One was shorter, and the slightest bit heavier. The other was younger, and was very pretty. She had raven hair down her back. They were dressed similarly. The older one had a tight, white short-sleeved blouse with a high collar. The younger, taller one had a white long-sleeved blouse with a high collar. They both had tight blue jeans with sequins on the pockets, and cowboy boots. Yee haw! They sat in the back row.

We were seated forward and across the room. The next time I glanced back, the older of the two was studying Eddie. She caught me looking. She averted her eyes, and didn't look at us again.

At 8:35, by the clock on the wall, they brought Billy in. The atmosphere in the court changed. This was a little more serious. A man in a suit and tie, whom I took to be the prosecutor, came to one of the tables in front. I'd never seen Billy, but there was a family resemblance. He was shackled, hands and feet. They had him in the standard prisoner's orange jumpsuit. He shuffled into the room and the bailiff sat him at the defendants' table. A large, balding man, in a wrinkled suit, had been sitting against the side wall. He stood now and joined Billy at the table. He was sweating, even though the temperature in the room was mild. He mopped his face and head with a handkerchief he carried in his hand. The man leaned to Billy and whispered to him at length. I glanced back at the two women in the back and they both were leaning forward, their eyes on Billy.

The judge finally nodded to the bailiff and the bailiff ordered Billy and his attorney to stand. As they did, the prosecutor began reading the charges. First degree murder. Less than a minute later Billy's attorney entered his not-guilty plea, and the judge denied bail, and set a court date that was over a month away. The attorney and a policeman led Billy away. The two women stood and left. Eddie sat for a short moment, then stood and I followed him out of the room. Once Billy had come in, the whole thing didn't take a couple of minutes.

The policewoman, from earlier, hailed us on our way out to tell us the chief wished to speak with us. She said she would escort us to his office. We followed her onto the elevator and rode to the second floor. As we stepped off there were chairs lining the hallway. She asked us to wait there. We sat. She disappeared into a closed door at the end of the hallway. A moment later she stepped out and beckoned to us. I followed Eddie.

The chief was taller than me. He had at least twenty years and twenty pounds on me. He carried a little paunch, but still looked fit and strong. His uniform was crisp, and creased in the right places. His light blond hair was cropped close, like a military cut. It was tinged with gray, his scalp gleaming through. His smile was easy, but his eyes were cop's eyes. Aware and watchful. They took us both in with a glance, and I could feel the processing. He was standing behind his desk. On the wall behind him was a large map of the city.

"Come in, gentlemen," he said, waving a hand at two chairs that faced his desk. He didn't offer a hand. We sat down.

He settled behind his massive desk.

"I'm told you are related to Patrolman Bragg?"

"I'm his uncle," Eddie said. "My sister's boy. My name's Eddie."

"Last name?"

"Bragg."

"Bragg? Bill is your sister's boy?"

"Emily changed their names back to the family name when she finally divorced the son of a bitch she had been married to."

The chief leaned forward, his elbows on the desk. "Bill has said he has an uncle that once was on the Chicago police force?"

34

"That would be me," Eddie said.

The chief smiled. "And you, sir?" he said, looking at me.

"My name is Jackson. I'm a friend. Just giving Eddie a ride up from Phoenix."

"First name?"

"Just Jackson."

He studied me with a smile. His eyes weren't smiling.

"Like you and Cher and Prince and Madonna?"

"Something like that."

He was looking at me with a friendly look, but I wasn't fooled. His eyes were the eyes of a man that didn't suffer fools. He didn't like me not giving a first name, but he let it ride. I guess I could have made one up, but the Colonel didn't give us first names. His eyes lingered on me, then he looked back to Eddie.

"So Mr. Bragg, I want you to know that I hold Bill in high regard. I'm doing what I can for him, but until we can get this thing figured out, I have to do what I have to do."

"Can you tell me what is going on? You can start with telling me why the boy is locked up."

"You were in the courtroom."

"Yeah," Eddie said. "First degree, but I don't know the circumstances. I don't know a damn thing. He called me and said he was in trouble. He didn't want to call his mom. They made him hang up before he could tell me much of anything."

The chief looked sympathetic. He had a folder on his desk. He picked it up and ran his thumb across the top, but he didn't open it.

He shifted in his chair. "Four days ago, one of our citizens was walking his dog, and the dog happened to be a beagle. If you don't know, beagles have very sensitive noses. Many are used for hunting and tracking. This one caught wind of something inside an old, abandoned city well site. The citizen let the dog off the leash and the dog went through a crack in the gate. The dog acted strangely enough to cause our citizen to move the chained gate enough to get in. In the tall weeds he found the decapitated body of a man. It was two days before State Homicide identified him. His name was Richard Mooney. He was well known around town. It's not a large town. People called him Dick and he lived up to the name. We had him down here more than once for assault drunk and disorderly."

"Who was the citizen?"

"Tom Waring. Retired city worker. Used to work for Parks and Streets."

"Why do you think it was Billy that did it?" I asked.

He had been talking mostly to Eddie, but now turned his eyes to me.

"I can't discuss all the elements of the case, but we had sufficient cause."

He looked at Eddie. "You being a retired policeman will understand that I can't talk about an ongoing investigation."

"You can't tell us anything?" Eddie asked.

The chief leaned back into his chair. "I can tell you what is commonly known. Two main things. One is that the last time Mr. Mooney was seen alive, he was fighting with Bill, and there are witnesses that heard Bill threaten to kill Mr. Mooney. There is some physical evidence, and the other thing is, according to some, Bill was involved with Mr. Mooney's wife. The Mooneys were separated, but legally still married."

"According to who?"

"Enough credible people to make it a concern."

"That's not against the law."

"No it's not, but it could be motive."

"What physical evidence?"

"I'm not at liberty to say."

"Mrs. Mooney, does she have a sister?" I asked.

Now his eyes lost any pretense of friendly. "I understood that you were new here. How would you know that?"

I shrugged. "Saw two women that looked alike, about Billy's age, in the courtroom a little bit ago. They left as soon as he put in his plea."

He studied me some more.

"The Martin girls. The oldest, Lucy, married Dick Mooney. The other girl, Dahlia, is single, and works at the library. Not twins but close in age."

"Not doing Billy any favors showing up in court like that," Eddie said.

I looked at him.

"Just fuels the gossip flame," he said.

"How long had the Mooneys been married?"

"Both were married before. Don't quite know how long it would be. Maybe ten years, probably less." He stopped to think. "I've been here eight, and they were married when I got here."

"You know everyone in town?" I asked.

"Like I said, it's a small town. Mooney liked to brawl. I met him early on." He looked at Eddie. "Despite you having been a cop, you need to know I have a very competent department. We will appreciate your concerns about Bill, but we won't appreciate meddling."

"Not here to meddle."

"Mind if we take a look at where the body was found?" I asked.

He looked at me. "That sounds like meddling. But it is in the paper, so it doesn't matter if I tell you."

He swiveled in his chair. Pointed to a spot on the map. "South end of town, off of Twelfth Street and Inca. Looks like a vacant lot with a fence around it. Has *No Trespassing* signs posted." He looked back at us. "It is a crime scene, don't doing anything foolish."

"What else can you tell us about Mooney?"

"Like what?"

"Like where he worked. You said he had been arrested before. Was there anything more than fighting? Did he do drugs? Things like that."

"I thought I made myself clear about meddling."

I leaned forward, "Chief Berry, you know Billy has a court appointed attorney. We don't know if the guy is even competent. If we can add anything to Billy's defense, we are going to do it."

He studied me for a long moment. He nodded, "Yeah, they assigned him Mr. Taggart. Billy's going to need all the help he can get." He pointed a finger at me. "Just don't do anything to piss me off."

"Wouldn't dream of it."

"Anything you can tell us?" Eddie said.

The chief nodded. "Dick Mooney had a small landscaping business. Had a small crew of Mexicans. Had the reputation for starting a job, then leaving his guys to finish. Spent a lot of time in the taverns. His guys were pretty good guys, so they carried him. Not much other work for them in this town. He drank too much, and when he was drunk he wanted to fight. Didn't matter who or why."

"Anything else?"

"I heard he did a lot of hunting, deer, elk and the like. He belonged to a so-called militia."

"Militia?"

He smiled, "Group of dipshits that never grew up. Put on their camos, and go out into the desert and shoot up a bunch of cactus, and play army. Getting ready for the Armageddon. Harmless bunch of nitwits."

"This militia have a name?"

"Not that I've ever heard of. We don't have to pay much attention to them. They usually take their silliness out of the city limits. Only trouble we've had recently was when a biker group came into town, and had some words with them at the Sunset Corral. Got into a brawl."

"When was that?"

"Month ago or so."

"Mooney was involved?"

"Of course. Lucy Mooney is a bartender out there. One of the bikers was talking to her, and even though they had been separated for a while, Dick picked a fight. In fact, Billy was one of the patrolmen that answered that call."

"These local bikers?"

He laughed. "Hell no. These guys are harmless. They weren't Hell's Angels or anything like that. Mostly accountants and dentists and middle management types from Phoenix. On weekends they take their Harleys out of their three-car garages, and put on their leathers, and group up and ride around thinking they are Marlon Brando."

"Think they could have had something to do with Mooney's death?"

"No."

"When can I see Billy?" Eddie asked.

"You can see Mr. Taggart about that. He can set it up. His office is on Main Street just north of the 89A intersection. A little blue building. Shares it with a barber shop." He stood. "If there's nothing else, I have work to do."

We stood. Eddie offered his hand, and the chief took it.

"Thanks for your time."

"Anytime."

I followed Eddie out. When I glanced back, the chief was still standing, watching us.

We stepped out of the building into the bright sunshine. Eddie looked at me. He was smiling.

"What's so funny?"

"Dentists and accountants on Harleys. What the hell is the world coming to?"

7

The library was just across the street. I decided to walk over and see if I could get a word with Dahlia Martin. Eddie sat to wait on a stone bench in front of the municipal building. I crossed the street and held the door for two teenaged girls with arms loaded with books. Inside it was every library in every city in the world. None of the women behind the counter were Dahlia. I waited in line. When it was my turn I used my most winsome smile. It usually makes women's knees weak but somehow didn't seem to affect the five foot by five foot woman behind the counter. She looked at my empty hands with disapproval.

"Can I help you?"

"I'm looking for Dahlia Martin," I said winsomely.

"She took the day off," she said. "Do you have anything to check out?"

"No, ma'am," I said.

"Next," she said, looking past me.

I walked back over and collected Eddie. He looked at me and I shook my head.

We got into the Mustang and I started the engine. "Where to?"

"Let's go look at the crime scene, then look up Lawyer Taggart."

"Which way?" I asked.

He pointed, "Just go south on 6th, all these numbered streets kinda go north-south."

I pulled out of the lot, and drove south. After a few minutes we came to a stop sign. The street sign read *Inca*. Travel wise, this was a small town. It only took a few minutes to get anywhere. There was hardly any traffic. We sat and looked up and down Inca. The area wasn't populated much. The nearest residences were over a hundred yards away and there was plenty of space between them. A quarter-block down, the fluttering, bright yellow crime scene tape caught my eye. I turned left, went to the tape and pulled to the curb.

The lot was an empty, weedy space surrounded by a fence that was old, droopy and ineffective. A small chained gate protected the place. The fence beside the gate was on the ground so the gate wasn't protecting much. Wasn't much to protect. Waist-high weeds and scrub sage and tumbleweeds. The trespassing signs lay discarded and face down in the dirt and weeds. Signs of police activity were apparent in the scuffed dirt and trampled weeds. In the center of the lot, hidden by the weeds, we found a concrete slab with a rusty capped water line rising from its center. The concrete had chalk marks. This is where the body had been.

Recently I had joined the twenty-first century and had obtained a cell phone. One of those *smart* ones. I pulled out the wonder, and started taking pictures with it. One of the features on the thing I really liked.

Eddie slowly walked around, taking everything in. He walked along the fence line studying the adjacent land. There was a lot of open space. It was a good place to stick a body. Except for the beagle.

Eddie crossed the street and stared back at the lot. I bent low, studying the impressions in the dirt. I could see the dog prints. Most of the dry ground was scuffed up by too many policemen. I could see the wheel tracks of the gurney that had been used to take the body away. I looked around, trying to understand why the body had been dumped here.

"Anything?"

"Most prints are alike. Cop shoes."

"Except for the civilian and his dog."

"Right." I pointed, "Also, tennis shoes over there. Smaller feet."

He looked to where I pointed.

"So what do you think? Kids?"

"Most likely. Saw the cops. Came over to see what was going on."

Eddie looked all around then turned to me, "Let's go visit Lawyer Taggart."

"Lead on," I said.

We climbed in the car and I did a U-turn and drove back down past the police station. A minute later we hit Highway 89A and turned toward Main. At Main we turned left, and a moment later we saw the blue building and the barber pole. Eddie had explained that as you travel down Main Street it curves from north to west. This meant that, depending where you were in Cottonwood, you could intersect with it by traveling east/west or north/south. Confusing to a stranger. I pulled into the small parking area. There was a small sign proclaiming *Egbert P. Taggart, Attorney at Law.*

The tires of the Mustang crunched on the rock parking lot, and I had my choice of all the empty slots. When I opened the office door a small bell tinkled above my head. Eddie followed me in. It was a small office. Two rooms, one behind the other. The first room was set up as a reception area with a desk and chair facing the door. There were two chairs against the wall. An empty water dispenser was in the corner. The cup holder on the dispenser was empty. Dusty plastic plants were on each side of the door. The desk didn't look like it was being used and had a fine film of dust on it. I ran my finger across a corner and it left a streak. There was a rustling in the back room, and Taggart appeared in the doorway.

He was still sweating. His jacket was off and his tie loosened. He was popping breath mints. He put on his best hail-fellow, Rotary Club smile.

"Come in, gentlemen, come in," he said extending his hand.

I took it. That was a mistake; it was wet with sweat. I wiped my hand on my jeans.

"This is convenient; my meeting just got moved back," he said. He turned and led us into the back room. Eddie wiped his hand on his gray work pants.

"Have a seat," Taggart continued. He moved his big

frame around his desk, and sat heavily in a swivel chair. It groaned under his weight.

We chose a chair and sat down.

"Now, just how can I assist you gentlemen?"

Eddie looked at me, so I took the ball. "Billy Bragg."

His eyes narrowed slightly in disappointment. The hail-fellow smile left.

"Most unfortunate circumstance. If I may ask, just what is the basis of your interest?"

"I'm Billy's uncle," Eddie said. "Only relative he has west of the Mississippi."

"I see." He looked at me. "And you, sir?"

"A friend," I said, taking a dislike to the guy. "We'd like to know what you know about the circumstances."

He studied me a moment. He drew himself up.

"Undoubtedly, you know I was appointed by the court to represent Mr. Bragg, and therefore, you must understand, everything between myself and Mr. Bragg is confidential." He spoke with an officious, self-important tone. "Now if you will forgive me, I have a scheduled appointment."

I looked at him until he shifted his eyes.

I looked at Eddie. "The hard way," I said.

He shrugged.

"Do you have a dollar?" I asked, turning back to Taggart.

"I beg your pardon?"

"A dollar, a buck. Do you have one?"

Now he was wary. "I don't carry cash," he said.

I looked at Eddie. "Do you have a dollar, Eddie?"

He reached into the gray work pants, and fished out a

crumpled wad of bills. He extracted a five dollar bill. "Smallest I got," he said.

"Loan it to him," I said.

Eddie tossed the bill on the desk.

"Now you have five dollars," I said. I picked it up. "And you just used it to hire us. And now that we are part of your investigative team you can tell us anything we need to know."

"This is preposterous," he said.

I stood, and closed his office door. I moved back and sat on his desk. I smiled down on him. He tried to back away but the wall stopped him.

"Billy is Eddie's nephew. His sister's only kid," I explained softly, taking the tone you would with a child. "Eddie is an ex Chicago cop with a fearsome temper, and he wants to help Billy. I want to help Billy, and I believe you want to help Billy. Now, if Eddie thinks you aren't helping Billy," I raised my hands and shrugged, "I can't guarantee what might happen."

He had moved as far from me as he could. He was flat against the wall. He looked from me to Eddie and back.

"Discretion is the better part of valor," Eddie said.

8

"Since he is family, I guess it will be okay to share information," Taggart said.

He pulled a handkerchief from his hip pocket and mopped his face. It was easier for him to look at Eddie, so he did. "A few days before Mr. Mooney's body was found, your nephew got into an altercation with him at the Sunset Corral," he said. "Your nephew was off duty, and they both had been drinking. Mr. Mooney's wife, Lucy, was behind the bar, and they had some words about her."

I was too close. I could smell him. An undercurrent of sour booze and body odor covered by the sickly-smelling mints. I slid off the desk and took the chair.

"Witnesses?"

"Several, including another off-duty patrolman."

"Name?"

"Joe Whitney.

"Tell us."

He looked at me. He wasn't happy.

"Patrolman Whitney says that it was pretty common

knowledge that after Lucy Mooney and her husband broke up, Bill started seeing her. Whitney said Mooney was a bad drunk and was pulled in a lot for fighting. Whitney said Mooney was drunk, and was using abusive language to Lucy and Bill objected, so they fought."

"Anyone else involved?"

"No, Whitney and the cook broke it up. Mooney left, but before he did they were shouting back and forth and Bill told him that if he ever talked to Lucy like that again, and I quote Whitney's deposition, *he'd take his head off.*"

He popped another mint.

"Then, Whitney says Mooney came back in. This scared Whitney because he thought Mooney had gone out to get a gun. Whitney says he was about to dive behind the bar, but instead Mooney just pointed a finger at Bill and shouted, "You'll get yours. You'll pay like the rest of them. There'll be a reckoning for all you cops. "

"A reckoning? What does that mean?" Eddie asked.

"Hell, I don't know what he meant," Taggart said.

"What was Billy's politics?" I asked Eddie.

"Didn't have any, I know of," Eddie said. "He was just a small town cop."

"You ever hear of any militia around here?" I asked Taggart.

Taggart shook his head. "Whitney says Mooney was a part of one but I never heard of it. 'Course my circles run more to the chamber of commerce and the country club."

"Where can we find Whitney?"

"He's probably on patrol."

"Who else witnessed this fight?"

"Besides Lucy?"

"Yes, besides Lucy."

He opened a drawer and pulled a manila folder out. It wasn't very full. He opened it and thumbed through the papers in it. He read a moment.

"The cook, Alfred Medina. A couple of construction guys, Dwyer and Ramirez, and a salesman, name of Howard Sieble. Buddy Dwyer works for King Construction. I think Ramirez is a drywaller but nobody knows much about him. He lived in a boarding house on Mingus. Not sure he's still there. Sieble comes through once a month and calls on our hospital. We have a really nice hospital. Best one around. Whitney says when Sieble's in town he goes to that bar to drink his supper allowance."

"You have contact information on them?"

"It's all right here," he said indicating the folder.

"Give me a copy."

He looked at me, and now he really wasn't happy. But he finally leaned over to the small, desktop copier against the wall and copied the documents.

"Give me a business card, and put a note on it that you would appreciate any cooperation for me. My name is Jackson. Sign it."

This time he didn't hesitate. He pulled a card from a drawer and wrote it down. He handed it to me. I took it.

"What happened next?"

"Lucy Mooney said after her husband left she chased them all out of there, including Bill and Joe, and closed the bar."

"The chief said I should talk to you about when I can see Billy," Eddie said.

"The arraignment was today," Taggart said.

"We were there," I said.

"Didn't notice."

"Does he have visitation?" Eddie asked.

"Not yet, but he is one of Bub Berry's favorites."

He opened a large official-looking appointment book.

"I can meet you there this afternoon. I'll be free around two." Upside down, I could see the page was empty.

He looked at Eddie. "It won't be official, but I'm pretty sure Bub will let us see him. It's a small town and Bill is one of his."

Eddie looked at me and I nodded. I stood. Eddie followed suit.

"We'll be in touch," I said.

We turned, and I opened the door, and followed Eddie out.

"You didn't have to strongarm me," he said to my back, some of the bluster coming back.

I turned and looked back at him long enough for his color to change. "I didn't," I said. I took the five and put it in his pocket.

9

Eddie and I drove to the Sunset Corral. He knew where it was, which didn't surprise me. It was a stone-faced building with a large parking lot, located on the west edge of town on the way to Clarkdale. Clarkdale is butted up to Cottonwood. There was only one vehicle in the parking lot. It was an old Ford F150. We parked next to it.

The sign in the window read *Closed.* The door was unlocked. We walked in. All the chairs were upside-down on the tables, and a push broom was resting against the wall next to a small pile of sweepings. The place smelled of stale beer and fried food. In other words, it smelled like what it was.

The kitchen was visible through an open, rectangular window in the wall behind the bar. Next to the window was a batwing door. We could see a man working there. He appeared to be slicing something on a cutting board. His movements were quick and precise. As I got closer, I could see he was slicing limes. He was engrossed, and didn't know we were there.

"Hello," I said by way of warning.

He jumped and spun around.

"Holy shit! You scared the crap out of me!"

"Sorry about that," I smiled. "Are you Alfred Medina?"

He wiped his hands on his apron. "We're closed right now. We open at eleven for lunch."

I took out Lawyer Taggart's card and handed it to him.

"We want to ask you some questions about Billy Bragg. Are you Alfred Medina?"

He read the card, then turned it over looking to see if there was more. Finally, he looked at me, and handed it back.

"Yeah, I'm Al Medina."

I indicated Eddie. "This is Billy's uncle. We're trying to figure out what happened with Billy and Dick Mooney."

Eddie stuck his hand out. Alfred wiped his hand on his apron again and took it.

"What would you like to know?" Alfred said.

Eddie looked at me.

"I guess, first of all, what happened the night they got in a fight," I said. "Did you see how it started?"

"No, I was in the kitchen, but as you can see it has this window here. When I heard the shouting I came over to see what was up. When I saw it was Mooney, I just figured it was the same old shit."

"Was his wife bartending?"

"Yeah, Lucy was on that night. I think that was what they were fighting about. Lucy and Mooney split up a while back, and Lucy got a job here and unfortunately Mooney started coming in two, three times a week. Nothing Lucy could do about it."

"Does Billy come in here a lot?"

"Since Lucy came to work, he does. Him and another cop, Joe Whitney, were in here together that night."

"Were they in uniform?"

"Hell no," he laughed. "Bub Berry would have their ass if they were drinking in uniform."

"Did you see how the fight started?"

"No, they were already at it before I came to the window. But it was probably because Mooney was running his mouth. Mooney was always running his mouth, even if Lucy wasn't here."

"Did you hear what they said?"

He looked at me a moment before he answered.

"I know what you are getting at. I already told the police. Mooney was calling Lucy names and Billy told him to shut up and Mooney just kept on and finally Bill shoved him and told him if he kept running his mouth he would take his head off."

"Billy would take Mooney's head off?"

"Yeah, that's right. But you hear that kinda crap a lot. One guy threatening to take another guy's head off. It's just a figure of speech."

"So you don't think he meant it literally."

"Hell, no. But I have to say it sure was a shock when Mooney showed up without his head."

"So, do you think Billy did it?" Eddie asked.

Alfred looked at Eddie.

"Man, I didn't know Bill very good. I mean, just when he would come in for a beer, but I sure didn't take him for the type to do something like that."

"After the shouting, it got physical?"

"Yeah, after Bill shoved him, Mooney started swinging."

"How did Billy react?"

"Well, it wasn't like Bill was tryin' to give Mooney a beatdown. More like a policeman would try to subdue a violent drunk. By that time I was out of the kitchen, and Lucy was screaming at them to stop, and me and Whitney got 'em separated, and got Mooney out the door."

"What did Billy do?"

"As soon as me and Whitney got control of Mooney, Bill quit fighting."

"Who else saw this?"

He looked thoughtful for a moment, "Salesman guy, comes in here once in a while. Calls on the hospital. And a couple of guys Mooney was drinking with."

"You know their names?"

"Buddy Dwyer and a new guy name of Ramirez. Quiet guy, don't say much. Kinda weird guy."

"How so?"

He shrugged. "I don't know. You know, just sits around with the other construction guys and don't talk much. Stares at Lucy. Just something kinda creepy about him. Not from around here."

"Where's he from?"

"Hell, I don't know. Back east maybe. Like I said, he's new. Does drywall, I think."

"How about Dwyer?"

"Buddy's a local. His dad's a barber. Got a shop up on Main."

"Blue building?"

"Yeah, that's the one. Buddy went to Cottonwood High. Played football."

"Were they close to Mooney?"

"Buddy was in the same class as Ed and Lucy. I think he was in their wedding."

"You said when you saw it was Dick Mooney fighting it was the same old shit. Mooney fight a lot?"

"When Mooney wasn't drinking he was okay, just laughing and joking and thinking he was the life of the party. Probably trying to impress Lucy. But the more he drank the meaner he got."

"I'm told Mooney was in a militia."

Medina smiled. "Militia. Makes it sound important. Him and Buddy, and a bunch of others would go out into the desert and play army. Shoot the shit outta the rabbits and cactus. Thought they were survivalists or something."

"How about Ramirez?"

"Don't know about him."

"Were you working when Mooney got into it with a bunch of bikers a while back?"

"Wasn't much to it. Mooney was doing his normal crap, getting loud and rowdy. He started it. All those guys were wearing leathers, but they weren't but a bunch of Phoenix guys that get together, and ride around in a bunch. Makes 'em feel good."

"What happened?"

"Mooney started in on this one guy. There were some that looked like they could handle themselves, but of course Mooney leaves them alone. He picks this short, bald guy and starts badgering him. Mouthing off. This poor guy feels like he has to stand up in front of his buddies so him and Mooney get it on. Then the balloon goes up and everyone's in it."

"Anyone get hurt?" I asked.

He laughed. "The furniture." He looked at me. "You look like you could handle yourself, you ever fight? In the ring, I mean."

"Not competitively, but I was taught how."

"I was Golden Gloves out of Maryvale twenty years ago," he said matter of factly. "If you were taught, then you know that most guys just shove, and flail around and maybe get lucky and bust a knuckle on the top of another guy's head. Mooney was like that. He started a lot of fights when he knew someone would step in and break it up."

"You break it up?"

He smiled, "Yeah, but I wish I hadn't have. When the little guy got going he was doing pretty good. I shoulda let him whip Mooney's ass."

"Anything come of it?"

"Naw, they moved on down the road, never saw them again."

"Anything else you can think of?"

He shook his head. "Not really." He looked at Eddie. "Didn't know your nephew real well, but he seemed like a good kid. Don't think he is the kind that would take a man's head. That's ugly stuff. Scares the hell outta people around here. But most people I hear talking in here, they don't know Bill very well. They're just happy to think the guy that did it is in jail." He picked up his chopping knife. "Look, I gotta get back to work. I got a lot of prep work to get done for the lunch crowd."

"Is Lucy working today?"

"She'll be on tonight."

We both thanked him, and I followed Eddie back out into the sunlight. We got into the car and I started it.

"Golden Gloves, huh." I said.

"He wasn't born with that nose," Eddie said.

10

For lack of any kind of a plan, we drove around Cottonwood just to familiarize myself with the town. The lawyer was right; they did have a very nice hospital. On a chance, I pulled into the front drive of the chain motel that was across the street from the hospital. I went in. There was a scruffy young man in a stained polo shirt and frayed jeans behind the counter.

He gave me a puzzled look. He evidently wasn't expecting customers.

"Can I help you, sir?"

"Is Howard Sieble still checked in?"

He didn't look.

"No, sir. Mr. Sieble checked out yesterday."

"Do you expect him back?"

"Probably not till next month. He comes once a month."

I thanked him, and went back out.

We drove around some more, had lunch, and by two we were back at the police station.

We sat in the lobby and it was two-thirty before Lawyer

Taggart made his appearance. The man was still sweating. He nodded at Eddie, but kept walking. He didn't look at me. He went to the desk. The same policewoman was on duty. He spoke to her in low tones we couldn't hear. She glanced at us, then said something. She waved a hand toward one of the doors. Without looking at us he went through it. There was a white, round-faced clock high up on the wall. Seven minutes passed very slowly until he reappeared.

He came up to us. He still wouldn't look at me.

"They have moved him to an anteroom," he said to Eddie. "We can see him for a short time there. If you will follow me."

He turned and started away, not waiting to see if we would follow. We did. The policewoman stepped out in front, and escorted us down a hall and opened a door. She moved aside as she held the door for us. We followed Lawyer Taggart in.

Billy was sitting in a straight back chair, at a table roughly the size of a kitchen table. He was still dressed in orange, his hands and feet shackled together. He looked up as we came through the door, and as he looked at Eddie his eyes filled. He didn't look any worse for wear except his hair was disheveled, and his eyes were bloodshot.

Taggart said, "Bill, you must understand this is not a sanctioned visit, but a favor from the chief. You must not tell these gentlemen anything you have not already told to me." He finally looked at me, then to Eddie. "As I have hired you to help me with the investigation."

"For five bucks," I said, and Eddie smiled.

"You must disclose," Taggart continued as if I had not interrupted, "anything and everything that Bill tells you, and anything else you may discover in the course of the investigation. If I learn you have withheld anything, I will have you thrown in here with your nephew. You have half an hour."

I didn't have a snappy retort ready, and that was disappointing. He turned and left the room.

Billy stood up and Eddie went around the table and hugged him.

"Have you talked to Mama?" Billy asked.

"Wanted to see you first," Eddie said. "I wanted to know more about this thing before I call her."

Billy sat back down, and looked at me. Eddie slid a hip up on the corner of the table. I sat in one of the chairs that were opposite Billy.

"This is Jackson," Eddie said. "He's a friend. I asked him to come with me."

Billy nodded.

"Hi," I said.

"Ain't much to know," Billy said. "I got in a fight with Dick Mooney, and two days later I come in for my shift, and the chief is telling me I was under arrest for killing him."

"When was Mooney killed?" I asked.

He shrugged, "Mr. Taggart said the state investigators thought he died the next afternoon, after the fight." He looked from Eddie to me. "I know; you are going to ask if I have an alibi, but I don't. Lucy Martin, a girl I'm dating, and I were going to go to Sedona for the day, but the other girl at the bar Lucy works at, called in sick, and the boss called Lucy in to do the lunch and night shift."

"What did you do?"

"Stayed home, watched TV; later on I took a bike ride."

"Bike?"

"I have a Harley Low Rider."

"Anybody see you riding?"

"Not that I know of."

"You wear a helmet?"

"It's the law."

"What color?"

"It's black with a visor."

"Tinted?"

"Yeah."

"You wear leathers?"

"Weather's cool enough for a jacket."

"So with the helmet and visor down and a leather jacket you pretty much look like any other rider?"

"Pretty much."

"Anyone stop by the house or call you?"

"No one stopped by. Lucy called my cell phone on her break."

"We hear that Mooney got in a lot of fights," Eddie said. "Why do they think you did it instead of some other guy he pissed off?"

"Well, there is the head thing."

"In the heat of the moment, you told him if he didn't shut up you'd take his head off?"

"Yeah. I guess I said it. Hell, I don't even remember. But it's just a figure of speech."

"Anything else?"

For the first time he ducked his head.

"What is it, son?" Eddie said gently.

He looked up at his uncle. "I just found out. They found my Kabar in my garage with his blood on it."

Eddie looked at me. A Kabar is a large military-styled fighting knife. "Physical evidence," he said.

"It is your knife?" I asked.

"Yeah, it's mine."

"And they know it is his blood?"

"They say it's the same type. Waiting for a DNA match. But I know it's going to be his."

"Why do you say that?"

He looked at me. His eyes were red-rimmed. "Because that's the way this thing is going."

"When was the last time you held your knife?" I asked.

"October, opening quail season, I took it with me."

"You use it to clean quail?" I smiled.

"No, of course not." He didn't smile at the joke. "I just like it, so I take it whenever I camp."

"When was the last time you saw it?" I asked.

"When I came back from hunting. I keep it in my camping tote."

"You packed it away?"

He nodded.

"Who knows where you keep it?"

He shrugged. "I keep all my hunting stuff together in the same place. Wouldn't take much to find it."

I looked at Eddie. Taggart had been holding out on us.

"Why didn't the chief tell us about the knife?"

"He's a cop," Eddie said. "Cops don't always tell you everything. Get a suspect, see if he knows something he's not supposed to." He shrugged. "I know that don't always make sense, but cop ways are hard to break."

I looked at Billy. "How many people know about the blood on the knife. Obviously Taggart?"

"Yeah, he knows, but we're not supposed to talk about it," Billy said.

"You told us."

He looked at me. "Fuck 'em. Eddie's my uncle and you're on my side, right? I didn't kill Mooney. I can't say that I'm sorry he's gone, but I didn't do it."

"You want to keep that sentiment to yourself," Eddie said.

"I didn't do it."

"So someone got into your garage and stole your knife, and hunted down Dick Mooney and took his head off with the knife, and brought it back but kept the head?"

"I didn't do it," he said for the third time, looking at his uncle.

Eddie looked at me. I looked back at him for a long moment.

Finally I shrugged. I looked back to Billy. "Who has it in for you enough to do something like this?"

"Damned if I know," he said. "I'm just a small town cop, for Christ's sake. The worst thing I do to someone is give them a speeding ticket!"

11

He didn't have much more to add. He couldn't remember seeing anyone he knew when he was riding his bike. He said he normally rode the back roads, through Clarkdale and up to Jerome, the old mining town that perched on the side of Mingus Mountain. He said sometimes he would eat a burger in Jerome, but for some reason he didn't this time. I had him specifically walk me through where he had ridden.

He asked Eddie about his mother, and they were talking family when the policewoman came in to tell us our time was up.

Sometimes I forget how old Eddie is. He was looking pretty worn down, so I suggested we find a motel and see if we could check in. Eddie knew of a locally owned place on the main drag, and the woman mopping the lobby floor told us they had vacancies. She checked us in. The Sunflower Inn. The name was precious but the room was just basic. It did pass the clean test.

The room held a distant odor of disinfectant. The good news was it didn't have the paper strip across the toilet, and the glasses in little paper bags. This told me that someone, probably the woman at the front, had actually cleaned the place instead of just wiping off the toilet seat and the drinking glasses with the wadded up towel the previous customer had left on the floor.

I left Eddie to take a nap, and I drove the Mustang to where Billy lived. The place was locked up. I was inside in two minutes. I walked though, just hoping to see something unusual. There wasn't anything. Dishes in the sink, the bed unmade. The camping gear was in the garage. The lid was off. There was powder residue on the lid. Someone had checked for prints. Careful not to disturb anything, I went back out and slid into the Mustang.

I retraced his route, as best I could, all the way to Jerome. I don't know what I expected to discover, maybe see something or someone that might verify his story. There was nothing. It was a pretty drive, though. Coming back down the road from Jerome a broad expanse of high desert unfolded in front of me. The air was clear, and you could see Clarkdale and Cottonwood and across to Camp Verde. In the near distance were the red cliffs and mountains of Sedona.

I decided to look up Dwyer and Ramirez. I stopped at a liquor store, and borrowed their phone book. I looked up King Construction. I drove to their offices. It was a low brick building with a large compound housing two large utility buildings, filled with heavy equipment. This was surrounded by a tall chain link fence. The girl behind the desk wore jeans and an NAU tee shirt. She was twenty pounds overweight and looked as though she had just stepped from the shower, combed her long hair and come to work. She didn't question me at all. She told me where to find Dwyer. She didn't know Ramirez. She gave me directions to the worksite where Dwyer was.

It looked like they were rebuilding an old Circle K. Probably going to be a check cashing store. They were framing it out. Tools and debris were scattered throughout its parking lot. There were five guys working. I parked and walked up to the closest one.

"Buddy Dwyer?"

He looked at me, then pointed at a guy with a Diamondbacks ball cap. The guy was bent over, fiddling with a nail gun. He looked up as I approached him.

"Buddy Dwyer?" He just looked at me. I handed him the card from Lawyer Taggart.

"I'm looking into the death of Dick Mooney," I said, trying to sound official. "I've been told that you witnessed the fight between Billy Bragg and Dick Mooney."

"Wasn't much of a fight," he said handing me back the card. "Mooney wasn't much of a fighter."

"Do you think Bill Bragg killed Mooney?"

He looked at me for a long moment.

"Hard for me to believe that."

"Why?"

"Bragg was a cop. He'd give you a speeding ticket, and bust your ass for DUI, but if he was gonna kill Mooney he'd have shot him, not cut his fucking head off."

"Was Bragg a friend of yours?"

"Fuck no. He was a cop."

"Cop is bad?"

"Just another government lackey."

"Did you belong to Mooney's militia?"

"It wasn't Mooney's."

"Whose was it?"

"It was a patriot organization. It belonged to all of us."

"Did Ramirez belong to it?"

"Yeah, for a while."

"How long?"

"Some guy brought him around. Said he had been in the Army. Only came a few times. I ain't seen him since I quit it."

"You quit?"

"I got this new job and hell, I didn't have time to go running around the fucking desert playing soldier. I was serious, I wanted things to change. One of these days the balloon is going to go up because someone has hacked the grid. Then this fucking country is going to shut down. We gotta be ready. That's what I thought we would be doing. But they were just a bunch of nitwits. Didn't take long to get tired of them anyway. They never did anything but spout a bunch of rhetorical bullshit, and get drunk."

"Was Ramirez like the dipshits, or more serious, like you?"

"Don't know if he was like me but he sure as shit wasn't like them."

"What does Ramirez look like?"

He looked hard at me. "What the fuck do you care? He

looked like every Mexican you ever saw. About your height."

"Where is Ramirez now?"

"Fucked if I know. Probably went to Phoenix. Ain't much work around here."

"Do you think he might have been involved with Mooney's death?"

He laughed, shaking his head. "Why? He didn't have nothing to do with Mooney. Everybody knew Mooney was a gasbag. Lot of people could have offed Mooney." He stood up. "Just the same to you, I gotta get back to work."

"Thanks for your time," I said.

He picked up the nail gun, and as he walked away I said, "Hey."

He turned.

"Who was it brought Ramirez into your group?"

He hesitated, thinking about whether he wanted to answer my question or not. "Ain't sure. Think it might have been Frankie. Frankie Wambaugh. They worked together," he said. "Why?"

"Just asking questions. Thanks for your time."

He turned and walked away.

I nodded to myself, walked to the Mustang, got in, and drove away.

When I got back to the motel Eddie was gone. There was a note on the table that read "*taking a walk.*"

I got my bag out of the trunk, and brought Eddie's sack in also. I took a shower. Eddie came back while I was dressing. He was carrying a paper bag. He set it on the dresser.

"Liquor store down the way," he said.

"How you doing?" I asked.

He hooked one of the cheap chairs with a foot and sat down.

"Startin' to get pissed," he said. "Somebody did this and they're stickin' it to Billy." He looked at me. "Did you find anything?"

I shook my head. "I thought I'd head to that bar, see if Lucy Mooney will talk to us."

"I'll come along," he said. "Let me clean up a little."

He took his paper bag into the bathroom and shut the door. A couple minutes later I heard the shower start. I found the remote control and started flipping channels to kill the time. Ordinarily I would have picked up a book, but I hadn't brought one.

Each channel I went through reinforced for me why I don't have a TV on the boat. I found this one channel that had a show where a man and a woman were dropped naked into the jungle, and had to survive for a couple of weeks. Is this what people watch? Right away they didn't know how to make a fire. They didn't know how to hunt or fish. They sure didn't know how to build traps. They froze at night because they weren't smart enough to build a waterproof shelter, and too stupid to cover themselves up with layers of dry underbrush. They whined about mosquitoes, but were too ignorant to cover themselves with a thickness of mud. When the man started whining more than the woman I turned it off.

When Eddie came out of the shower he was dressed,

shiny clean and sweet smelling. It was the first time I'd ever seen him clean shaven.

"Damn, you are a vision," I grinned.

"Give you a run for your money, boy."

"The ladies won't even glance my direction," I said.

"Damn straight."

"You ready?" I asked, moving toward the door.

"Need a favor," he said.

"Sure."

"I need to talk to Billy's mama. Can I use your phone?"

I pulled it from my pocket, and handed it to him.

"She as hard as you are letting on?"

"Worse. Was the main reason Billy went into the service. Had to get away."

"People say family can be hard. I've never had the problem."

"Family is funny," he said. "They can do things you put up with that you wouldn't with anyone else. Somebody else robs a bank and goes to prison, you can just walk away. If it's family, you're taking them cigarettes."

I smiled.

"I'll wait outside," I said. I opened the door and stepped through. He didn't need an audience.

I could hear the muffled tone of the conversation. Not the words, just the tone. Sounded like Eddie was losing. I was leaning against the Mustang when he finally came out. He handed me the phone.

"Everything okay?" I asked as I slid into the driver's side.

"No," he said. "She thinks I should have done something.

Like it was my fault or something. Thinks I should have stopped him."

"She thinks he did it?"

"She always thinks the worst."

"Wasn't your fault. What could you do?"

He shrugged. "She don't think that way. Never did."

12

The sun was hitting the western mountains, causing deep blue shadows on the western slopes. Looking east, the light bathed the high desert far into the distance, adding a golden magical twinge to the land. It was postcard photography time.

It was still relatively early, but the parking lot at the Sunset Corral was more than half full. As I pulled into the lot it dawned on me that it was Friday. Happy hour. I parked next to Alfred Medina's old Ford. The two old Fords could co-mingle, maybe get a thing going while we were inside.

Eddie followed me in. There were enough customers to make the place seem smaller, more intimate, that it had earlier. Through the window to the kitchen I could see Alfred Medina working. There was another smaller man working with him. One of the two girls I had seen in the courtroom was coming through the batwing doors balancing a tray of food-filled dishes. Her sister was sitting at the bar, at the end, by the cash register. She had a beer in front of her and empty stools beside her. Eddie followed me over, and we sat down beside her. She didn't look at us.

A few moments later Lucy Mooney finished serving a table of men, and came back behind the bar.

"What will you gentlemen have?" she said without really looking at us. Then she did.

"Hey, I know who you are," she said to Eddie with a smile. "You are Billy's Uncle Eddie. He told me all about you."

Eddie nodded, "Yes, ma'am."

"I'm glad you are here," she said. "Billy can use some family around him right now."

"This is my friend, Jackson," he said, indicating me.

She reached her hand across the bar. "Pleased to meet you," she said.

"Likewise," I returned. She had a good grip.

Her sister had hitched around, and was looking at us now.

"This is my sister, Dahlia," Lucy said.

"Hi," she said. She smiled and it was enough to invade Troy for.

I smiled back, and Eddie leaned forward to look across me. He nodded.

"What can I get you gentlemen?" Lucy asked. "First one is on the house."

"That's mighty kind," I said.

"PBR," Eddie said.

Lucy smiled. "Old school. How about you?"

"Dos Equis, if you have it."

"Green or brown," she said.

"Green," I said.

"Coming right up," she said and turned away.

I looked at Dahlia.

"I saw you guys in the courtroom," she said.

"Your sister's right," I said. "Billy can use some support."

"He didn't do it," she said, looking at me and I noticed that her eyes were as deep and dark as the hair that flowed to her shoulders.

I could tell Eddie couldn't hear very well; the bar talk filled the room with a wall of noise.

"Would you mind moving to a table with us so we can talk with you about Billy?"

"Sure," she said. She picked up her beer and a napkin and slid from the stool.

I turned to Eddie, "We're moving to a table to talk."

"Good," he said.

We followed her. She was tall and trim and wore a chambray shirt with a small red scarf around her neck. Her jeans were the same as in the courtroom. Elena wore the same kind. They were known as "skinny jeans," and you had to be skinny to pull it off. They were tucked into a pair of boots that were fashionably wrinkled around the ankles. These were different from the ones she wore in the courtroom.

It was a pleasure to follow her to the table. Not all women can pull off walking away from a man. She chose one toward the back corner. As we passed a table of men, all those facing her watched as she walked by. One of them, a smaller man with a stubble of beard and a camouflaged cap, watched her intently. It looked more like anger than appreciation. He looked a little out of focus. Like he had been drinking for a long time.

She reached the table and turned to look at us.

"This okay?"

I looked at Eddie and he nodded approval. I angled around so I could sit with my back to the wall, facing the room. An old habit. If Wild Bill Hickok had done the same, things might have turned out better.

Lucy found us and brought the beers. We thanked her.

"Do you get a break?" I asked as she placed the bottles in front of us.

"I can take one when Janine comes in. She should be here shortly. We can talk then."

Another group of men entered and sat at the bar. She moved away to serve them. I looked at the table of men with the little guy with the cap. He was still staring at us.

"You know that guy with the camo hat at the table?" I asked Dahlia.

She looked over, and the guy averted his eyes.

She snorted, "That's Calvin. He's a regular here. He usually closes the place. He's Ed Mooney's cousin. Ed's mama and his mama are sisters."

"He doesn't seem happy."

She looked over at him again. She shook her head, "He ain't. He's not very smart either. Does odd jobs around town. Always seems to have beer money. Since they found poor Ed he's been getting more and more vocal. Especially after a few beers. He's here almost every day. Drinks until he can barely walk, then one of his buddies will take him home."

"Lucky he doesn't drive."

She smiled, and I liked that a lot. "Not since Bub Berry shook a knot in his tail."

"Sheriff Berry runs a pretty tight town?"

"He's fair, but you don't cross him."

I took a drink of the beer. It was good so I took another one. "You said Billy didn't do it?"

"Billy is a cop, but he's a pussy cat. Not soft, but you know, he's a sucker for a sad story. Got a big heart. He's always in trouble with the chief because he gives out more warning tickets than actual tickets. I didn't really know him until he started seeing Lucy. Compared to Dick Mooney, he's a saint."

"Do you know of any way to prove he didn't do it?"

She shook her head, her hair moving on her shoulders. She looked like a young and sexy Linda Ronstadt. "If I did, Billy wouldn't be in jail."

"How long have Lucy and Billy been seeing each other?"

"Not long enough. I wish Lucy had met Billy first. Lucy married Ed about ten years ago, and I've always been sorry I stood up with her. But who knew what a miserable son of a bitch he would turn out to be. I think they separated at least five times, and each time he would talk her into coming back. But this last time was it."

"What happened?" Eddie asked.

"Ed never was what you call a success in business. He pretty well got let go from every job he ever had. Finally he started the landscape business, but he screwed that up too. He just couldn't stay away from the booze. And the more he drank the meaner he got. Lucy finally had enough of him beating on her, so she came to move in with me. I told her this was the last time, and that's the way it turned out."

"Did your sister love Mooney?"

She shrugged, "At first I think she did. But you know how it is, you fall in love with a pair of shoes, and you put them on every day for ten years and somewhere along the line you don't think about them anymore. But when they start beating you up, it's time for them to go."

"Don't believe I ever fell in love with a pair of shoes," Eddie said.

Dahlia and I laughed.

"When did Billy and Lucy get together?"

"You'll have to ask her. I first knew about it after she had moved in with me." Dahlia looked across the room. "In fact you can ask her in a minute; that's Janine." She nodded toward a middle- aged woman that had come through the door, and was going behind the bar.

I watched Lucy as she spoke with the woman. The woman looked our way, then pulled on an apron. Lucy made her way over. She snagged a chair from an empty table and pulled it up beside Dahlia. She reached over and took a drink of Dahlia's beer. Behind her I saw a tall, angular, young man come into the room. Like most of the men in this town, he wore a ball cap. It was tilted back trying to contain a shock of unruly hair. He stood inside the door looking around. I watched as he looked at us, then started over.

He came up, and touched the brim to his cap, "Ladies," he said.

"Hey Joe," Lucy said. She tilted her head toward us. "This is Billy's Uncle Eddie and his friend Jackson. This is Joe Whitney. He works with Billy on the force. He is a friend. Join us?"

He nodded, "Thanks." He hooked a chair from a neighboring table and Eddie and Lucy scooted to let him in.

The waitress, Janine, came up behind him and expertly sat a napkin and a bottle of Coors on the table. He dug into his pocket and extracted some crumpled bills. He handed it to her.

"Keep it," he said.

"Thanks, Joe," she said, moving away.

"Jackson was asking us about Billy and Ed," Dahlia said to Whitney.

He looked at Lucy. "Lucy, you know I'm sorry Ed is dead."

Lucy nodded, "I appreciate that. I know we called it quits, but I spent ten years of my life with the guy, and it still hurts."

Dahlia reached across the table, and took her sister's hand and squeezed it.

"Is there anything new on it?" I asked, looking at Joe.

"Don't know if it has anything to do with Ed, but we got a call about noon from County. Hunters found another body out in the desert." He shrugged. "It's probably a hundred year event when we have a local citizen show up without a head. I can't remember another murder since I've been on the force. Maybe a long while back when Bernie Wisdom shot-gunned his wife. Said he thought she was an intruder."

"He thought his wife was an intruder?" Eddie smiled.

"That's what he said, even though she was sitting in her rocker on the porch."

"You're kidding," Lucy said.

"Be a cop long enough, you'll see everything," Eddie said.

"Was the guy in the desert a murder?" I asked.

He looked at me. "Don't know. Quail hunters found the guy five miles from the nearest paved road. He had a hand chopped off. Based on the blood, the guy bled out. No car, no tracks, no hand and no nothing. Out in the middle of nowhere."

"Who was it?" Dahlia asked.

"It was Frankie," he said, looking at Lucy. "Frankie Wambaugh."

Lucy looked shocked.

"You know him?" I asked.

"He was a friend of Ed's," Lucy said. "One of them Ed would go out into the desert with. They called themselves the Sons of Thunder," Lucy said. "Some kind of Bible thing."

"Two of the Apostles," I said. "James and John. They were the sons of Zebedee."

They all looked at me.

"He reads a lot," Eddie said.

"Were these guys religious?" I asked.

Lucy laughed.

"Only time Ed saw the inside of a church was at his dad's funeral. We were married at the town hall."

A tall, slender, dark-haired woman came through the

front door. She caught my eye. She stood quietly, looking around, letting her eyes adjust. Eddie and I looked at her, then each other, then back to her. We watched her start toward us. Joe, Lucy and Dahlia saw us looking, and turned. They watched as the woman came up to us.

"Detective Boyce," I said, coming to my feet.

13

The bar was thinning and Boyce and I sat across from each other. We each had a half a glass of beer in front of us. Lucy had gone back to tending bar. Dahlia and Joe had moved back to Dahlia's previous spot at the bar. I had given the keys to the Mustang to Eddie so he could drive back to the motel. Boyce said she could get me back to the motel.

She looked at me, her eyes calm and knowing. She could always look right into me. I was remembering how very much I liked this girl.

"Are you mad at me?" she asked.

"Of course not," I said. "Are you mad at me?"

"Of course not," she said.

"There you are. Two grown-up people not mad at each other."

She took a drink of her beer. "How did your job go?"

She meant the op for the Colonel. One of the rules was that we never talked about ops with anyone. All she knew was that I had been gone to do something for the Colonel.

"No worries," I said. "Are you out into the field yet?"

She shook her head.

"Rules say I have another two months." She looked at me. "You haven't asked why I'm here."

"I figured you just couldn't stay away from me."

She snorted. "Yeah, that's it."

"Why are you here?"

"Mendoza offered me up to Homeland Security."

"Offered you up?"

"I think he got tired of me hanging around, so when the Feds came and asked for some bodies he offered me up. Short time assignment."

"What do they have you doing?"

"Can't tell you." She leaned forward with a smile. "But most of us they have down at the border because of all the illegals coming across. I'm on my way to Sedona because of some unusual activity on an IP address. Somebody's been online a lot with radical ISIS websites."

"That's against the law?"

"No, but we gotta check it out. Exciting work."

"So glad you didn't tell me. How did you know I was here?"

She smiled. "Stopped by El Patron. Blackhawk told me."

I smiled now. "Did you see Elena?"

"Yeah. Jesus, Jackson, she was acting like I had terminal cancer or something. She was almost in tears."

"She gave me hell."

She finished her beer. "You deserve it." She looked around the bar. Her gaze landed on Dahlia. She looked back at me.

"Pretty girl," she said.

"Just met her," I said.

"Not bad for first day here," she grinned.

"You know me, a regular babe magnet."

"Blackhawk told me why you are here. You think Eddie's nephew is innocent?"

I shrugged, "Don't know. He had motive and opportunity, and we just found out it was his knife that did the deed."

"Proved?"

I shrugged, "Staties are checking the DNA, but Billy thinks it's his. Maybe they'll find somebody else's DNA too."

"Somebody set him up?"

I shrugged again, "Nobody is on the radar. But we just got here." I nodded at Dahlia and Joe. "Skinny kid with the hair is a police officer, and friend of Billy's. He just told us another body was found out in the desert. Hunter's found it. Missing a hand. Bled out."

"Lot of missing body parts around here."

I finished my beer. "Another one?"

She shook her head. "I still have to drive to Sedona. I can't imagine," she continued, "that this kind of thing is common in a small town."

"Helluva coincidence."

"Anything connect the two?"

"They both belonged to the same militia."

"Militia?"

"What they call themselves. Police chief says they're just a bunch of nitwits that run around in the desert in their four-wheel drives, and like to play army."

"Boys are boys."

She stood. So did I.

"Place to start," she said. She looked around and noticed that Dahlia and Joe were watching. She came around and kissed me lightly on the lips.

"See what the babe thinks of that," she said with a twinkle in her eye. "Come on, I'll give you a ride to the motel."

"Yeah, thanks. You know what this looks like?"

"Of course I do," she said, taking my hand. She led me out of the bar.

14

It was full-on dark and the parking lot, which by now was half empty, was illuminated by lights attached to the roof line of the bar. She had parked her city-issued boat of a vehicle next to where the Mustang had been. The streets were empty. I think they rolled them up at ten. As we reached her car she moved to the driver's side, then stopped, and turned to look at me. I had my hand on the passenger's door. I stopped.

"You know, things don't have to be much different," she said.

"True," I agreed.

"I am very fond of you," she said.

"And me of you," I said.

She leaned on the roof of the car and stared across at me.

"You know, one thing I have been thinking about for some time." She hesitated.

"What have you been thinking about for some time?"

The dim light softened her features. She was quite lovely. This made her even more so.

"All the time we were together we never used the word love."

"Really?" I said.

"Really," she said.

"Commitment issues?"

"Probably."

She turned her gaze across the parking lot and I turned to follow it. The dipshit that had been staring at Dahlia had come out of the bar and was staring across the lot at us. Two of his buddies joined him.

She looked back to me.

"You know I'm a cop through and through."

I smiled. "I know that. I understand that. And I guess I am whatever I am."

"Bon vivant, raconteur, man of the world."

"Unemployed boat bum."

"Speaking of that, you never did tell me where you get your money." Again her gaze moved to behind me. I turned and the three men were making their way toward us. Boyce moved around the car, and came up beside me.

"Friends of yours?"

"Not hardly. Saw them for the first time tonight. The short one is named Calvin. He's a cousin to the guy that lost his head. I think they have been drinking a long time."

"I'll handle it," she said.

I laughed. "The last time you said that you got shot."

"I'll duck this time."

The three men spread out a little as they came up to us. We waited. When they got close, Boyce said, "Calvin, you don't want to bite off more than you can chew."

He peered at her. "Do I know you?"

"Not yet," she said. "But if you have more in mind than just getting in your cars and going home, you will."

"What the fuck does that mean?"

"It means you really need to turn around and go away," I said.

He glared at me.

"We don't need you Phoenix pukes coming up here and getting in our business."

"Calvin, go home now," Boyce said.

He turned his head and spit on the ground. "Shut up, bitch!"

When his head came back around, Boyce slammed him in the nose with the heel of her hand. She stepped into it, the punch traveling about fourteen inches. In a punch like that, the thing is to try to punch through the target. His head snapped back, and he went backward, and sat down hard. Blood was gushing from his nose. The other two were so stunned they didn't move. When they did, they looked back at Boyce and she had moved her jacket aside to show the badge on her belt and the pistol on her hip.

"Get him up," she said.

They stood stunned, looking at her.

"Now!"

They each took an arm and pulled the dazed Calvin to his feet. His eyes were glassy and he was very unsteady.

"If you boys don't want to spend the night in jail, I suggest you take good old Calvin and yourselves out of here."

The two wouldn't look at her. They started the stumbling Calvin across the lot. She looked at me, and I was grinning.

"That's all it takes to amuse you?" she said. "Give a guy a shot in the beezer and you're a happy camper?"

"Maybe I do love you."

"Shut up."

15

The next morning Eddie and I were sitting in the hallway outside of Chief Berry's office. He wasn't in it. We were told this by the same policewoman we had met before. Now she knew us and smiled and told us that Chief Berry would be in shortly. He was. He walked by us and entered his office without looking at us. I looked at Eddie; he smiled.

"Guy's in charge," he said by way of explanation. "That's the way they let you know."

A few minutes later the policewoman came up to us.

"The chief will see you now."

We stood and filed into the chief's office while she waited by our chairs to ensure we didn't dawdle. Don't want to keep the man waiting. The chief was busy at his desk, and didn't acknowledge us. Eddie made himself comfortable in one of the chairs and I followed suit. We sat in silence for longer than was necessary. Finally, the chief looked up at us.

"What can I do for you?" he asked brusquely.

"Why, a pleasant good morning to you, sir," I said with a winning smile.

He looked at me for a long moment. His uniform was crisp and neat but he hadn't shaven today. He looked like it had been a long night.

"I talked with Lieutenant Mendoza in Phoenix," he finally said. "He said you were a pain in the ass, and had a mouth on you."

I had nothing to say to that.

He leaned back. "He also said you had a trained set of skills, and could be helpful. He said you sometimes worked outside the boundaries, but if you did, you kept law enforcement out of it."

"Well," I said. "That was better than I expected."

"So I repeat," he continued. "What can I do for you?"

Eddie made a slight wave of his hand, putting the ball in my court.

I took it. "We heard another body has been found. This one missing a hand. Is this related to Billy's case?"

He looked at me for a long moment, then shook his head. "Hell, we don't know. We are, just now, trying to piece this thing together. I had a very early conference with the mayor and the City Council. I had nothing to tell them either and believe me, they are not happy, so forgive me if I am less than hospitable."

"Hell of a coincidence," I said.

"There are no coincidences," he said tightly.

"Would it be possible to talk to the ME, and maybe see the scene where the body was found?"

"Jesus, son. Is this your idea of not meddling?"

Eddie straightened up in his chair. "Sir, no one else is

helping my sister's boy," he said. "We aren't going to mess with any evidence, but we need to know."

Chief Berry looked at Eddie for a moment, then said, "The crime was outside my jurisdiction. I don't have anyone on it. Why don't you two wait outside?"

Eddie and I stood, and moved out the door. As it closed the chief had picked up his phone. We walked down the hall and resumed our seats and waited. A slow half an hour passed, then finally Joe Whitney came down the hallway. He was in uniform. He came to a stop in front of us, and we stood.

"Chief says I'm to take you guys over to the hospital."

"Tell you why?" I asked.

"He says you want to see the medical examiner," Joe said.

"Lead on," I said.

He led us down the hallway and down the stairs, and then down another hallway until we went through an outer door into the back parking lot. He led us to a patrol car and waved us in.

It was a short jaunt to the hospital. He pulled the patrol car around to a no-parking area, and we followed him into the building. Once inside, it was every hospital, everywhere.

The morgue was appropriately in the basement.

After a long walk, we rounded a corner and beside the sign announcing the morgue stood a tall, cadaverous man in a white lab coat. He had a dark complexion, a prominent Adam's apple, with thick dark-rimmed glasses. He held a clipboard. If this had been filmed in black and white, and there had been thunder and lightning, I would have expected him to be shouting "It's alive! It's alive!" He seemed impatient.

Joe Whitney said, "Doctor Patel, this is Mr. Bragg, Patrolman Bragg's uncle, and his friend, Mr. Jackson."

"How do you do," he said formally. "Chief Berry called to ask that I give you gentlemen a moment of my time, and let me assure you, a moment is all I have. I still have rounds to make."

"Your time is greatly appreciated," I said. "We have been told that you have the body of a man by the name of Frank Wambaugh. We would like to see the body, and if possible have you tell us what you think happened to him."

"The body is this way," he said, pushing the large handicapped button that automatically opened the double doors. "But I cannot give you speculation. I don't speculate. I can only offer conclusions based on my observations."

We followed him into a cold and clinical room. There were three tiers of closed body drawers on either side. He looked at a chart, and then led us to one of the drawers. He took it by the handle and slid the tray out. The body was covered. He pulled the sheet off. The body was shrunken and chalky white. It wasn't much of a specimen. One of the hands was indeed missing. There didn't appear to be other severe trauma. I walked around the body slowly. There were light abrasions on his upper arm, his shoulder and the back of his neck.

I looked at the doctor. "What are the conclusions from your observations?"

Eddie smiled, and looked away.

Doctor Patel pushed his glasses up on his nose.

"The blow that took the arm was a very clean cut. A singular blow from a very sharp instrument. Whoever took it didn't hack at it."

"I've seen men that lost a limb," I waggled my foot, "including me, and they didn't die."

He looked at my foot, then back up at me.

"Yes," he said. He looked at the tag on the door. "Mr. Wambaugh died from loss of blood." He picked up the arm missing the hand. "No sign that he tried a tourniquet." He shook his head. "He just bled out."

"What are these marks?" I asked, indicating the abrasions.

"Contusions that occurred just before he died," he said, replacing the sheet and sliding the tray closed. "Blood rushes to bruised areas. So the abrasions occurred before he bled out."

"Did you, by chance, see the body of Dick Mooney?"

He nodded.

"Were there any marks like this on him?"

He shook his head. "Not on the body. I haven't seen the head."

He turned and we followed him to the door. He allowed us to leave first.

"Thank you for your time," I said.

"You are welcome," he said, starting down the hall. He stopped and looked back at me.

"I don't speculate," he said. "But it certainly appears that the abrasions happened at the same time that he lost his hand. I would say that it is probable that whoever took his hand had someone forcibly holding him down."

"Murder?" I asked.

"Hard to be an accident. There weren't any guillotines in the vicinity," he said.

"Sword?" I asked. He shrugged, turning to walk away.

We watched him walk down the hall and turn a corner, out of sight.

"Was that a speculation?" Eddie said.

"It was."

16

It took an hour to get to the place where the hunters found
the body. The squad car was a big, floating Impala, and Joe
had to carefully traverse the unimproved dirt road that led
us back into the high desert. There were parts of the road I
didn't think we were going to make, but Joe expertly kept
the car moving forward. Whenever I glanced to the back
seat, Eddie looked half asleep.

The turn off the highway onto the dirt road had offered
no advertising. If you weren't familiar with it, and traveling
at highway speeds, it would have been easy to blast right by.
Joe was familiar with it, and took the turn, hardly slowing at
all. It was a rutted dirt road. As we moved along it, there
were a series of offshoot roads, branching off at odd angles
into what seemed to be nothing but open desert. The main
road was just two tracks. The desert was flat and wide with
mountains off in the distance. There was absolutely nothing
out here. I wondered who had made the road, and why? I
mean, there was nothing. Scrub cactus and desert plants.
Staghorn, saguaros, cholla and ocotillo. The ocotillo had

their bright orange flowers on the tips of the tall slender thorned branches that rose straight up. There was an occasional saguaro with its arms reaching. My mind went to the militia racing around yelling "Hands up or we'll blast you!"

Bunch grass was everywhere. Where there weren't other plants there was creosote. The smell of creosote was heavy in the air. And alongside the trail were wire fences that spoke to cattle.

I tried to pay attention. Third right, second left, fourth right, straight for five miles. Finally, Joe pulled the car off the track between two fence posts that bracketed a cattle guard, and I realized we had pulled beside some kind of fence corral. There was half a salt block surrounded by an impressive collection of cow patties. He stopped and got out. We followed. To my right was open desert with not much more that creosote bushes, but to my left was salt cedar and palo verde trees so thick you couldn't see through them.

Joe started walking, paralleling the thicker brush. Eddie and I followed. We had gone a few yards when through the thick brush I caught the glint of water.

"What is this, a pond?" I asked.

"Earthen cattle tank," he answered. "Ranchers lease the state land for their cattle to graze. They dig out the tank and run water in from their well."

"From where?"

"Got a well dug a couple miles on down the road."

"So this is a cattle ranch?"

Joe laughed. "It's state land but it's leased to the ranchers."

"How the hell do they round up the cattle?"

He shrugged. "Beats me."

I followed him, careful not to step in something I would regret. As I walked, I saw random, spent shotgun shells on the ground. I stopped and picked one up and smelled it. It was old.

Joe watched me.

"This is a popular place for quail and dove hunters. Been here myself," he said.

"That's why you know about the well. Wasn't it hunters who found the body?"

He nodded. "A group of guys from Prescott were hunting quail." He pointed. "Body was found up ahead."

He started forward and we followed. We were now on a narrow path that had been made by the cattle coming and going from the tank. The brush was getting thicker when suddenly we spilled out onto the bank of a broad wash. The bank was steep and deep. The wash had to be a hundred feet across.

"Supposed to be the largest wash in Arizona," Joe said.

"Ever see water running in it?"

"Never have. It would be a sight to see. Watch yourself," Joe said as he hopped down into the wash. I followed him down and turned to Eddie. He was smarter: he had moved down a way to an eroded spot. He slid down on his rear.

"Body was found across the wash, up on that knoll," Joe said, pointing. He started across and we followed. I was surprised to find the wash filled with fine sand. I could see a path of indentations, either caused by men or cattle, you couldn't tell which. On the other side he chose a spot where the bank was crumbling and the footing up was easier. They were just dimples in the sand. We scrambled up the other side. Joe picked his way through the brush and we stayed right with him. We walked single file. Ahead I could see police tape glinting yellow in the sunlight. It had been run in a broad circle. As we reached it, Joe lifted it and held it overhead. We went under.

"The body was found there," he pointed. The spot he pointed at was in a thicket of underbrush. The matted-down grass was stained dark with blood as was a large flat rock.

"How the hell did they find it?"

He pointed back the way we had come. "The hunters had flushed a covey of quail on the other side of the wash by the tank. Birds will almost always fly across a wash to put a barrier between themselves and danger. One of the hunters got a bird as it flew and it went down on this side. They were hunting for it when they found Frankie."

"Dumb luck."

"Yeah. He could have been here forever. You can hunt ten yards away and still not see him. If they hadn't been searching for the dead quail they'd never have found him."

"Awful lot of work for such a small bird," I said.

"They don't have quail around Prescott?" Eddie said.

Joe smiled. "Quail hunters," he said, as if that explained it all.

Eddie was studying the ground.

"They trampled this place up pretty bad."

He was right; the brush and grass were crushed down and the ground was scuffed and torn.

"The chief had me bring you out here because he knows I know the area," Joe said. "But it's not our jurisdiction. This is the Yavapai sheriff's scene. In fact I'm surprised someone isn't out here."

"I'm going to look around," I said.

"I'll come with you," Eddie said.

"They've already searched the area," Joe said. "But knock yourself out. I'll wait here."

With Eddie following I went back to the wash. We began to work our way methodically along the bank. I didn't know for sure what I was looking for, but it was an odd place to leave a body. With the amount of blood sign, poor old Wambaugh had to have come out here on his own power. Then for some reason, somebody whacked his hand off, and left him here to bleed out. Why here?

We carefully picked our way for about two or three hundred feet, following the wash. When I thought we had gone far enough we turned east, putting our backs to the wash. Tracking is simply paying attention. If there is no track you draw a large mental circle, and follow it meticulously, searching for sign of anything that has crossed it. Anything that doesn't ordinarily belong. A print, a broken twig, a thread or hair in the brush, anything.

The further we went, the higher we climbed. After another hundred yards I stopped, and turned. We were much higher. The wash below us meandered until the trees obscured it. Below, I could see flashes of Joe's blue uniform as he moved around. Joe's vehicle was easy to spot back by the water tank.

I wanted to climb a little higher. Eddie followed. Now it was cholla and Joshua trees that sprung from the hard, tan dirt. At the top we were with a stand of saguaros. One was huge, a good thirty feet high. Next to it was a strange one. It was bent forward, one arm turned toward the sky and the other bent across its middle, like a man bowing. Next to it was a huge ocotillo tipped with orange blossoms. We turned north and resumed picking our way through the desert.

"Dammit!" Eddie said. I turned to look and he had gotten too close to a cholla. They aren't called jumping cactus for nothing. A ball of barbed spines had snagged his pant leg.

He started to reach for it.

"Don't!" I said. "Don't touch it. Those spines are barbed: you get one in your skin, you have a problem. Do you have a comb?"

He pulled a comb from his back pocket. I took it and carefully slid the teeth of the comb between the cactus and his pant leg and pulled it loose.

"Thanks," he said. "That's a good trick, with the comb."

"You didn't learn about jumping cholla in Chicago?"

He didn't bother to answer. I started off again, searching for any sign.

Twenty minutes later we were back with Joe, and we had found nothing. No sign at all. Just a walk in the park. Whoever had whacked the guy's hand off had come and gone the same way as the police. The same way as us. We made our way back to the car.

The ride back to the station seemed quicker, and was

mostly in silence. I don't know what I expected to find, but we sure as hell succeeded in not finding it. I was disappointed. If we could tie Dick Mooney's head with Frankie Wambaugh's hand, the timing would take Billy off the hook.

Joe Whitney dropped us at the Mustang and we drove back to the motel. I went to get some ice, and when I got back to the room Eddie had the television on and was studying it intently.

"You need to look at this," he said.

17

A bomb had exploded in Sedona at a shopping area crowded with tourists.

It looked like chaos. It had happened within the hour and they already had camera crews there. The pictures showed bloodied survivors being loaded into ambulances. The on-camera talking heads said there were fatalities, but didn't know how many. I dialed Boyce's number. It went to voicemail. I asked her to call me.

They were already speculating it was a terrorist attack. I told Eddie about my conversation with Boyce.

"Radical Islam in Sedona?" Eddie said. "I thought Sedona was for crunchy, bark-eating tree- huggers that sat around holding hands in the vortex waiting to be beamed up."

"All it takes is one whack job."

He looked at me. "What do you want to do?"

"Let's go to Sedona," I said.

Fifteen minutes later we were checked out and on the road. The shopping center where the bomb exploded was named Tlaquepaque - pronounced too-lockee-pockee – and was a very popular shopping area with galleries and small artist boutiques. I pushed the Mustang and it took no time to get there. We came in from the west side of the town, and as we got closer to the site the traffic was jammed up. We had to find parking three blocks away. The place was swarming with police, state police and first responders. Tourists were milling around, with shocked frightened faces.

I locked up the car. We walked toward the hastily erected barricades; most of the people were heading the other way. I said, "Sometimes there are two bombs. One for maximum damage, and the second to take out the first responders."

"Hell of a time to bring it up," Eddie said. He looked around. There was still the inevitable small curious crowd gathered at the barricades, straining to see something. "These people, obviously, hadn't thought of that."

I thumbed my phone out and tried Boyce again. This time she answered.

"Boyce."

"It's me. Are you okay?"

"Yeah, I'm fine. I'm busy."

"Just checking on you. I'm in Sedona. I'm at the north end of the center, at the barricades, if I can help."

"Gotta go," she said and hung up.

I put the phone away and Eddie looked at me. I shrugged. "She's busy."

"Hell yes, she's busy," he said.

Twice the local patrolman moved us out of the way to let ambulances out. I was beginning to wonder if this was a good idea when I spotted Boyce making her way through the crowd. She came up and moved one of the barricades and waved me through.

"He's with me," she told the cop.

"I'll wait here," Eddie said but she had already put the barricade back in place. She turned without a word and I followed her.

The place had been built to look like an old-fashion Mexican plaza. The bomb had exploded in the open courtyard, located at the center. I could still smell the faint odor of the explosion in the air. It brought back memories I would just as soon not have. Most of the parking was on an outer rim around the center. Vehicle damage was minimal. Walking in, I had noticed a lot of the license plates were from out of state. This time of year a lot of people came to Arizona to escape the snow and cold back east. It was a beautiful area.

I followed Boyce as she worked her way into the center of the complex. The injured had been removed to the local hospital. Two bodies, obvious fatalities, were left, covered with blankets. The investigators had not released them yet. A dazed old man sat on the bumper of a fire truck, a blanket across his thin shoulders. A paramedic was sitting next to him, her hand covering his. His haunted eyes were fixed on one of the covered bodies. I looked around. There wasn't as much devastation as there could have been.

Boyce led me to a corner of the courtyard.

"What do you see?" she said.

I nodded at the bodies. "Where were the bodies?"

"When I got here, they were lying where they are now."

As she said this, a large, balding man and his sunglasses came up to us. His suit was stained with dust and he carried a little paunch but he carried it well. He looked like he had played football a long time ago. I had noticed him standing with a group of suits. The way they had been hanging on his every word, he must be in charge. He looked at me with disapproval.

"Detective Boyce," he said. "Who's your friend?"

"Mr. Renfro," she said. "This is Mr. Jackson. Mr. Jackson is a special consultant for Phoenix P.D. Mr. Jackson, this is Evan Renfro; he is with the National Security Team. He is in charge of the site. I have been assigned to him."

I offered my hand and he briefly took it.

"Just exactly what is it you do for Phoenix P.D., Mr. Jackson?" His face was smiling, but his eyes were not.

"I just happened to be close by when I heard of this, Mr. Renfro," I said. "I have had experience with bombing sites. I thought I would come and offer my assistance. Detective Boyce happened to see me and brought me in."

"What kind of experience?"

"Experience with bombs and bomb sites. I have disarmed bombs, placed and detonated bombs, and have seen and investigated many sites where bombs have exploded," I said.

"Where was this?"

"Mostly in the Mid-East."

"You were in the service, Mr. Jackson?"

"Yes, sir."

"Which branch?"

"The Navy."

"Seals?"

I thought about how to answer that, then finally just nodded. I could sense Boyce watching me.

He looked around. "So what do you see here, Mr. Jackson."

"The same thing you do, Mr. Renfro. Usually, when something like this happens, the first thought is a natural gas explosion, but this was a satchel bomb."

"How do you know?"

I looked at him. "I know because of the location of the explosion. If there were gas lines in the center of the courtyard and they exploded, it would be obvious."

"What else?"

I looked around. "I'm a little puzzled."

"Puzzled?"

"I don't know what the motive is here but devastation isn't it. A different type bomb could have caused a lot more damage."

"What do you think the motivation is?"

I thought of the medical examiner in Cottonwood and how he doesn't speculate. I didn't mind speculating because this guy wouldn't listen anyway.

"This seems more like a statement to me."

"What kind of statement?" Renfro said.

"Someone is telling us they are here, and no one is safe."

"Anything else?"

"Two things strike me. I have seen satchel bombs that could take down large buildings. This one was small. And there was no shrapnel. Usually, if the goal is to kill as many as possible, these things are packed with nuts and bolts and ball bearings and anything else that would tear people apart."

He looked around. "You are right. The two we lost were just unlucky. They were standing close to the explosion. If there had been shrapnel, there is no knowing how many we would have lost. Lucky for us, I suppose."

"Yes," I said. "Lucky. Has anyone claimed responsibility yet?"

He shook his head.

"They will. Are there surveillance tapes?"

"We are processing them. I'm told that they were mostly pointed at the parking. Not much crime here; they were expecting vandalism, not terrorism."

He looked at Boyce. "Speaking of which, Detective, I'd like for you to go find Agent Murray and look at the tapes. Get copies. See if we can put a timeline on anyone coming in just before the explosion. And look at who left right afterwards."

"Everyone left right afterwards," I said. "As quickly as they could."

He looked at me. I had been dismissed.

"I know what to do," Boyce said. She turned so Renfro couldn't see her face and stuck her tongue out at me. She walked away.

"Mr. Jackson," Renfro said. "You have no clearance here so I would appreciate it if you would leave the rest of this to us."

"Sure," I said. "I understand completely."

He turned and walked away. I watched him walk away and wondered again why I had always had so much trouble with authority. I had picked a funny life to have an attitude like that. I thought about the Colonel.

"Some people earn respect," I said aloud. I shook my head, thinking that I just met this guy, how could I know to respect him or not. His dismissive attitude, I suppose. I turned and took a long moment, taking everything in. I looked at the old man, sitting in his pain, and I knew it wouldn't ever go away. I headed back to Eddie.

He wasn't at the barricades. I stepped over them and walked back to the car. He wasn't there either.

18

I stood beside the car for a moment, looking around. I got in and drove, slowly looking for him. Up the hill was an old school saloon. I took a chance and grabbed an open parking spot. I went inside. The saloon had a long bar, pool tables, a stuffed grizzly bear, and Eddie. The stool next to him was empty. I slid up on it.

"Got thirsty," he said. "Thought you'd be a while."

The bartender slid up and I pointed at the PBR in front of Eddie. "Same thing for me, and get him another."

He nodded and moved away. He was back in a second, setting the two longnecks on the mahogany bar in front of us. I set a twenty on the bar and he palmed it, made the change and placed the change in front of me. There were three televisions up high behind the bar. One was in front of us and they were showing the same images we had seen earlier.

"Find anything?" Eddie asked, watching the screen.

I shook my head. I told him about Renfro.

"Assholes," he said. I was pretty sure he meant the

bombers, not Renfro. I sipped the beer and watched the screen. Suddenly a *Breaking News* banner scrolled across the screen. The bartender reached up and turned the volume up.

"…CBS affiliate in Phoenix is sharing what is a purported to be an exclusive video of a group that is calling itself Khorasan America and is taking credit for today's horrific bombing in Sedona, Arizona. We are going to show the video and please note that parental discretion is advised. This may not be suitable for younger children."

The screen went blank then opened again to a shaky image that swam around before it steadied. I recognized the inner courtyard of Tlaquepaque. The fuzzy image of an older couple came into view. They stopped and the man turned and went back out of the picture. I recognized him as the old man I had seen at the scene. The woman stood looking back at where he had gone out of the picture, then the screen erupted in a white flash. The station cut the video at the flash.

"That explains it," I said.

"Explains what?"

"The type of explosion. Minimum effect and no shrapnel so they could stay close enough to film it. The courtyard is enclosed. If they could have filmed it from further away, they might have used a different device."

The bartender turned the volume back down and the news station played the film again and again. Maybe they were expecting different results.

"You think this has anything to do with Billy?" Eddie asked.

I shrugged. "Could be. Somebody took off Mooney's head, and the other guy's hand. Something assholes like this would do without blinking. And we both know Billy didn't do it."

Eddie looked at me, "You do believe that."

I nodded, "Yes, I do."

"What do you think this militia shit is all about?"

I shook my head. "I honestly don't know. My gut says it's involved somehow but damned if I know how. None of the guys we know were involved with the militia seemed dangerous enough to do this. Let alone smart enough."

"You're giving them too much credit. Any coward can plant a bomb."

"True. But to make a bomb as specific as this takes knowledge."

"What do we do now?" he said, then his eyes shifted past me. I turned to look and there was Dahlia coming in the door. She was followed by a young girl with a strong family resemblance. The girl looked to be fourteen or fifteen.

They came up to us. "Hey, you two."

Eddie and I slid off our stools.

"Ma'am," Eddie said.

"Why, hi there," I said.

"I saw your car outside. I'm parked up the street so we were walking by, thought we'd say hi," Dahlia said. She turned to the girl. "This is my one and only, Megan. Megan, say hi to Mr. Bragg and Mr. Jackson."

"Hi," the girl said shyly. She had her mom's dark hair.

"Just Jackson," I said. "Can you join us?"

"Just for a second. When we saw the news reports on the bomb we had to come check on Aunt Betty."

"Your aunt lives here?" Eddie asked.

"She has a dress shop at Tlaquepaque."

"She okay?" I asked.

"Yes, thank you. She was at the bank when the bomb went off. She is cell phone challenged, and I couldn't get her to answer, so we drove up."

"I'm glad she's okay," I indicated the bar stool, "Can I buy you a drink?"

"No, we can't stay, just saw your car and wanted to say hi. We have to get back. It's a school night and Megan has homework."

The girl was studying me.

"Mom says you have a cop girlfriend," she said.

Eddie smiled.

Dahlia looked at her daughter. "Megan!"

"Well, you did."

I laughed. "Your Mom is almost right. Detective Boyce is a policewoman, and she is my friend." I looked at Dahlia. "But we are just good friends."

"She walked out on him," Eddie grinned. I just looked at him.

"Regardless of what my comical friend here says, it was a mutual parting. We are still fond of each other."

"Is she up here to find out who killed Uncle Dick?" Megan said.

"Not really," I said. "She's up here on assignment. Today she's part of the team that is investigating the bombing."

Dahlia frowned. "Did they know there was going to be a bomb up here?"

I shook my head. "Don't know what they knew. Must have known something, they sent her up yesterday."

"I'm scared," Megan said.

"Do you think there will be more?" Dahlia asked.

"I think whoever it is, is making a statement. They'll probably make more."

"That's not very comforting."

I shrugged. "You never know what people like this will do. Usually, the next step is to claim responsibility and make more threats and beat their chest. They are trying to scare us. Trying to tell us that no one is safe. Most Americans think this kinda thing only happens somewhere else. It was just a matter of time. The good news is that we are a much more sophisticated country than most. These guys will get caught."

"You think so?"

I looked at Megan, "My friend, the detective, is looking at surveillance tapes even as we speak. They'll catch these guys; *when* is the question."

"Mom says you are trying to find out who killed Uncle Dick. She says it wasn't Billy."

"We agree on that," I said.

"I never did like Uncle Dick, but I like Billy. He didn't do that."

"Megan," Dahlia said.

"What?"

"It's okay," I said. "She's just echoing what I've heard all over town. Mr. Mooney was not well liked."

"He was a prick," Dahlia said. "Excuse my French."

"Why do grownups use a bad word, then think saying 'excuse my French' makes it okay?" Megan said.

"Detective Boyce saved Jackson's life," Eddie said.

Now I really looked at him. "You are a bucket mouth," I said.

"Saved your life? How did she save your life?" Megan said.

"It's a long boring story," I said, "that doesn't need to be told." I said this directly to Eddie.

"It won't bore me," Megan said.

"Me neither," Dahlia said.

Eddie was grinning. "Couple of dirt bag gangbangers," he said, "wrapped up a young girl, not much older than Megan here, in a plastic sheet and dumped her in the lake. Lucky for her they did it right beside Jackson's houseboat. He dove in and brought her back up and CPR'd her till she was breathing again."

"You have a houseboat?" Megan said.

"How did Miss Boyce save his life?" Dahlia asked.

"I'm getting to that," Eddie said. "He warned you it was a long story. How 'bout we grab that table there and I'll finish it."

Eddie turned to the bartender, who was pretending not to listen, "Two more beers," he said. He turned to Dahlia. "Sure you don't want just one drink?"

"A margarita and a Coke for Megan," she said.

Once we were settled and the drinks came, I said, "I'm serious. You really don't want to hear this."

A beautiful smile covered Dahlia's face, "No, I really do want to hear this."

"You have a houseboat?" Megan asked again.

"He lives on it," Eddie said.

"You live on a houseboat?" Megan said. "I never heard of anyone living on a boat."

"At Lake Pleasant in Phoenix," Eddie said. "So anyway, to show how grateful she was to Jackson saving her life, the girl runs away the next day. Lo and behold, what Jackson found out was, that the girl was the granddaughter of the Columbian ambassador, and a drug cartel was trying to use the girl to get at the grandfather."

"Shut up!" Megan said, looking at me.

"You're joking," Dahlia said.

"It gets better," Eddie said.

"Enough," I said.

He looked at me, smiling.

"Okay, I'll shorten it down. So, long story short, the bad guys that had the girl wanted to sell her back but Jackson being Jackson, he was becoming a pain in the ass." He nodded to Megan. "Excuse my French."

Megan grinned at him.

"So," he continued, "they decided to get rid of him and they sent a bad guy to shoot him and Detective Boyce sees what's going on and shoves Jackson out of the way of the bullet and gets herself shot. And there it is. Detective Boyce takes a bullet and saves Jackson's life."

"Wow," Dahlia said. "That is quite a story. The detective looked pretty good to me. For someone that got shot."

"She healed up fast," I said.

"With help, I'm sure," Dahlia said looking at me. "What happened to the girl?"

"Jackson got her back," Eddie said.

I looked at Eddie and he was looking smug.

I shook my head. "I've known you for over three years and that's the most words I've ever heard come out of your mouth. I like it better the other way."

Megan looked at Eddie. "Did you make this up?"

"Why do you think I made it up?"

"Some of it just sounds made up."

"Which part?"

"Nobody lives on a boat."

We all laughed. Dahlia turned and looked outside. The sun was behind the mountains.

"We have to go," she said, standing.

"I'll walk you to your car," I said.

"Thanks," she said. "I'll take you up on that."

"I'll wait here," Eddie said.

I followed them outside. They were parked around the corner and up the street. When we reached the car, Dahlia dug into her purse and took out a pen and a notepad. She wrote on it and handed it to me. It was her phone number. I told her mine and she wrote it down.

Megan was looking around. "I don't like this place."

"They'll catch whoever did this," I said. "Don't be afraid."

She looked at me, and in the fading light I could see her mother's dark eyes.

"Easy for you to say," she said. "You have that cop looking out for you."

She was serious.

19

Eddie didn't want to check into another motel, and since we were just a couple of hours from the lake, we decided to drive down and sleep in our own beds.

We barely got to cruising speed when Eddie said, "Sure is a pretty girl."

"She doesn't believe I live on a boat," I said.

"Well, yeah. Her too. But I meant her mama," he said.

I knew what he meant. "You're a born troublemaker," I said.

I drove awhile.

"This thing has Megan scared," I said.

"This thing has a lot of people scared. Have you talked with your detective?"

"She's not *my* detective."

We moved out on the freeway and the traffic was light. I glanced at him and the dash lights accented the deep life grooves on his face. It was a strong face. "I tried to call her. No answer."

"You know son, the more I think about Billy, the more I

wonder why they've charged him in the first place. Makin' a threat to take a man's head off, even if it did come to pass, don't seem like enough to throw him in jail."

"There is the knife."

"Yeah, there is that."

"You know when you were resting and I took a ride up to Jerome?"

He looked at me.

"I started that ride at Billy's place. He has an electric garage door with keypad security on the outside."

"Yeah, I've seen it."

"If a guy knows how, he could be in Billy's garage in seconds."

He looked at me again. "You mean a guy like you."

"Just saying."

"And Billy was locked up when that other guy lost his hand."

"There is that."

"I was a beat cop for a lot of years," Eddie said. "I didn't have to play detective but I've been at a lot of murder sites and I know the first thing the good cop asks is 'what's the motive.' Find the motive and you almost always find the killer."

"Let's call Joe Whitney and see what he knows about Wambaugh. See if we can't link them up."

"Tomorrow," Eddie said.

"Yeah, tomorrow."

He settled back, slid his cap forward over his eyes and soon appeared to be sleeping. He didn't rouse until I pulled into the parking area above the marina.

The boat was like I had left it. I reset all the alarms, took a shower, fixed a scotch and sat on the stern watching the moonlight trail across the water. I had read that this lake was almost ten thousand acres of water. I knew that below me was eighty feet to the bottom. That was a lot of water. Most people think of Phoenix as hot and dry and sometimes it is, but there is a string of fine lakes that capture the snowmelt from the mountains and provide the people with the water they need. Most people also think of Arizona as nothing but desert but that couldn't be farther from the truth. I have traveled the state, and inside Arizona I have found places identical to parts of Utah, Idaho, Montana, Wyoming and even Colorado. I once heard a proud citizen brag that he could snow ski in the morning, come down the hill and play golf in the afternoon and be in the hot tub by dark.

I don't play much golf, and I'd need a special prosthetic for skiing, but the hot tub thing sounded good.

I went to bed.

I awoke early. I lay in the oversized bed looking out the double sliding glass doors and watched the slow-moving morning light climb its way up the western slope. I watched some gulls fishing. I finally climbed out of the rack, put on trunks and my swim foot, and dove in the icy water. I swam steadily to the *No Wake* buoy, then back. I did it three times. When I climbed out, the water seemed warmer than the air. I took as hot a shower as I could stand. I dressed, then fixed an omelet and a pot of coffee. After I cleaned the galley I worked for a couple of hours on the new brackets. It had been awhile since I had fired up the big Hercules diesels. I checked them over, fired them up and let them idle for a while. I cleaned the cabin and swabbed the upper deck.

I went out on the stern deck and dialed Joe Whitney's number. He picked it up on the first ring.

"Whitney."

"It's Jackson," I said. "I've been wondering about the Wambaugh guy. Can you think of any connection between him and Mooney?"

"Sure," he said. "You already know he was in that militia with Mooney."

"Anything else?"

"Not that I know of."

"Everyone says they were just a bunch of nitwits running around playing guns."

"Yeah, pretty much."

"Taking a man's head and a man's hand doesn't sound like nitwit work."

"That's what the chief says."

"Since Wambaugh showed up dead, has the chief been rethinking Billy?"

He was silent, then he said, "I'm not supposed to talk about what the chief thinks, but if you were here now, you would see me nodding my head."

"I get the impression you know most of the guys in this militia."

"I grew up with some of them. Never ran in their circles. Never seemed dangerous to me, however...."

I waited.

"Have you been watching television?"

I didn't want to go through the whole explanation of why I don't have one, so I said, "No."

"Turn it on. Some dude with his face wrapped up in black, just his eyes showing, is in a video claiming credit for the bombing."

"What do the Feds say?"

"They don't. Not to us. They think we are backwater pukes and want us to get out of the way. They treat the chief like a red-headed stepchild."

"It's on now?"

"Been on all morning. But," he hesitated, "I'll give you a tip I'm not supposed to. We haven't even told the Feds. Fuck 'em, let 'em find out on their own. If you watch the guy closely, and get a good look at his eyes, I swear to God, it's Ramirez."

20

I drove to El Patron. The customer parking was empty. Blackhawk kept his Jaguar covered and parked by the door where the area was marked *Employee Parking Only*. There were other cars there also. I parked beside them and punched the access code into the keypad beside the door. It buzzed and I went in, then punched the security code in when the door closed. It buzzed again. Now we were all safe and sound.

Blackhawk was in his apartment.

"Coffee's on," he said. As usual, he was immaculate. White silk shirt, tailored slacks, no socks. Mahogany colored loafers with the tassels hanging to the side, as his feet were crossed and at ease on the coffee table. He was reading the paper.

I poured a cup, added some sweet 'n low and creamer.

"Mind if I turn on your TV?"

He looked at me. "TV? When did you become human?"

I told him what Whitney had told me.

He picked up the remote and turned the set on. There

was a soap opera on. He went through the channels until he settled on a 24-hour news station. It was showing a bombing but it was halfway across the globe. The world had become a crazy place. I sipped the coffee. As with everything of Blackhawk's, it was excellent. Even his taste in women.

Elena came into the room wearing an oversized terrycloth bathrobe and had her hair wrapped in a pure white bath towel. It looked like a turban, and she looked like the Queen of Sheba. My phone rang.

"Jackson."

"Hi," Dahlia said. "Are you watching TV?"

"Yes, I am."

"Channel 264?"

I signaled Blackhawk. "Channel 264," I said.

He thumbed it in. It took a second to switch over. When it did, the picture revealed a turbanned man with all his face, except his eyes, covered. There were other men in the background. Their faces were covered also. Blackhawk turned the volume up, but though it was apparent the man was talking, the voice was that of a news anchor. There was a scroll under the picture explaining that the man was claiming responsibility for the Sedona bombing in the name of a group, Khorasan America. Blackhawk turned the volume back down.

"Do you have it?" Dahlia said.

"Yes."

"Lucy thinks that guy is the guy that was at the bar when Billy and Dick fought."

"Ramirez?"

"Yeah, that's the guy."

"I don't want to get Joe Whitney in trouble but he told me that just a bit ago. Is Lucy sure?"

"Lucy is never less than sure, that's how she ended up married to Mooney in the first place."

My phone beeped at me. I looked at it and it was Boyce.

"Can I call you back? I've got another call coming in. Three calls all month and now two at the same time."

"You are just a popular boy. No need to call back, I'm heading to the library. Just thought I'd tell you."

"Thanks, I'll call later."

I punched the screen on the phone to roll to the other call and it hung up. I was trying to figure out how to call Boyce back when it rang again.

"I didn't think you liked phones," Elena said.

I hit the button. "Jackson."

"You watching TV?" This was getting redundant.

"Yeah, just now."

"Any ideas?"

"I think the guy's name is Ramirez."

There was a pause. "How'd you know that?"

"Don't get him in trouble, but Joe Whitney, the cop in Cottonwood, Billy's buddy, he called to tell me."

"Who's Ramirez?"

"He was at the bar when Billy Bragg got in a fight with Mooney. The guy that lost his head."

"You sure?"

"Mooney's wife, Lucy, thinks so too."

"The waitress? The dead guy's wife."

"Yeah. Go scoop your boss."

"Can you tell where the video was taped?"

"I see grass and trees, so it's not the desert."

"We think it's in Phoenix."

"What is he saying?"

"Same bullshit. America is an infidel state and is going to suffer the wrath of Allah."

Elena came over to me. "That is Boyce? I want to talk to her." Before I could stop her, she took the phone out of my hand. I looked at Blackhawk. He just shook his head and turned back to his paper.

"How are you doing, girlfriend?" Elena said into the phone. She turned and walked out of the room, my phone firmly in her ear. I looked at Blackhawk again and he had the newspaper up, hiding behind it. The paper shook with his laughter.

Nacho came in the door, went through the room, and immediately came back in carrying a beer.

"Make yourself at home," Blackhawk said.

"Thanks," Nacho said. "Who's Elena talking to?"

"How is that your business?"

"Is it that girl detective?"

"She is a detective, and she is a girl," I said.

He took a long pull on the beer and flopped into a chair. "That's who I thought. Man, I'm glad I'm not you."

"Besides the obvious, why would you say that?" Blackhawk said.

He shrugged. "Elena is giving you the business. What did you do to that poor girl?"

"I didn't do anything," I said.

"Okay," he said. "If you don't want to talk about it, that's cool."

"I didn't do anything," I said again.

Now the TV had Nacho's attention.

"What'cha watching?"

"Asshole's claiming to be the one that set off the bomb in Sedona," Blackhawk said from behind the paper.

"There was a bomb in Sedona?"

"Yeah, yesterday," I said. "You don't watch the news much, do you?"

"Not if I can help it. Never anything relevant to us ex-con, reformed gangbangers. What are they doing at the park?"

"The park?"

"Yeah, the park."

"How do you know it's a park?"

"Hell man, fifty percent of the drug deals in Phoenix go down right there. Right where they are standing."

"Where are they standing?" I asked.

"I told you, at the park."

"Which park?" I said, trying not to punch him.

"You been there," he said looking at me like I was his really slow cousin.

"Tell me."

"Remember when we rousted Benny Yoon?"

"Margaret Hance Park?"

"I think that's it. The one downtown."

I got up and started out of the room.

"Where you going?"

"To see if I can get my phone back."

21

I was leaning against the wall in Mendoza's office, sweating. Typical Phoenix this time of year. This morning it had been just a tad over fifty degrees and now it was in the eighties. The city managers had the air conditioning off to save money. Mendoza was immaculate in a crisp white shirt and maroon tie. The shirt was damp under his arms. He didn't seem to notice.

I had a hand in my pocket, absentmindedly rubbing the thumb drive Blackhawk had made of the video of Ramirez. Boyce and Evan Renfro came in, followed by two men in suits. Renfro carried a briefcase. Boyce moved across the room and leaned against the wall opposite me. She didn't look at me. The other men took the two chairs that were already in the room. The last one in snagged a chair from one of the desks outside the office and brought it in with him. They both wore suits and left their jackets on, despite the warmth. The older one was thick, but moved well. He had his hair cropped close and his scalp shined through. Instead of a neck he had a roll of flesh at the base of his skull.

The other one was taller and sandy-haired.

Once they got settled, the sandy one looked at me.

"Who is this?"

Mendoza looked at him for a moment. His eyes were cool and non-committal.

"This is Mr. Jackson. He has brought some information to me that might be of use to you."

"What is it?" the man said curtly.

Mendoza leaned back, his eyes still on the man. I was hoping the man would piss Mendoza off. I'd like to see what would happen. But as always, Mendoza was cool.

"Mr. Jackson and a colleague were watching the news feed of the alleged Sedona bomber, and the colleague identified the location of where the video was filmed."

"We have an entire agency working on that," Renfro said. He looked at me. "What makes you think you know?"

I looked at Mendoza and he nodded.

"I'll let my, uh, colleague answer that," I said, pushing away from the wall. I leaned out of the office and signaled Nacho. He was sitting across the room drinking a Coke. Looking uncomfortable. He stood and came across. In the openness of El Patron, his bulk seems almost normal. Here, in this closed space, surrounded by desks and chairs, his shoulders looked enormous. I stepped aside and motioned him into the room. He stepped in; his eyes flicked across the men in suits, then stayed on Mendoza. I stepped around him and went back to my spot on the wall. He stood beside me.

"This is Nacho," I said.

"Nacho?" the sandy one said.

"Ignacio Pombo," Mendoza said. "He is an old acquaintance of mine." Boyce was hiding a smile.

"An acquaintance of yours?" Renfro said.

"He put me away," Nacho said.

They all just looked at him.

"Two years for dealing," Nacho said.

"Mr. Pombo paid his dues and is now an upstanding member of the community," Mendoza deadpanned.

A broad smile broke out on Nacho's face, and Boyce had to turn away.

"Very commendable," Renfro said.

"What makes you think you know where that video was filmed?" the sandy one said.

Nacho's smile went away.

"Would you recognize your own backyard?" Nacho said. "That was filmed in my backyard."

Renfro looked at Mendoza, "I'm afraid I don't understand."

"Before Nacho did his time and saw the error of his ways, he was dealing drugs at Margaret Hance Park. Here in downtown Phoenix. That's where he thinks the video was filmed."

"Thinks?" the sandy man said.

"Play the video," I said.

Renfro looked at me. He reached down and opened his briefcase and took out an old electronic tablet. He fiddled with it for a couple of minutes, then I could hear the video start. He paused it and set it up on Mendoza's desk where we could all see it. Mendoza stood and moved around to where he could see it too. Renfro tapped the screen and the video played.

When it ended, Nacho said, "Play it again. Show me how to pause it."

Renfro started it again, then immediately tapped the screen to pause it. "Just tap on this," he said to Nacho. Nacho reached over and tapped the screen and the video began again. He watched it intently, then halfway through he tapped the screen and it paused. He pointed over the talking man's shoulder.

"See that tree with the bush trimmed around it? I can take you to it. Just to the right and back a ways, just out of sight, is a little jungle gym for the kids."

"That could be any tree," Sandy-man said.

Nacho looked at me and shook his head, like *see*.

Renfro looked at Mendoza. "So there are drug dealers doing business right in the heart of Phoenix. Dozens of policemen patrolling the area, right next to a children's playground?"

"The safest place for the fly is on the flyswatter," I said.

Mendoza took his jacket off the hat rack. "Let's go look at a tree."

22

We were standing in the middle of the park and Renfro played the video a half-dozen times. It was the tree. Mendoza already had the SWAT guys there before we arrived, and they were swarming the park and the surrounding neighborhoods.

"They don't really expect them to still be here?" Nacho said.

I shook my head.

"I'm surprised I didn't recognize at least one of them," he said.

Boyce was standing a few feet off. She heard him and came over.

"Why is that?" she asked.

He shrugged, "Why would they choose this spot unless one of them had been here? Knew the place. Probably did some business here. And I already know most of those guys."

"Drug dealers blowing up shit in Sedona in the name of Allah?" I said.

"Lot of so-called Muslims in the joint," he said. "Somebody

goes to the joint, if they don't have a gang they get one. If they don't have a religion, they get one. It's how you survive. Lot of the black guys become Muslims. You know, Malcom X and Mohammad X and that kinda shit. Some Mexicans too, unless they belong to MS13 or the Mafia. Guys get really radicalized in the joint. You become a skinhead or a mafia guy or a Muslim, they teach you to hate everyone. Everyone that ain't like you. With the Muslims you had to be the right kind of Muslim, and you know who the Muslims are 'cause they get on their knees and pray several times a day."

"How did you survive?" Boyce asked innocently.

He smiled that smile of his. He'd had all his teeth capped and they looked like they belonged to a movie star.

"'Cause I was the meanest motherfucker in the joint."

"Of course," she said without smiling. She looked at me. "We have a line on the room in Cottonwood where your guy Ramirez was staying. We have a team there seeing if they can lift some prints, maybe get some DNA. Find out who the guy really is."

"You'll let me know?"

"Sure."

"Might get you in trouble with Renfro."

"Fuck Renfro," she said, and my phone rang.

It was Blackhawk.

"You and Nacho going to be much longer?"

"Don't have to be."

"Good, I have a situation here."

23

When Nacho and I got back to El Patron they were sitting in the main room at the bar. It was Blackhawk and Elena and a smallish man with long, greasy black hair that curled around his ears. His suit and shoes were black and shiny like his hair. He looked like a pimp.

As we came out of the hallway and into the bar, Nacho said, "Crap," under his breath.

"You know this guy?" I asked as we moved across the dance floor.

"Elena's cousin," he said under his breath. "He's a shit bag, but she loves him. Family." He said all this without moving his lips. The last word was said with a certain disgust. They watched us approach.

They were seated at the bar at the spot where Nacho normally read his morning paper. Blackhawk sat on the corner. Sat isn't the right word. He occupied the stool like a dancer occupies a stage. Elena was next to him; she was half turned looking at her cousin and the cousin sat, perched on his stool like a canary, his feet not touching the foot rail.

When Elena turned to look at us, I realized that I had never really seen her angry. Now she was angry.

I took the seat on the other line of the corner, next to Blackhawk. Nacho remained standing.

"This is Elena's cousin, Luis Diaz. He's got himself in a little bit of a pickle," Blackhawk said, his face not showing anything. The man didn't look up.

Elena looked at me. "Blackhawk has convinced me to include you in this," she said. "I don't want to, but my cousin has done something stupid and if he doesn't fix it, he will be killed."

Her eyes welled up.

The little man, Luis, started to say something and she turned and slapped him so hard it almost took him off the stool.

"Estupido!"

Diaz covered up, afraid she'd hit him again. She slid off her stool and went up the stairs. She didn't look back.

Blackhawk had turned and watched her go. He turned back to me.

"Luis is a mule. He drives a truck across the border at Douglas. He brings marijuana and coke, and sometimes heroin, into Phoenix. He carries cash back across."

He turned to Luis. "Tell Jackson what happened."

The man had a red spot on his cheek and his eye watered from Elena's blow.

"I was tricked," he said.

"Tell me," I said.

He looked at Blackhawk. "Can I get a beer, or something?"

"Tell him before I slap you," Blackhawk said.

He swallowed and looked at me. "I had a run back south, and I had chorizo and eggs for breakfast."

Nacho snorted, "Nobody gives a shit about what you had for breakfast."

"It's the reason I had to stop. I think the chorizo was bad. I got out of Tucson and all of a sudden I had to drop a deuce. I mean real bad, so I know of this place between Benson and St. David. It's like a Circle K. It has toilets on the outside of the building so you don't have to go in. I pulled in and parked to the side. I barely made it."

Blackhawk glanced at me, a tired look on his face. "Get on with it."

"When I got done I couldn't get out," he continued.

"You couldn't get out," I said.

"The door was jammed. I panicked. I thought someone was jamming me in so they could fuckin' rob me, which at the time, I thought was stupid because if someone stole money from the people I work for, they're dead."

"But that's what happened," I said.

He nodded. "I started yelling and a guy that just happened to be there waiting to use the john opened the door from the other side."

"But you were robbed."

"I didn't know it at the time. I checked the truck and the cash is hidden really good, and I didn't dare tear everything apart to check on it and I couldn't see that anything had been moved, so I kept going."

"But you were robbed," Blackhawk said again.

He nodded. "When I got to our warehouse and they unloaded, the money was gone. I about shit my pants."

"The guy that let you out, do you know him?"

"Just some guy. Never saw him before."

"Why are you still alive?"

He was sweating now. He reached across the bar and picked up a paper napkin. He mopped his face and neck. "They gave me a week to get the money back."

"That was generous, who stole it?"

He shrugged. "I don't know; if I did, I'd go and get it back."

Nacho snorted. Almost a laugh, but not quite.

"Who do you work for?" I asked.

"Emilio Garza is the main guy."

"Who does Garza work for?"

He shrugged. "He works for the family."

"The Valdez cartel."

He nodded.

I looked at Blackhawk. He was studying his fingernails. I looked at Nacho. He shook his head, disgusted with the whole thing. I looked back to Diaz.

"You got someplace to stay, they don't know about?"

He looked at Blackhawk. "I thought I would stay here."

Blackhawk didn't look up. "You thought wrong." Blackhawk looked at Nacho. "Take him to the Best Western by I-17, check him in under your name." He looked at Diaz. "There's a restaurant attached, eat all your meals there. Don't leave the room except to eat."

"What the hell am I going to do all day?" He was whining.

"Play with yourself, watch TV, what the hell do I care?" Blackhawk said. "But if you leave, you are on your own."

"What are you going to do?"

"Whatever Elena wants me to do, which, luckily for you, will probably save your life."

24

After Nacho and Diaz left, I followed Blackhawk upstairs. Elena had a lighted mirror set up on the ottoman and was applying her makeup. I flopped on an overstuffed leather chair and hung one leg over the arm.

Still applying her lipstick, Elena said, "Are you going to help Luis?"

"No," I said.

She looked up at me, her eyes flashing.

"I'm going to help Blackhawk and I'm going to help you, but I don't give a damn about Luis."

"I don't give a damn about him either. But he is family and I do give a damn about Aunty Lorraine. He is her oldest. If he dies, it will break her heart." She pursed her lips in the mirror, studying her handiwork.

I pulled out my phone and dialed the marina store. Eddie and I had a lot in common, one of which was an aversion to electronic devices. They had swarmed across the world like a horde of locusts and while I had succumbed to the phone, Eddie had resisted it, and all else. He figured if you wanted to talk to him, come and sit, have a conversation. If you wanted to be entertained, go fishing. He absolutely hated the fact that you couldn't repair a modern automobile without a diagnostic computer. He figured that if you wanted to know what was behind you while backing your vehicle, you could turn and look. What are mirrors for? I once asked him if he liked the access to information the internet gave him. He replied that at his age he already knew everything he needed to know. He said old people don't forget things, they just have so many more memories to sift through. It takes longer.

One of the new kids answered the store phone, and I gave him my number and asked him to pass it on to Eddie when he came in. He said he would. I had my doubts.

I dialed Boyce. To my complete surprise, she answered.

"Boyce."

"It's me."

"I know."

"Have you heard any more about Ramirez?"

"I'm working right now," she said. "We'll talk later."

I started to hang up when I heard Renfro's tinny voice say, "Who was that?"

"My sister," Boyce said, her voice fainter. She had not disconnected and was obviously holding the phone so I could hear. Boyce didn't have a sister. "So what were you saying about the fingerprints at the boardinghouse?"

"We lifted clean prints in the bathroom. Ramirez is really Ali Ibrahim Atef," said Renfro's tinny voice. "He was born in the U.S. while his Jordanian father was part of a diplomatic mission here. So he has citizenship. When he was a child, his father was assigned to a mission in Venezuela, and he learned to speak Spanish fluently."

"That's why he could pass for Hispanic, and why he can travel in and out of the U.S." Boyce said.

"Exactly. When he came of age he returned to the U.S. and subsequently began to get in more and more trouble, eventually doing three years for assault, drug running and money laundering. That's why we have the prints."

"Sounds like a sweetheart."

"While he was inside, he converted, or should I say, re-converted to Islam. The radical version. After he got out, he disappeared. The last the State Department had was that he was trained by militias in Iraq and fought with the IS in Syria."

"How do we find him?" she asked.

"How would you find him?"

"Put his face out everywhere. Somebody knows where he is."

"Soon as we do that, he'll go to ground."

"He's already gone to ground," she said. There was silence, then a rustling sound. I could hear some more rustling. She was moving away from him. Then I could hear his faint voice. He was talking to someone else.

"Guy's an asshole," she said in my ear, in a low tone. "Did you hear what he said?"

"Yes, don't know what I'll do with it, but I appreciate it."

"I'm sending you a picture of Ramirez. Hang up and look at it, then call me back."

I disconnected. A moment later, my phone buzzed. I managed to thumb the appropriate places to bring the picture up. The picture was cropped in tight to Ramirez's face. He wasn't smiling. He was a handsome, dark-haired man. His eyes were baleful, dark and empty. I called Boyce back.

"You get it?"

"Yeah, it might help."

"I hope so," she said. "If my phone is bugged, I'm out of a job and probably in prison."

"They'd bug your phone?"

"Jackson, you have no idea what they will do."

"What about freedom of speech?"

She barked a short laugh and disconnected.

25

I showed the picture to Blackhawk, but his mind was on something else.

"You think it's Dos Hermanos took the money?" Blackhawk asked.

"Dos Hermanos?" Dos Hermanos – two brothers - was a heavy rival cartel to Valdez. The Consul General of Columbia, the girl's grandpa, was heavily connected to Valdez.

"If it was Dos Hermanos, it would start a war," I said. "They don't want that."

"Someone else then," he said. "Wonder who?" We both looked at Elena. Elena had packed up her mirror and cosmetics, and was starting out of the room. She turned to look at us. Each. One at a time.

"You help him," she said. She left the room.

Blackhawk watched after her for a moment, then turned to me, shaking his head. "I don't think she knows what she's asking."

"She knows. Any ideas?"

He shrugged, "Maybe go see if Mr. Escalona knows anything. They owe us a favor."

The Columbian Consul was in Los Angeles, but they had a consulate office in Phoenix that worked with Arizona on South American issues. Santiago Escalona was the ambassador's man in Arizona.

"Not sure I want to waste a favor on a pissant like Diaz," I said, watching the door Elena had disappeared out of.

"The old Don said if you ever needed anything...."

"Do you want me to? For Elena?"

"No. How about our old friend Emil?" Emil was Escalona's muscle. He had helped in snatching the girl back from Dos Hermanos.

"Yeah, I like that. He won't tell us anything that Escalona doesn't want him to. But it won't be like calling in a chit from the ambassador."

Blackhawk's phone buzzed and he pulled it from his pocket.

"Hello," he said formally. He was always formal on the phone. Please and thank you and how do you do. He listened, then, "I'm going to be gone. I need you at the club." He hung up and put the phone in his pocket. He looked at me. "Nacho. He got Diaz checked in."

Elena came back into the room. She wore a wide straw hat and bright red sunglasses that covered half her face. They matched her huge red purse.

"I'm going to Scottsdale for shopping. I'll be back for the first show." She leaned down and kissed Blackhawk on the cheek. She went out the door without looking back.

"When do you want to go see Emil?" I asked.

Blackhawk stood. "No time like the present."

We took the Mustang. Escalona's office was in the same place. A tall, fancy high rise office building in downtown Phoenix, on Adams. There was a convenient spot open on the street next to a fire hydrant. I pulled the Mustang in and parked.

The consulate office occupied a half a floor. Stepping off the elevator, nothing had changed. The same seal of Columbia was on the glass of the doors. We pushed them open and stepped in. The receptionist was new. Just as striking as the last, but new. She had the same uniform. A black skirt and crisp white blouse. Like the old receptionist, her white blouse was straining to contain her. Also like the old one, her eyes barely left Blackhawk. I guess I'm going to have to get me one of those two thousand dollar silk suits.

"May I help you?"

"We are here to see Emil," I said, giving her the killer smile. It didn't seem to faze her. Mostly because she wasn't looking at me.

Watching Blackhawk, she said, "I'm afraid we don't have anyone here by that name." She sounded almost disappointed.

"Big guy. Bald. Muscles. Likes to shoot things."

She shook her head, her eyes flitting on me, then again resting on Blackhawk.

"I'm sorry," she said. "Is there anything else?"

Blackhawk turned his back and began studying a painting on the wall.

"If anyone that answers that description happens to

wander through here, please tell him that Jackson and Blackhawk are across the street at the Einstein Brothers eating a bagel."

"Jackson and Blackhawk?" she finally looked at me.

"Yes ma'am, Jackson and Blackhawk."

"You are making that up."

"Only the names, ma'am, the bagels will be real."

She wasn't amused. "I'm sorry, as I have already told you, there is no one here named Emil."

"We'll be waiting," I said, winking at her, but it was wasted. I'd lost her attention again. Blackhawk turned and looked at me, a small smile on his face. I hoped the girl didn't see it. If she did, she might wet herself. We turned and left.

In the hallway, as I punched the elevator button, I looked back through the glass doors. She was still watching Blackhawk.

Einstein Brothers was like Starbucks; there was one on every block in every city in the world. This one was across the street, and down mid-block. We went in and ordered plain coffee, which threw the girl behind the counter for a loop. We redeemed ourselves by buying two parmesan bagels. We sat at a table for two at the window. Halfway through the coffee and bagel, I saw Emil come out of his office building. He stood on the curb and looked across at my car. He wore a tailored dark suit and a red tie. Emil was built like a redwood. Tall, wide and solid, without an ounce of fat. His bald head gleamed in the sun. We knew him to be a very dangerous man, and an excellent shot. He jaywalked across, dodging the traffic, moving like a dancer. A moment later he was coming in the door.

Emil was smiling. "I thought Rain was joking," he said. "You made an impression."

"Rain? The receptionist?"

"Yeah, I think her name is Betty or Beverly or something, but she wants everyone to call her Rain."

"Does she know how to joke?"

"Probably not." He snagged a chair from an adjacent table. "She's too young to not take herself seriously."

"Is that a double negative?" I said.

"She's new," Blackhawk said.

Emil reached across and took my coffee cup. He took a sip, made a face and set it back down.

"Never took you for a sweetener guy," he said. "Mr. Escalona changes receptionists like other men change their socks. He keeps them for his amusement until they start thinking they deserve to be a permanent part of his life. He is a very happily married man. This a social call?"

"You think?" Blackhawk said.

He smiled. "What's up?" He had been born and raised in Columbia but he had no accent. He could have been born in Toledo for all you could tell.

"You know Blackhawk's woman, Elena?" I said.

"Beautiful woman."

"Indeed. She has a cousin that has been muling dope out of Mexico and smuggling cash back for the Valdezs."

"Diaz?"

"You know him?"

"I know what the street knows."

"What else do you know?"

"Somebody heisted the money."

"You know who?"

"The street thinks it's Diaz. If Valdez thought that, your woman's cousin would be dead now. As it is, I don't think your woman's cousin will live very long."

"It would make Elena very sad," Blackhawk said. "Jackson and I want to get the money back and cut a deal to exchange it for the mule's life."

"Admirable. How do you intend to do that?"

"We were hoping that you might have some idea. Diaz came to us, or rather, came to Elena with his sob story. If he had stolen the cash, why isn't he running as fast as he can?"

Emil reached over and picked up the remnant of my bagel. He tore off a piece and began munching on it. He set the remainder back on my napkin.

"Good question," he said.

"Not Dos Hermanos?" Blackhawk said.

Emil looked at him with a faint smile, "We would know." He leaned back in his chair and crossed his arms. "You boys are smart," he said.

"Meaning we can figure it out," I said.

Emil just looked at me.

"Okay, I'll play. I would guess," I continued, "very few people knew about the run and fewer still would know how the money was hidden."

He nodded.

"And if someone did lift it while Diaz was in the crapper

they would have to know where it was, to get it out so fast."

"Does he know how it was hidden?" Blackhawk said.

I looked at Emil. "Do the drivers know how the money is hidden?"

"What do you think?"

"That would be pretty stupid, wouldn't it? So he might be telling the truth," Blackhawk said.

"It's possible," Emil said. "But I doubt if that helps him."

"If we got the money back, would they trade for him?"

Emil shrugged. "They are hard people. It is hard to say."

"Would Diaz's boss man know how the money was stashed?"

"Possible."

"Emilio Garza?"

He looked at me for a long time. Finally, he shrugged.

"Diaz worked for Garza," I continued. "Think you can introduce me?"

"You mean like a networking mixer?"

"Can you set it up?" I said.

He stood.

"Your funeral," he said.

26

Elena was a good singer, but she was a great entertainer. Her main music was salsa but she'd mix in other popular music. She had the crowd captivated with her own slowed-down and sultry rendition of the Stones' *Satisfaction*. There was blood flowing to every male groin in the place.

Not mine, of course, Blackhawk was my friend.

Maybe I was wrong; I felt a vibration down there.

It was my phone. I thumbed it out of my pocket. It was Eddie.

"Hold on while I get out to where I can hear you," I said. I had been leaning against the bar. I stepped out into the busy hallway. It was a little quieter.

"So the kid did give you my message," I said.

"What message?" His voice had a tinny, echo-like sound.

"I called the store and asked the kid to have you call me."

"Shit no, he didn't tell me. I'm at the store, and the nosepicker didn't tell me anything."

"Figures. What's up?"

"Wondering if you talked with Joe Whitney?"

"I did. Nothing new except both those dead guys were in the same militia, and we already knew that. But the Sedona bombers released a video claiming credit. Call themselves Khorasan America." I spelled it.

"Same assholes, different name."

"Radical group out of Syria and Iraq. They hate America so I guess they want to bring it to us, up close and personal."

"Dirt bags."

"Yeah, but something interesting. You remember Nacho?"

"Hard to forget."

"Yeah," I smiled. "Anyway, he took one look at the video and identified where it was shot. Called it his backyard, Hance Park in Phoenix. He used to deal drugs there before he did his time. But the really interesting thing is that the shit bag in the video was ID'd by two separate people. Whitney and the headless guy's wife, Lucy."

"They know him?"

"Said it was Ramirez, the guy that was at the bar when Billy and Mooney fought. And Ramirez was in their militia."

There was silence on the other end and I thought I had lost him. There was thunderous applause from the other side of the door. Evidently Elena had finished *Satisfaction* satisfactorily.

"Are you still there?" I said.

"Yeah," he said. "That is damned interesting."

"Better yet, Boyce's federal guys have identified Ramirez as the son of a Jordanian diplomat. His real name is Ali Ibrahim Atef."

"Jordanian, not Mexican."

"Spent time in South America. Speaks Spanish fluently. He apparently was radicalized in prison."

"Passing for Mexican."

"If you had a cell phone, I'd send you his picture."

"Fuck cell phones."

The hallway was filled with El Patron customers roaming between the three nightclubs. Over the milling heads I saw a large, perfectly bald head that was a good four inches taller than anyone else. Emil had two guys with him. Except for standing next to Emil, they would have seemed to be very large themselves. One had a full head of curly black hair and a swarthy, droopy moustache. The other was as bald as Emil, but his wifebeater shirt showed his thin and muscular body. Both were marked with homemade pin and ink prison tats.

"I gotta go," I said. "Call me once a day to check in, okay? Just so I don't have to talk to the nosepicker."

"Will do," he said and disconnected.

Emil saw me and started forward. The crowded hallway parted for him like the Red Sea parted for Moses.

I put my phone in my pocket and leaned against the wall. When they reached me, I opened the door and waved them into the main room. Emil barely acknowledged me as he moved past, but the other two looked at me with naked curiosity.

I moved past Emil and they followed me to the bar. Blackhawk and Nacho were behind it, helping Jimmy with the large crowd. I caught Blackhawk's eye. He came over.

I leaned across the bar.

"Can I use your office?" I said above the din.

He looked at Emil and the other two, taking his time. He nodded. "It's open."

I looked at Emil and nodded toward the stairs. They followed me. The crowd didn't part for me the same as for Emil. I took them through the landing doorway. The hallway that went the length of the building sported his two doors. One to his living quarters, the other to his office. The office door opened into a foyer. The foyer was a small waiting room furnished much more richly than Lawyer Taggart's. I wondered who Blackhawk would keep waiting in here. Beer salesmen probably. The back wall sported a closed door and his office was behind it. As usual it was tastefully furnished. He had expensive-looking paintings on the walls and a plush, burgundy rug. The wall behind the desk sported a one-way window overlooking the bar below. I moved around the large mahogany desk and glanced down to see that Elena had started another number, and the dance floor was full. The room was soundproof, and for all the activity below, I couldn't hear a thing. I sat in Blackhawk's chair. I felt like the pretender to the throne. Emil's two friends remained standing until Emil waved at the leather couch that stretched across one wall. They sat. Emil sat in the leather brass-studded, high-backed arm chair. Without moving much, I placed my hand on my right leg, then lifted it so the back of my hand touched the Sig Sauer that was held in place by a magnet. Still there.

"Can I get you a drink?" I asked.

Emil nodded, "Whiskey."

I looked at the other two. "Sure," said the curly-headed one.

I got up and went to the wet bar. He had a half-empty bottle of Jack Daniels. I normally see a glass as half-full. When it's a whiskey bottle I see it as half-empty. I got four glasses and poured an inch in each. I carried them over and handed them to Emil's friends. I gave Emil his, and took mine back to the desk. I sat and took a small sip.

"Introduce me," I said to Emil. He seemed amused.

He indicated Curley. "This is Emilio Garza." He nodded at baldy. "That is Rojo."

"Red?" I said.

Rojo emptied his glass, looking at me with unfriendly eyes. I was disappointed. I'd hoped we could be friends. He was tall and stringy, his skin the color of coffee with cream. He wore a diamond-studded crucifix on a slender gold chain.

Emilio Garza stared at me with dark-eyed intensity. He held his glass but didn't drink.

"This is Jackson," said Emil.

"Yeah, you told us," Garza said.

Emil turned slightly to look at him. "Don't underestimate him," he said flatly.

Garza took that in, but didn't respond. He looked at me. "You wanted to talk," he said. "Talk."

"I like a man that gets right down to business," I said. "The lady you saw singing downstairs is a very good friend of mine."

Garza turned to Emil. "We come here for him to talk about his *Puta*?"

"Her mother's sister has an eldest son," I continued. "His name is Luis Diaz."

154

I had his attention.

"A dead man," he said.

"Maybe," I said. "I would like you to answer some questions. I intend to find your money and bring it back to you."

He studied me. "Why the hell would you do that?"

"In exchange for Diaz's life."

"You're crazy. For some *Puta's* cousin?"

I looked at him. I didn't even try to look tough, "You call her a *Puta* again and I will shoot you."

He slid his shirttail back to reveal a pearl-handled pistol in his belt. He was giving me that stare-down look that he thought made him look like a really bad man.

"You will be dead before you even touch it," I said. My hand was already on the Sig Sauer.

Emil tossed his whiskey back. "Maybe you two can stop playing big dick, little dick, and," he looked at Garza, "why don't you answer his questions."

Garza stared at me for a long time, then looked at Emil. He shrugged. He pulled his shirt back over the pistol. He looked back at me.

"What do you want to know?"

27

I moved my hand from the Sig Sauer, but left it lightly on my thigh.

"Did Diaz know where the money was hidden on his truck?"

Garza smiled. "We are not stupid. The mules know nothing. They don't come to the truck until it is time to drive."

"Is it always hidden in the same place?"

"No."

"Is there an infinite number of places for it to be hidden on the trucks?"

Rojo said, "What's that mean?"

Garza held up a hand.

"I know what you are asking. It is a good question. No, there are only three ways we have moved the money."

"How many men are aware where the money can be placed?"

"Only one man knows. But we have others to load the trucks."

"How many trucks?"

Again, he looked at Emil.

Emil nodded.

"Five," he said.

"Does the same man hide the money on each truck?"

"No," he said. "Each truck has its own man. These are our most trusted."

"But usually only three places on the truck?"

"Yes."

"So four other men had a one in three chance of knowing where the money was placed on Diaz's truck?"

Garza didn't answer, but I could see him thinking.

"Was Diaz late? Did he have time to stop and find the money, then put everything back?"

"There is a window of time," Garza said. "If a driver is detained, like there is a road closure or mechanical trouble, or any reason at all they will be late, they are to call immediately. Their life depends on it."

"And Diaz didn't call."

He shook his head.

"So Diaz was within acceptable limits?"

Garza nodded.

"So, how long would it take Rojo, here, to find the money on the truck?"

"Rojo worked on Diaz's truck."

I looked at Rojo. He stared back.

"So another truck. How long for him to find the money on another truck?"

"He wouldn't."

"Never? Let's say he has all the time in the world. He could empty the truck and take everything on it apart, piece by piece. Then start on the truck itself."

"Unless he was fuckin' lucky, it could be hours."

"Did Rojo place the money on Diaz's truck?"

"No."

"What about the guy that placed the money. How trustworthy is he? Has he disappeared?"

For the first time, he smiled.

"The only guy in the whole world I completely trust."

"Really? Who is that?"

"Me," he said.

I leaned back and studied him. Emil stood and went to the bar and poured some more into his glass; he offered me some. I shook my head. He didn't offer any to the other two. He returned to his chair and sipped his drink. They didn't look as if they expected to be offered any.

"How long were you in the joint?" I asked Garza.

He studied me. "Which time? I've enjoyed several vacations."

That made me smile. "A friend of mine once told me that if you go inside and if you don't have a religion, you get a religion; if you don't belong to a gang, you get a gang."

"Your friend has been inside."

"He said that some men became Muslim. He said they were different. If you were Muslim, it depended on which kind of Muslim you were as to which gang you joined."

"Yeah, it ain't like the blacks or the skinheads. There were two groups of Muslims. Muslims would turn on each other."

"There is a man I am interested in. It has nothing to do with Diaz. It is a different matter. He passes for a Mexican but he is a Jordanian. While he was inside he was recruited by the Muslims. Recruited to be a terrorist. If you were looking for this particular man. A Muslim that had been inside, but was out now. If you were looking for such a man, where would you look?"

He looked at Emil. "This guy a cop?"

Emil smiled and shook his head.

"Why should I help you?" Garza said.

"That is a legitimate question," I said, taking another small sip from my glass. I set it carefully on the coaster. "Maybe the day will come that I can do you a favor."

He studied me, glanced at Emil, then studied me some more.

"This man did his Excellency a very large favor that he didn't have to do," Emil said, indicating me. "His Excellency was very grateful."

"The answer is easy," Garza finally said.

"Easy?" I said.

"Sure. A guy like that, out in the world, won't stay away from a mosque or some kinda mosque for very long. Not if he is truly into it. Their religion is tough, no booze, no women, of course which is bullshit. They break those rules all the time. But they stick together. More than other guys. He'll find his own kind. They were the most fucking paranoid men I ever saw."

"So he will show up in the Muslim community?"

"Some time or another."

"These two different kinds of Muslim. Could you tell them apart in the joint? One group dresses differently or something. How do you tell one kind of Muslim from another?"

"Fucked if I know."

I looked at Rojo. "What was loaded on Diaz's truck?"

Rojo looked at Garza. Garza looked at Emil.

"Oranges," Garza finally said.

28

Father Correa ran a downtown shelter for homeless, battered and troubled women. I found a parking spot a block and a half away. The weather was typical sunny Phoenix weather. It promised to be hot later. The building was a nondescript brick structure of undetermined age. It had no windows facing the street which made me believe that at one time, it had been a warehouse. It still had the small *Safehouse* sign by the front door. The door was unlocked. It was always unlocked.

The good Father was in his office, which had not changed at all since I had been there. He sat behind a metal industrial desk on a secretary's chair. The coffeepot was still the old stained one, still half-full and still on the dented file cabinet. I couldn't look at Father Correa without thinking he was a cross between Sancho Panza and Friar Tuck. If anything, he was a little rounder, his gray hair a little whiter, since the last time I saw him.

He looked up and broke into a broad smile. He came around the desk and grabbed me in a bear hug.

"Jackson! It is so good to see you again." He waved at a folding chair. "Sit, can I get you some coffee?"

"No thanks, Father," I said. "I've already had a pot."

He moved back around the desk and sat. He was beaming at me. I think he spent most of his day beaming. It was a little disconcerting to know someone who was so damned happy all the time. Especially when he was surrounded by other people's misery.

"So you have finally come around to accept my undying gratitude?"

I smiled. "I have no idea what you are talking about."

"Of course not. An anonymous donor to the end."

His Excellency, the Consul General of Columbia had been very grateful and very generous when Blackhawk and I had returned his granddaughter. To Blackhawk's credit, he had said not one word when we came to Safehouse, and left a satchel of money on Father Correa's desk. It's a long story.

"Is this a social call?" he asked, a twinkle in his eye.

"Afraid not. You have heard of the bombings in Sedona?"

The twinkle went away. I can find a way to ruin a happy mood. "Yes. Terrible things. I was doing laundry when I noticed all the girls gathered around our new television set. A nice flat screen, I might add. Courtesy of our anonymous donor. They were showing videos of the bombing."

"I'm looking for a man. A converted, radicalized Muslim, who is involved. I believe he's in the Phoenix area and will probably be associating with others like him. I'm wondering if you know anyone of the Muslim persuasion connected here that might help me find him?"

He thought about it. He clasped his meaty hands and leaned forward on the desk, "I belong to the All Faith Ecumenical Council of Arizona," he said. "I have worked with Mullah Ghazi on various committees. He is a good man and works and believes in peace between all peoples. This man you seek, tell me more about him."

"Not much is known. His name is Ali Ibrahim Atef. He is the son of a Jordanian diplomat and spent a lot of his childhood in South America where the father was stationed."

I thumbed my phone out and brought Atef's picture up. I showed it to him.

"He speaks fluent Spanish and has passed himself off as a Hispanic and called himself Ramirez. He has spent time in prison and while there he was radicalized, and joined a group calling itself Khorasan America. It's an offshoot of ISIL."

"Terrible people," he said.

"Not sure they are people. He has been trained in Iraq and Syria and has fought with militias in both places. He's the guy that set off the bombs here. Him and his buddies. I think he is the guy that took off one man's head and another man's hand up in Cottonwood."

"I read about that. I didn't put the two together."

"I'm pretty sure they are connected."

"If you know this, then I would guess that the authorities know it. Why are you involved in this?"

I told him about Eddie and Billy.

He leaned back and rubbed his chin. "It's a long way from Syria and Iraq to Cottonwood."

"Here's what scares me: I think he and his buddies are practicing for something."

"Practicing for what?"

"I was at the Sedona bombing right after it happened. It could have been much worse. Much, much worse. It was like they weren't trying for maximum murder. They videotaped it. You don't usually see that. Usually any video of a bombing is made by surveillance cameras, or a lucky tourist. This was like a dry run. They wanted to study their handiwork."

"That's a very frightening thought."

"Yes, it is. And I don't think for a moment that Billy Bragg took Mr. Mooney's head off. My primary goal has been to find who murdered Mooney and now that's led me to Atef. I have been told that Sunni Muslims stick with Sunni Muslims and Shias stick with Shias. If your friend can shed some light on where Atef might show up, maybe we can stop this."

"Why do you think your man is in Phoenix instead of still up north?"

"Did I ever introduce you to Nacho?"

"The Indian gentleman?"

I laughed, "No, that's Blackhawk. I don't think you met Nacho. Nacho works for Blackhawk. Nacho is an ex-con. He did the crime and did the time. He doesn't want to go back. Did you also see the video released by the assholes claiming credit for the bombing? Excuse my language."

He smiled, "No, assholes is about right. Yes, I saw that also."

"Back in Nacho's bad times he dealt drugs at Margaret

Hance Park. He IDed the park as where the video was shot. It proved to be right. These guys are in Phoenix."

"Do the police know this?"

"Of course. They are keeping it low. Don't want to spread panic."

He rubbed his chin. "Yes, I can see that." He leaned forward, his elbows on the desk. "Jackson, you may be the most unusual man I've ever met. Why are you involved in this?"

"Eddie is a friend of mine."

He smiled and nodded. "Yes, with you that would be enough."

He was silent a moment.

He said, "Mullah Ghazi is a Sunni. I believe most Muslims are. Do you know which side of the aisle Mr. Atef sits on?"

"No. That might be good to know."

"Probably. There has been a rift between the two sides since six hundred something AD when the Prophet Mohammed died. I will introduce you to the good mullah." He stood. "Can I show you around? Show you how some of the money our anonymous donor left has improved the lives of our girls? If you have time?"

"Always," I said.

29

Father Correa wrote a letter of introduction to Mullah Ghazi and I drove away from Safehouse feeling better than I had felt in a while. He had proudly displayed his new stainless steel kitchen with its oversized refrigerator and the large freezer which helped the donated food last much longer. There was new exercise equipment in the community room, and all the pieces were being used. There were also new changing tables throughout. He had been able to put in a new shower room. He also had a new, oversized washer and dryer. Both were running while I was there. I suspect they ran 24/7.

Mullah Ghazi's mosque was north and I grabbed the Black Canyon and sped toward the 101. It took a half hour. I saw the mosque while I was still some distance away. The building itself was white alabaster with a copper-gold dome. Actually, there were two buildings but that wasn't apparent until I pulled into the parking lot. From a distance, they looked like one large, blindingly white, building.

The parking lot only held a few cars. There was a small

sign at the end of the parking lot with the word *Office* and an arrow pointing toward the corner of the building. Since I had been meticulously trained in connecting even obscure dots, I headed that direction. Sure enough, around the corner was a double door with the word *Office* next to it. So smart and ever-aware.

I went through the doors and stepped to the counter that ran the length of the room. The girl behind the counter was dressed like any American girl anywhere except she was wearing a hijab. Not sure what I was expecting.

The girl looked up from her computer screen with a bright smile and a freckled nose and I noticed the small gap between her two front teeth. I'd bet she's a good spitter. I call her a girl because she looked to be thirteen. She had a wedding ring. The older I get, the worse I get at guessing ages.

"Can I help you, sir?"

"I'm here to see Mullah Ghazi," I said with my winning smile. Maybe it would work better here than it had worked on Rain. It should; I didn't have Blackhawk as a distraction. The girl managed to withstand it without a change in expression. Stoic.

"He's at prayer right now," she said. "Do you have an appointment?"

I held up the envelope with the letter of introduction and smiled as if it explained everything. She glanced at it and then turned to look at a clock on the wall.

"He should be available in a few minutes. Would you care to wait?"

"Certainly," I said.

"May I tell him your name please?"

"Jackson," I said.

"Oh, yes. He's expecting you."

"Father Correa called?"

"I have no idea, sir. He just said to expect you. If you'll have a seat, Mr. Jackson."

Okay, older than thirteen.

There were chairs against one wall. I turned and sat down. I stretched my legs out and emptied my mind. I was good at waiting.

It didn't take long. Without, seemingly, anything happening, the girl suddenly stood and looked at me over the counter.

"The mullah is ready for you now."

She directed me through the interior door. This led to a hallway. His office was the first one on the left. He was standing as I entered.

He was a tall, angular man with olive-colored skin, a strong nose and piercing dark eyes. Each eye had its own matching, bushy, dark eyebrow hovering above it. The eyebrows matched his dark and bushy beard. He was dressed in white linen; the shirt was collarless and was covered with a sleeveless vest that was open and hung below his waist. He wore a white skull cap. His feet were bare.

The room was bright and casual. There were chairs and a small table with a laptop on it. There was no desk or any other office furniture. The floor was covered by a thick, rich looking rug with a pleasant pattern. It looked to be just an easy room to sit and read in. He held his hand out to me. I took it.

"Mr. Jackson. My friend, Father Correa, called to say to expect you."

I held up the letter as we released each other's hand. "He gave me a letter of introduction."

"I'll read it if you wish," he said with a smile. "But he had enough good things to say about you, I don't really need to."

"I think I'll blush now," I said.

"No need, the good Father is not given to false praise," he said waving me to a chair. We both sat.

"How can I be of assistance?"

"I won't take a lot of your time." I stopped. "I'm not sure how to address you."

"My parents called me Hassan. That will do."

"Thank you. I'm looking for a man. A Muslim. He was involved in the bombings in Sedona. I'm sure you are aware of them."

"Yes, Mr. Jackson. Quite aware. Unfortunate. Unfortunate for those in Sedona and unfortunate for the whole Muslim community. When these things occur, it seems we believers are all painted with the same brush."

I pulled out the thumb drive Blackhawk had made.

"Can I plug this into your laptop? I'd like to show you the men I'm looking for."

"By all means," Hassan said.

He turned the laptop so I could access it. He tapped the center pad and it came awake. I plugged the thumb drive in.

"You are more familiar with this one, maybe you could access the drive?" I said.

"Certainly," he said and began moving the mouse. He accessed the external drive and moved the cursor to it. A couple of clicks and the video started.

"Do you need the sound?" he asked.

"Not really. I'd like for you to look at this man in front."

"Is this the man, Ali Ibrahim Atef, Father Correa told me about?"

"We think so."

He leaned forward and studied the screen intently. When the video finished, he replayed it. When he looked up, he was shaking his head.

"I'm sorry. I have seen this before on the television, but I don't recognize any of these men."

I pulled the phone and brought Atef's picture up. I showed it to the mullah. He looked at it intently, then leaned back, shaking his head.

"Sorry," he said.

"Worth a try," I said. "Too much to hope. There are a lot of Muslims in the area."

"And I know most of them," he said. "If they were Shia, then I might not know them. Most likely they are just radicalized outsiders."

"If you were looking, where would you look?"

He leaned back, stroking his beard.

"I have been told of a small group on the west side. I've been told that they adhere to a more radical point of view than we do. But I've never heard of any violence from them."

"Where on the west side?"

"Somewhere on Avondale Boulevard in a strip mall, I

believe. I can't be certain. I've never had a reason to be in contact with them. The ones I'm familiar with are just regular people."

He stood. The meeting was over. I stood and extended my hand. He took it.

"Thank you very much for your cooperation," I said.

"Anything for a friend of Father Correa's."

As I stepped through the door and into the office, there was a man leaning against the counter. He had his wallet out and was showing his credentials to the young woman with the freckles. He looked at me with surprise. It was the sandy-haired agent I had met in Mendoza's office.

"What are you doing here?" he said.

I kept moving toward the door.

"Just morning prayers," I said. The girl looked confused. "What are you doing here?" I continued.

"My job," he said curtly.

"The mullah is free now," the girl said.

I had the outside door open.

He pointed at me. "You stick around. Wait for me in the parking lot. I want to talk to you."

I saluted and shut the door behind me.

The official Fed car was parked next to my Mustang. It was running. I slid into the front seat of the Mustang and looked across to the agent that was behind the wheel. I shot him with my forefinger and thumb and backed out and drove away.

30

I parked in the crowded asphalt lot in a space directly under
the light that illuminated that corner of the lot. I was next
to an older van. It looked tired. A light was on in the condo
I was interested in. I had never been here before, but I knew
where it was. It belonged to Boyce. It was where she had
moved when she moved off of Tiger Lily. It was a ground
floor unit in a middle-income complex. It was neat and tidy,
with enough grass to make it seem friendly.

I saw her little Miata parked under the cover of the reserved
parking that was numbered to coincide with her unit number.
It wasn't late. But late enough that most of the residents were
home and watching their TV shows, and eating their
microwavable dinners. Most all the parking slots were filled.

I walked across the still-warm asphalt and up the walk to
her door. The blinds were drawn. I rang the doorbell. I could
hear it chime faintly behind the door.

A moment later the door opened. Boyce had her hair
back, a glass of red wine in her hand and an apron on. Her
eyebrows went up.

"Jackson," she said.

"Boyce," I replied, ever the wit. "I thought I'd stop by and see how.." my voice trailed off as a man came into view. He too was holding a glass of red wine.

She turned to look.

"I'm sorry," I said. "I didn't know you had company. I should have called."

She smiled. "Come on in, I'll introduce you."

I felt like turning and running, but instead I stepped in. The man was about my height. He wore a light blue shirt and tie with the tie loosened and hanging down around his neck. He seemed young. He was good looking and seemed somehow familiar.

He stepped across the room with his hand outstretched, smile in place. A born salesman.

"Ronnie Hawkins," he said. I accepted his hand. He had one of those bone-crusher grips. The easy way to defend against that is to move your forefinger up on the wrist. This protects the bones in your hand when someone is trying to make them dust.

"Jackson," I said. "I'm sorry to interrupt."

"Not at all," he said with a smile that didn't tell me anything.

"Can I get you a beer?" Boyce asked.

"No, thanks, I truly was just close by and thought I would stop and check on you. See if you guys have made any progress." I didn't say progress in what, but I didn't have to.

"In the bombings?" Ronnie said.

"You've probably seen Ronnie on the morning news," Boyce said.

His smile got brighter and I realized that I had seen him making the report on the bombings while Eddie and I sat in the bar in Sedona with Dahlia and Megan.

"Yes, I believe I have," I said.

"Senior correspondent, Channel Five news," he said. He looked at Boyce, then at me." He smiled. "Maybe you can get more out of her than the local press can."

"I doubt it," I said.

"My lips are sealed by the U.S. government," she said, watching me with a twinkle. "I've invited Ronnie to enjoy my world-famous pasta and marinara sauce. Would you care to join us?"

"Oh, no thanks, I can't stay. I have dinner plans."

What I wanted to do was to tell good old Ronnie to turn and run fast. I've had Boyce's marinara sauce. Okay, I admit, I had lied and told her I really liked it.

"You sure you don't want to stay, dude," Ronnie said. "I'm sure the girl has made plenty."

Girl, I thought, remembering the shot in the shnoz she had given little Calvin in Cottonwood. I looked at Boyce and she was smiling very demurely.

"Very tempting," I said. "But truly, I can't."

"Who are you having dinner with?" Boyce asked.

My turn to be demure, "Not a who, a where."

"Where then?" she persisted.

"El Patron," I said, for lack of a better answer.

"Be sure to give my best to Blackhawk and Elena," she said.

"Blackhawk?" Ronnie said. "There's actually someone named Blackhawk?"

"A very real someone," Boyce said. "I'll tell you about him someday."

"Well, dude, don't let us keep you."

Dude?

I withstood the urge to smack him, and Boyce knew it and she thought it was funny. I looked at her. She returned a very innocent gaze.

"See you around," I said.

"Tell everyone I said hi," she said.

I turned to leave and did everything I could to not make it look like a full retreat.

31

As I drove out of Boyce's parking lot, I was muttering to myself. I had intended to head back to the boat, but now, since I had said I was going to El Patron, the Mustang just headed that way.

I felt a little foolish. It must be a male thing. When I had pulled up to Boyce's I had been perfectly content to enjoy our friendship, with no expectations of anything. At the same time, I could acknowledge the reasons we were no longer together. Everything was cool. But now, with old Ronnie in the picture I was suffering those irrational male competitive urges. Having proprietary feelings on things that weren't mine. How could I want something that I had already decided I didn't want? It wasn't rational. And besides, if I got it, would I want to keep it? Yeah, that was dumb. I pushed Boyce out of my mind and instead started concentrating on an icy cold shot glass of clear, pure, Arta tequila. That would do the trick.

El Patron was crowded but I got lucky and a blue Ford was pulling out of a spot in the middle of the lot. Once inside, I had to wait for a stool. That irritated me. Some gal in a tank top and very short shorts was sitting on my stool. Nacho and Jimmy were behind the bar. Nacho saw me and I mouthed the word *Arta*. A moment later handed me a rock glass with an inch of Arta in it. He reached it out, over the heads of the seated customers. I took it, gratefully. Nacho kept it refrigerated and it was cold and delicious. But I was still irritated at the girl on my stool. I glared at the back of her head. That'll teach her.

I had forgotten what night it was, but it had to be a night Elena was performing because the place was packed. A spot at the bar finally opened up, and I grabbed it. Nacho brought me another Arta and a glass of beer. A moment later, I waved the empty shot glass at him. He took it, refilled it and as he sat it in front of me he gave me a look.

"Something on your mind?" I asked above the noise of the crowd.

He shook his head, and moved away, a slight smile on his lips. I sipped my tequila, then the beer. The guy next to me turned, and looked up toward the landing that led to the living quarters. I turned to look, and Elena was descending the stairs. She was wearing a shimmering red gown that flowed behind her. She seemed to float down the steps. All she needed was a few half naked, muscular young men to be fanning her with palm fronds. Everyone in the room was watching. If she knew it, she didn't show it.

She reached the floor and her eyes locked on me and she came directly at me.

Uh oh.

I slid off my stool as she reached me. She leaned up and kissed me on the cheek.

"I am still very angry with you," she said in my ear. She took me by the upper arm and pulled me after her. I grabbed my beer with my free hand. All the men were watching.

She walked me through the crowd, and they parted for her like they had for Emil. She took me to a group that had three tables pulled together. There were nine people crowded around it. Four couples and an extra girl. They were all young, good looking and Hispanic.

"This is Jackson," she said to the group at large. She then moved me toward the extra girl. "Get him a chair." One of the men stood to fetch me a chair.

"This is my friend, Anita," she said. Anita was smiling up at me. She was pretty with long, very dark hair, brown eyes and a pleasantly plump figure. Her dress was very short and if her round thighs hadn't touched half way up there might have been trouble.

Everyone scooted around, and the extra chair was placed next to Anita. I turned to Elena but she was already moving to the band stand. I turned back and there were nine smiling faces all looking up at me. I sat my beer down, and took the seat.

"Hi," I said.

Still smiling, they all looked at Anita. Then they turned toward the band stand. The rest of the crowd had grown quiet in anticipation of Elena.

"Is Jackson your first name or your last name?" Anita said brightly. We were packed in so close my leg was firm against her thigh.

"Both," I said.

She laughed, "Jackson Jackson?"

Before I could respond, Nacho leaned over me and set another tequila in front of me. Jimmy was right behind him with drinks for everyone else.

"On Elena," Nacho said with no expression, but his eyes were howling with laughter.

Anita raised her new bottle of Modelo and said "Saluda." I touched her bottle with my glass.

As usual, Elena took off like a rocket and in seconds every available dance floor space was filled with dancers. Our table emptied as the couples got up to dance. This left Anita and me.

"You want to dance?" she shouted at me.

The thing about tequila is that it flows directly to your legs, which drains your brain and you start thinking you can dance.

"Be fools not to," I said. Such a wit. I stood up and dumped my chair over. Anita laughed and set it up. She took my hand and led me onto the floor. The good news was, no one but Anita was paying me any attention. And she turned out to be a really good dancer. She moved her round little body like a professional. We danced and danced until we were drenched and glistening. At last we took a break, and went to our table. Awaiting us was a bottle of fresh Modelo for Anita and two more tequilas and a fresh beer for me. Waste not, want not. In a moment of booze-infused clarity, I knocked the tequilas back.

I turned to look for Blackhawk but he wasn't there.

Nacho was busy and Elena had the crowd, and her red dress, moving. From then on it became a blur. We danced a lot more and at one point I remember looking at my feet as they moved in strange and wondrous ways. I marveled at why I had not known they could do that.

32

I knew I was badly hung over before I even opened my eyes. You feel it like you feel your soul. Dante's Inferno. On fire. A really cold, unforgiving fire. It's really deep. Like someone dug a hole in crap, and you are the hole. And your head is the crap.

A well-earned hangover has properties of its own. It's not so much a headache but more like the air around you has become ugly rocks, and very dense, and is pressing from the inside on all your sensitive places. Like your head. Like your stomach, and your chest and your arms and legs, and even your balls hurt. And your mouth is drier than you've ever experienced. So dry your teeth might turn to dust. And you wonder how you could have possibly got sand in your eyes.

Slowly, I realized I was lying face down. I tried to roll over and the only blessing was, whatever I was lying on had a back I could roll against. I half opened one eye and the room was dark. I realized I was on Blackhawk's couch in his office. There was a soppy wet spot where my face had been. I groaned as I sat up. I put my feet on the floor and the floor seemed to shift. I put my head in my hands and sat very still for a very long time. Finally, I stood and realized that I was still drunk.

I made my way to the small refrigerator Blackhawk kept next to his wet bar. I pulled a bottle of water and drank it all. I got another and drank it, then pulled another and drank half. I replaced the amount I had drunk with vodka. I shook it, took a drink and gagged. I waited until my stomach had ceased the revolt, then took another sip. It would take some hair of the dog to get me home. There was a mirror behind the bar, and a strange and ragged looking creature stared back at me. There was something wrong with my mouth. I rubbed the back of my hand across it. The back of my hand turned red with lipstick. I don't remember how it got there.

I took a deep breath and made my way out into the hallway and down the stairs, my hand trailing on the wall to keep me upright. To keep me on track. It was very early. No one was stirring yet. At the front door, I disarmed the alarm. I let myself out and rearmed the alarm. The Mustang was sitting in the faint dawn light. Right where I had left her. Out in the middle of the parking lot. All alone. The headlights and the grill were looking at me and she disapproved. She was not happy.

Despite her attitude, she started right up and I pointed her toward the Black Canyon. I gently sipped the life-giving water and vodka. I moved through the side streets quietly and carefully. Once on the highway the sun broke and it was painful. I drove very cautiously.

No one was stirring at the marina so there was no ride down the hill. The walk almost killed me. The boat was warm and musty and I cranked the air up on high and opened the bow and stern doors to get a cross breeze. I undressed and slipped my foot off. It didn't look so magical now. I looked longingly at the bed but slipped on my trunks, hopped out onto the stern deck not bothering with the swim foot, and before I could change my mind, I dove overboard.

It was awful. I made myself start swimming. I could see the headlines. *Unidentified body surfaces at lake. Drunken crawdads nibbling on it.* I gutted it out and kept swimming until I felt the body get into the old rhythms. Finally, I climbed the stern ladder, slipped out of the wet trunks and dried off. Tiger Lily had cooled off and I shut the doors, leaving the air cranked. I shook two aspirin out of the bottle, and washed them down with a beer. I looked at the water bottle with the vodka- water concoction where I had set it on the counter, and suppressed a gag reflex. I pulled the blackout curtains, set the alarms and fell on the bed. I was going to live.

33

When I opened my eyes, I lay for a very long time taking inventory. Except for being terribly thirsty and hungry, I was okay.

I picked up my trunks from off the floor and they were still cool and damp, but I put them on anyway. I started for the head when I stopped. You live on a boat for a long while and it becomes as familiar as a longtime lover. Its moves and creaks and attitudes are familiar. And now there was something wrong. I stood quietly for a long time. Finally, I turned and reached back for the Ruger I keep on the magnet on the back of the headboard.

I checked the alarms and they were armed. I pulled the curtains back and the outside world appeared to be enjoying mid-afternoon sunlight. I disarmed the alarms and went out the back. There were no boats nearby. I went up the ladder as quietly as a cat and my eyes followed the Ruger over the top.

Blackhawk was stretched out on a lounge chair. As usual, he was immaculate. Dressed in four hundred dollar slacks.

Tan loafers with tassels and no socks and a blindly white, crisp, shirt. So completely at ease, but so completely out of place in this marina. Especially on this old scow.

"Make yourself at home," I said.

"Thanks," he said.

I went back down and went to the head, then drank a glass of water. I put the Ruger back. I put on my foot, grabbed two cold beers from the locker and went back up. I handed him one of the beers. They had twist-off lids so we twisted them off. I drank half of mine in one swallow.

We sat in silence for a while. A good distance across the water, closer to the dam, an aluminum skiff bobbed on the waves the rising breeze was creating. A single man in the boat was fishing.

After a while, Blackhawk said, "Your phone is off."

"Probably dead," I said. "I don't remember when I charged it last."

"That'll do it."

I looked at him, "You nursemaiding me?"

He smiled. I could see my reflection in his sunglasses. "I had instructions to check on you."

"Elena?"

"About the only one I take instructions from. Everyone else makes suggestions."

"I'm fine," I said.

He nodded, "Sure. I was told to check anyway. You had a real good time last night."

"I'm fine," I said again. It sounded lame.

"Anita sends her regards."

"Shut up."

He grinned. "Elena said she has never seen anyone dance in quite that fashion."

"Shut the fuck up."

He laughed again. We sat in silence for a while.

"How'd you get up here?" I finally said.

He smiled. "You aren't the only trained operative that knows alarm systems. And you were snoring so I decided to wait up here."

"I don't snore," I said, finishing my beer. I collected his empty and went back down. I returned with two more. I handed him his and he twisted off the top and took a small drink.

"First for thirst, second for taste," he said, looking across the water. "That guy's been out there in the same spot since I've been here. I haven't seen him catch a fish."

I shaded my eyes and studied the fisherman.

"That's Eddie," I said. "If he thinks that is where the fish are, he'll sit there for hours."

"There are fish in the supermarket," he said.

"You miss the whole point."

"I never miss anything," he said.

I smiled, "Copy that."

"His nephew still in jail?"

"Far as I know."

"You think it was that Jordanian you're looking for?"

"Pretty much. Got no way to prove it."

We sat in silence some more. The afternoon breeze was building and the chop in the lake had started.

"How's Elena's cousin, Diaz?" I said.

"Nacho says he's gone."

"Take the money and run?"

"If he has the money. If that's what he's doing, he better run hard, run long, and run low to the ground."

I studied him.

"You don't think so?"

"Nacho doesn't think so. He thinks he's out scoring one of the ladies that work the streets in that area."

"So he'll be back?"

"If he's smart. If he isn't smart or he did take the money, he's a dead man and Elena will mourn for her aunt, but she'll get over it."

"Nacho looking for him?"

He took a drink. Out across the water Eddie caught a fish.

"There you go," Blackhawk said, watching Eddie. "Nacho has better things to do. I've asked him to check again tonight. If he's still gone then we talk to Elena and find out where he might hole up. Diaz isn't smart enough to hatch some elaborate plan."

"And we go get him."

"And we go get him."

He finished his beer and set the bottle aside.

"Another one?"

He shook his head. "How's the bomb thing going?"

I told him about Father Correa and the mullah.

"So the asshole is probably Shia?"

"Probably. The mullah suggested I check a strip mall

mosque on the west side. Says he doesn't really know many of the Shiite rank and file."

"You know where it is?

I nodded.

"So you are going to go check it out?"

I nodded again.

"When you going to do that?"

"No time like the present."

Across the water, Eddie had pulled up anchor and was moving.

Blackhawk shook his head. "All that for one fish."

"Fishing by definition is an end unto itself. People don't go catching, they go fishing."

He was looking at me. He smiled. "You are one strange white man, kemosabe."

34

Blackhawk decided to go with me. This time of day, Danny was running the shuttle. We hopped into the golf cart and he took us up the hill to the parking. Blackhawk's sleek, black Jaguar was parked in a reserved spot. It wasn't reserved for him. Except for the Mustang, the other cars and trucks parked there seemed to be faded and lacking.

"They will tow you," I said.

He shrugged, "Special modification. All the wheels lock. They'd have to get a crane and pick it up to move it."

I looked at him. "You park illegally a lot?"

"Did a favor for a guy once and got towed in the process. He owned a Jaguar dealership. He did it pro bono." He pulled the remote control from his pocket and pushed the button. The car unlocked but no beeping and no flashing lights.

"Sometimes it's better to unlock at night without advertisement." He smiled at me. "Same guy."

"You drive," I said. I popped the Mustang trunk and snagged the gun case that held the Kahr 45 and two clips. We took the Hawkmobile.

Driving with Blackhawk was like driving with Jeff Gordon. Everything was smooth, economic and fast. He glided through the traffic like a trout headed upstream. He could anticipate an opening in the traffic before it happened. If he couldn't avoid stopping at a light he would always pull up behind the line of cars that ultimately would be away faster than the other lane. Sometimes that is easy. You pull up behind the Corvette instead of the old sedan with Wisconsin plates. With him it was effortless.

I directed him to the 101 and we headed west. Ghazi had said we would find the place in a strip mall on Avondale Ave. If I remembered correctly that was how you got to Phoenix International Raceway. Where they had Nascar races. It shouldn't be too hard to check out the strip malls along the way. Blackhawk and I had the same smartphone so I plugged into his car charger. Since it was completely dead it took a moment for it to initialize. When it came awake, I looked at the map. Avondale Boulevard wasn't very long. How many strip malls could there be?

I met a guy at El Patron once. A big Nascar fan. He talked about going to the track like a kid would talk about Christmas. He said he would take his woman and pull their RV out to the track. They have a special lot set aside for RVs and he said people would come out and park a week before the race. It was a good quarter mile from the track. He said he had been going for years, and now there was an entire group that all came and parked next to each other, and had their Nascar reunion. They'd set out their camp chairs and grills and coolers of beer. When race day came they'd gather 'round and someone would fire up a portable TV and they would all watch the race without actually going to the track. He said there was more actual beer drinking than race watching. He asked me why in the hell should he go, pay big money, sit on a hard bleacher, stand in line to take a piss, and pay eight dollars for a measly cup of beer. He had bombastically said he only watched the race at the track once and that was once too many. I asked why he didn't just stay home and watch it in the comfort of his own home. He looked at me like I was an infidel.

We merged onto Interstate 10 and within a few minutes we were at the Avondale exit. I had not been out here for a while and it had grown tremendously. All the streets, retail outlets and business complexes looked brand new. There was a sameness that growing cities have, and are proud of. The chamber of commerce takes pictures and puts them in brochures.

Blackhawk kept to the slow lane and we drove the entire length of the boulevard without seeing a mosque, or anything that resembled it. When we reached the dry Salt River we turned around for another pass.

It was Blackhawk who spotted the bearded man in the mauve tunic and round Islamic cap. He was leaning against the stucco wall of a shop, smoking a forbidden cigarette. He was shaded by the veranda overhang that was built across the asphalt parking lot. We were already moving past, so we kept moving, staying with the traffic. When he had a chance, Blackhawk turned around and we drove to a gas station and pulled in. We were a half block away. Blackhawk positioned the Jag so we were facing toward the smoking man.

It was a long single building divided into a number of small businesses. The man was leaning against the wall in the middle, next to a door that had no lettering. A bay window next to the door was covered from the inside by a dark material. This made it a mirror. There was nothing to announce this was a mosque. A dog groomer was on one side and a small Mexican restaurant on the other. The lettering on the restaurant was in Spanish. I usually found this to mean the food would be authentic and good.

The man flipped his cigarette butt out into the parking lot and disappeared through the door.

"What's the plan?" Blackhawk said.

"Damned if I know," I said. I looked around at the gas station. It was more convenience store than gas station.

"I don't think well on an empty stomach," I said.

I got out and went in the store. I let my stomach rule my head and came back with a dozen donuts, two hot dogs, and two large bottles of Gatorade. We ate the hot dogs first, then started on the donuts. Blackhawk had shut the motor off and rolled the windows down. It was warm but not killer.

One of the things they had taught us was how to wait. An active mind is a killer, so the job is to empty the mind. For the next three hours, the sun got lower and lower in the sky and nothing happened. I completely ignored thinking about Boyce, and her pretty boy news anchor. People carried their little fluffies in and out of the groomers, and the restaurant had a decent flow.

"We could just go in there," I finally said.

"Be going in blind," Blackhawk said.

"If Atef is in there, be a chance to get him."

"Be a chance for him to get us."

"He doesn't know who we are."

"I'm not sure I know who he is."

"He's the guy in Boyce's picture and the video."

"Guy in the video had a head scarf and sunglasses."

"Scarf was red."

"You're right. Dead giveaway."

"Never expected him to be here, anyway."

Blackhawk looked at me. "What exactly did you expect?"

I ignored him. "If these are the bad guys and Atef isn't here, they won't tell us anything. If they are the good guys, they don't know Atef and won't tell us anything."

Blackhawk was still looking at me. "And we're sitting here, why?"

I didn't answer. I had lost track of how many donuts each of us had and there was one left. I took it out of the sack, and took a bite.

"That was mine," Blackhawk said. I broke it in half and handed him the part with the bite when Buddy Dwyer walked out of the mosque.

35

"Ho, ho," I said. "The game's afoot, Watson."

Blackhawk disgustedly threw the donut back into the bag. "You are truly weird."

He followed my eyes. "You know that guy?"

Dwyer walked across the parking lot to a well-worn white Ford F250.

"Buddy Dwyer. He was in the militia, up in Cottonwood, with Dick Mooney and Atef. He told me he quit because they weren't serious enough."

"How serious is enough? Take a guy's head? We following him?"

"A bird in hand."

"You think so?"

"Yeah, I think so."

He started the Jaguar.

Dwyer had to wait to pull out in traffic.

"Don't let him spot us. This isn't exactly a Toyota."

Blackhawk shook his head in disgust. "He's not going to spot us." When Dwyer pulled out, Blackhawk waited for a few seconds then followed. He was three cars back.

"Maybe it's supper time," he said.

"Mexican right next door," I said.

The light was fading. Dwyer's truck had a taillight out. It made it easier for us. Blackhawk floated along behind. He judged the lights just right without being obvious. Dwyer stayed in the right-hand lane and drove north. His right turn signal came on. He pulled into another strip of small retail shops. A drive-through liquor store was separated at the end.

"Out for booze," I said.

Blackhawk turned the corner, executed a U-turn, dodged the traffic skillfully, then pulled into a business parking lot across the street. We watched as the liquor store attendant handed a sack and a twelve pack of beer out the drive-up window.

"I didn't think Muslims drank," Blackhawk said.

"Or smoke," I said. "Earlier evidence to the contrary. But we don't know that Dwyer is a Muslim."

"Hanging with them."

"I'm hanging with you, don't make me Cochise. Hell, I'm not even sure you are Native American."

"Some of us prefer the term *Indian*. You'd have to ask my mother."

I looked at him. "You had a mother?"

"Rumors to the contrary."

We watched the attendant make his change, then Dwyer pulled back out onto Avondale Boulevard. He headed north.

"Not going back," Blackhawk said. "Do we stay with him?"

"When in doubt, do something," I said.

Blackhawk slid back out into traffic. Dwyer drove to Interstate 10 and up the eastbound ramp.

"Stick with him?" Blackhawk asked.

"Let's see where he's going."

"Yowzer boss."

"That doesn't sound like an authentic Indian phrase," I said.

"Native American to you."

"Don't confuse me," I said.

Interstate 10 is an American main artery that goes from the west coast of California across the underbelly of the country all the way to Jacksonville, Florida. No matter what day or time of day, it is loaded with those behemoths of commerce, the 16-wheel monster trucks. Blackhawk nestled in behind one and dogged the white Ford. When Dwyer reached the 101 loop I expected him to take it north, but he didn't.

"Interesting," I said. "Guess we'll find out where he's going."

"Brilliant," Blackhawk said. "You just come up with that on the spur of the moment."

"Quick," I said.

Blackhawk took advantage of the traffic and stayed with him. At the Black Canyon Freeway interchange Dwyer angled onto the northbound exit lane. The exit ramp narrowed to one lane, so Blackhawk dropped back, letting a couple of cars move between us.

Swinging down and merging with the freeway, Dwyer

stayed in the slower, right-hand lane. Blackhawk dropped back a little more.

"Not going far," Blackhawk said.

Sure enough, a few minutes later at Dunlap Avenue, Dwyer's turn signal came on.

We got lucky on the light and we followed him east. Now the broken taillight was really handy. The sun was down, the street lights were up, and the late commuters were packing the streets. Still, Blackhawk glided behind the white truck with ease.

Dwyer stayed in the left lane. He caught us by surprise at 19th Avenue by not using his turn signal. He moved into the left turn lane and took the turn on yellow. Blackhawk cut across the front of a van, and had to stop as the left turn light turned red. He waited for a break in the traffic then ran the light. The Ford was two blocks ahead. Blackhawk made up a block, then eased up. Dwyer pulled into the left turn lane at Mountain View. The left turn was red but the through traffic had a green. Blackhawk had to go through or pull up behind him. We went through. I turned my head to look away from Dwyer as we passed.

Blackhawk slowed and watched his mirror until Dwyer got his light and turned. He twisted the wheel and we did a sharp U-turn. Again, we caught him with a couple of blocks between us. Dwyer turned right on a side street and Blackhawk hung back to put more distance between us. We made the turn and dropped further back.

The white Ford turned off the street and into a business driveway. He pulled up to a black wrought-iron gate. There was a block building, on his right, attached to the gate. Behind the gate, the fenced lot went back a long way. He honked. As we went by, the gate opened and he drove forward. I could see a number of bays behind the building. Some were open with the lights on.

As soon as Blackhawk felt we were out of view, he pulled to the curb. He touched a button on the dash and when I opened the door, the light didn't come on. I opened the gun case and took the Kahr. I snapped one clip in the pistol and put another in my pocket. I ratcheted a shell into the chamber and stuck the Kahr into my back pocket.

The building was down the street and hidden by two huge Eucalyptus trees. I crossed the street and took to the shadows. I moved cautiously. There was a parking lot across the street from the building. It had two tall lights. This type of light spilled a cone of light around the base which illuminated what it was pointed at, but made the shadows darker. I found a dark spot where I could see the front of the building, and through the gate into the back lot. There was a medium-sized white sign by the front door that sported black letters that read *S&K Rigging*.

I sensed movement behind me and I turned, my hand going to the pistol. It was Blackhawk.

"Now what?" he said.

"Hell if I know," I said.

"Maybe he works here," Blackhawk said with a low tone. "Maybe he has a friend that works here. Maybe there's a poker game going on. Maybe he's a customer. Maybe it's where they hatch their sinister plots."

He was amusing himself. I was studying the building and the back lot. The parking and drive area behind the gate had pallets, loaded with materials, spaced down the length of the fence.

"Yeah, I know," Blackhawk said.

"Know what?"

"When in doubt, do something."

"Damn straight," I said and started to move.

"But," he said, taking my arm to stop me.

"But what?"

"We should look before we leap."

I looked at him.

"What do you know that I don't?"

"Well, now that you ask, I know they have a guy on the roof."

36

"Up next to the air conditioning unit," he said.

I could see the dark rectangle of the unit against the slightly lighter sky. Then the guy moved and I saw him.

"Sho 'nuff," I said.

"Now that's pure Native American speak," Blackhawk said. "I saw him moving while you were moving."

"Think he made me?"

"Nope."

"Think you can take him out?"

"Yep."

"Brevity is all."

"Sho 'nuff," Blackhawk said and moved back further into the shadows. He moved away to my right and disappeared.

I squatted down, halfway into a bush, and waited. If you are wearing dark clothes, like I was, and you remain immobile inside a shadow, you can be invisible. I didn't have to wait long. Across the street there was shadow and dim light, and then there was Blackhawk climbing a fence and up on the roof like a cat. I waited. There was no sound, no sign of a struggle, no nothing. Then Blackhawk stood beside the air conditioning unit and waved, the streetlight gleaming against his white shirt.

I sprinted across the street. Following Blackhawk's lead I went up the fence and onto the roof. The man was face-down and out cold. Blackhawk held up an AR-15. He pulled the clip and jacked the shell out of the chamber. He walked silently to where we had come up and dropped both pieces off the side. They landed with a soft thud.

I silently moved to the edge of the building that was attached to the long, covered roof of the bays. I could hear muffled voices. The roof over the bays was corrugated tin and I knew we couldn't walk on it without noise. I felt Blackhawk move up beside me.

I went to the corner of the building where the gate was attached. Below me was Dwyer's truck. I dropped silently to the ground, inside the gate, behind the truck. The bays were around the corner. A second later, Blackhawk joined me. I could see light flickering off the fence and could hear the hissing, burning sound of someone welding.

"What do you think they are doing?" Blackhawk said in a very low voice.

"Hatching sinister plots," I said.

"I knew that," he said.

"Let's find out," I said.

"You know we're trapped in here."

"So are they," I said.

"They know how to open the gate," he said.

"I didn't think of that," I said and looked around the corner.

There were four of them, including Dwyer. Two were standing to Dwyer's right and they all were watching another guy welding. It looked like he was welding a lid to a fifty-five gallon drum. They weren't expecting company. They didn't notice us until we were at the bay door. Then they saw us. The welder must have sensed something. He stopped welding and raised his protective mask.

"What the fuck," Dwyer said.

"We heard you were hiring," I said.

I was to Blackhawk's left. In front of me was a big guy, but in a sloppy, weightlifter-gone-to-seed way. He had a thick dark beard and sideburns up to the top of his ears. After that, his head was shaved. Next to him, the other guy had a striped shirt and tattoos up to his ears.

The welder was dark with cropped black hair, a wifebeater shirt with tufts of wiry black hair bursting out the top, with a bushy beard. He was looking hard at Blackhawk. Blackhawk probably looked the way he always did in moments like this. Disinterested and half asleep.

The big sloppy guy took a half step forward.

"What you talking about? Ain't nobody hiring here."

"How'd you get in here?" Dwyer said.

Blackhawk and I stepped in closer, spreading apart.

"Guy on the roof let us in," I said.

Behind them, a corner of the bay had been built out with unfinished drywall and a cheap door. Behind the door, we all heard the sound of a toilet flushing. The door opened and Ali Ibrahim Atef stepped out, buckling his belt. He froze when he saw us.

"Who are you?" he said.

"I know you," Dwyer said, staring at me. He turned to Atef. "Saw this asshole in Cottonwood. He was asking questions about Mooney."

Atef finished with his belt. "Get rid of them."

The big guy started to reach behind his back and I hit him a straight left in the nose. As he went back I followed, hitting him two rapid rights. One to his jaw and one to his neck. He didn't go down, but he was stunned. I kicked Striped-shirt in the chest with my prosthetic, and he went down. Blackhawk slapped the welder's mask down, and kicked the welder in the knee. The welder fell into Dwyer who was struggling with a pistol from his back pocket. Blackhawk ripped the welder's helmet off and smacked Dwyer across the face with it. Atef had a pistol in his hand and pointed it at me. I grabbed Sloppy by the lapels and swung him around as Atef fired twice. I felt the slugs punch into the big man's body, and felt a sting in my side. On one knee, the welder grabbed Blackhawk and tried to wrestle him down. With a full arm swing, Blackhawk smacked him with his own helmet, and he fell senseless. Atef took off at a flat run, and Dwyer scrambled behind him. The big man had fallen into me, and I shoved him out of the way. I pulled the Kahr. Atef and Dwyer disappeared around the corner, then Atef leaned back around and fired at us. I dived behind the fifty-five gallon drum. I threw two shots over the top of it in his general direction. Blackhawk had thrown himself against the wall of the bay. I heard someone gagging. It was Striped-shirt. He had caught one in the throat. Atef was on a roll. He kept this up, he'd be out of men.

We heard the dual sounds of the gate opening and the truck starting.

Blackhawk said, "Cover me."

I came up over the drum and put the sights on the corner of the building. Gun fight, front sight. Blackhawk sprinted to the corner and dropped flat. I could hear the engine racing and the squealing of tires. Pistol extended, Blackhawk looked around the corner at ground level. He came to his feet and waved me forward.

The gate was open. The only thing left of Atef and Dwyer was dust, and the smell of burning rubber.

I looked back at the bay. Three men down and two of them looked really dead. The welder was out cold but his foot rocked back and forth.

I looked at Blackhawk. His beautiful shirt was a mess.

"You really should get that dry-cleaned," I said.

Blackhawk was looking at me.

"You hit?" he asked.

I looked down, and my shirt was covered in blood.

37

"Holy crap!" I yelped, as Elena spread the antiseptic on the furrow in my side.

"Hold still, you big baby," she said.

Atef's bullet had passed through the big guy's blubber and scorched a furrow in my right side. Most of the blood on my shirt had been the big guy's.

We were in Blackhawk's apartment in the bathroom where he had hustled me so I wouldn't drip blood on his good carpet. Blackhawk was leaning against the far wall with his arms crossed. He looked amused. Elena began applying butterfly bandages, pulling the skin together. Once that was done, she put on an antiseptic pad and taped it into place. She picked up my shirt from where I had dropped it, and holding it delicately, between forefinger and thumb, she dropped it into the garbage can.

She wrinkled her nose in disgust and looked at me.

"Anita will be here Friday night."

Now I know Blackhawk was amused.

I started to say something sarcastic, then thought better of it. I just nodded.

"Anita is a very nice girl, and she likes you."

"That's nice," I said humbly.

"I have told her that you are not normally a drunken maniac."

It was all Blackhawk could do to keep from falling down.

"That's nice of you."

She looked at me hard.

"Don't be a smart ass!"

"But…"

She waved a dismissive hand at me.

"Stop! I know what you are doing. You think we don't know that men are born insincere." She looked at Blackhawk. He was a stone wall. "Anita is a sweet girl."

Blackhawk didn't blink.

She turned back to me. "You had better not hurt her."

"I don't…."

She waved her hand again. "I'm going to rehearsal," she said and turned and left the bathroom.

I looked at Blackhawk. I started to speak. He held his hand up, stopping me.

Elena stepped back into the doorway. She looked at me, then at Blackhawk. She looked at us for a long moment, then turned and left.

I looked at Blackhawk, and he was smiling.

"How did you know she was going to do that?"

He shrugged.

I shook my head in wonder. "Is this what a long-term relationship looks like?"

He was still smiling. "I've never had so much fun in my

life," he said. "I'll get you a shirt, then I'm going to clean up."

He went to the bedroom, and I went to the living room. He brought me a black tee shirt, and with a grimace I slipped it over my head.

"Is there a payphone around here?" I asked.

He looked at me, "Why do you need a payphone? There's not many of those left."

"I want to call Boyce and give her a heads-up, before someone else does. But I don't want my cell to show up on her phone."

"No trace?"

I nodded.'

"Follow me," he said.

We went out into the hall and down to his office. Inside he moved to his desk and pulled a drawer open. He took out a cell phone and looked at it to check the battery. He handed it to me.

"Clean?"

He nodded. "It's a throwaway I bought for Jimmy. But he's a kid and now he's full-time he has to have one of the fancy smartphones. I'm going to clean up."

He left and I sat behind his massive desk. I dialed Boyce. She answered on the third ring.

"Boyce."

"S&K Rigging at 27th Avenue and Mountain View," I said.

There was a long pause, then, "Where are you?"

"El Patron."

"S&K Rigging at 27th Ave and Mountain View," she repeated. "Do I go alone or take help?"

"Take help. Atef was there. It looks like a bomb factory. You may find some bodies."

Another long pause.

I continued, "Atef is with a guy from Cottonwood named Buddy Dwyer in a white Ford F250. It's missing a taillight but it's most likely been ditched by now."

"You know this how, and did you mention dead people?"

"You better hurry," I said and disconnected.

I went back over to the apartment. Blackhawk was out of the shower, and putting on another perfect shirt. My turn. I stripped down and washed around the bandages. Dried off and dressed, I found Blackhawk with Nacho at the bar in the living room. Blackhawk fixed me a scotch and soda, and set it up on the bar for me. Behind the bar was an exquisite oil painting of a distressed ballerina bathed in golden light. I'm not sure Nacho knew it was there.

"Tell him," Blackhawk said to Nacho.

"I hear you got your ass shot," Nacho said with a grin.

"Tell him," Blackhawk said again, shaking his head impatiently.

Nacho shrugged. "Diaz is back."

"Was he ever gone?"

He shrugged again. "Not really. Just out getting his pony ridden."

I could tell there was more.

"So we've been thinking," he continued. "The deal with Diaz had to be an inside job. And Diaz ain't smart enough and ain't tough enough to do it. He's just a worker bee."

He was drinking a Modelo. He took a drink.

"So Blackhawk had me pick up Diaz and make him walk me through the whole deal. Like made him show me where they load the trucks and shit. So we parked down the street and watched a while. We saw that asswipe Rojo going in and out, and Diaz kept saying that Rojo had to be in on it. I was just getting tired of sitting there when all of a sudden Diaz got so excited he just about pisses his pants."

He was grinning at me now, waiting for me to ask the question, so I did.

"And?"

"A guy came out with Rojo, and Diaz thinks it was the same guy that got the door open when he was stuck in the toilet on his way south."

38

"So you're saying the guy jammed Diaz up until someone got the money out of his truck?"

"If that's the guy."

I looked at Nacho.

"Diaz is sure?"

He shrugged. "As sure as Diaz is about anything. He did get agitated when he saw him. Wanted to confront the guy. Or said he did. Diaz ain't about confronting anyone, but he talks a good game."

"And this guy is part of Garza's bunch?"

Nacho's eyebrows went up.

"He was there, man. Had to be one of them, or he wouldn't have been there."

"Where's Diaz?"

"Back at the motel watching porn."

I looked at my watch. "Diaz say when they make their last run of the day?"

"Hours ago."

I finished my drink and looked at Blackhawk.

"I'm tired. I'm going home. Maybe tomorrow we go see what this guy has to say."

"What suits you, tickles me plumb to death," he said.

The night was warm and the traffic heavy. The Mustang was hot but the good thing about the Mustang was that the air conditioning was almost immediate. Two blocks down and it was starting to blow cool. By the freeway it was blowing cold. It seemed to take forever to get to the marina. I had time to think. I thought about Elena and how she made Blackhawk happy, and how, if it were her and me, she'd eventually drive me nuts. I thought about Boyce, which led to the pretty TV anchor, which led to me shutting that thought down. Eventually, I thought about the fact that I lived on a boat a long way away. But then, when I reached the gate, I thought that wasn't too bad.

Danny was running the shuttle and he dropped me at my gate. The only life in evidence was a few relentless bugs slapping against the dock lights. I unlatched the dock gate and eased it shut behind me. Clanging is rude.

As I walked down the pier toward Tiger Lily I noted the same thing I always noted. Everyone else's boat seemed to be bigger and nicer than mine.

Yeah, but mine was cheap.

I walked by the 80-foot Stardust that had been the Moneypenny. Eddie had told me it had been bought by a retired television writer. He had named it *13 Episodes*. I had not met him yet. I don't know if he lives on it or not, although it was definitely set up to be lived on.

I stepped aboard the Tiger Lily and reengaged the alarms.

The inside was musty and warm. I kicked the air on, opened the blackout blinds, and opened the bow and stern doors to get a cross breeze. I kicked off my clothes, put on the swim foot, pulled up my trunks and hesitated, thinking about my new bandages. The heck with it; I went over the side.

The moon was riding high, was huge, and the sky was mostly clear. I swam steadily to the buoy that bobbed gently in the moonlight. My side stung but I ignored it. I rationalized that the high moon offset the pain. When I reached the buoy, I treaded water and took in the view. I was enjoying something that probably no other person had ever been in this exact spot to enjoy. The lake was quiet and beautiful.

I felt a series of small bumping tickles against my stomach and chest, and a school of tiny shad swarmed around me. Hundreds upon hundreds, splitting behind me, going around, and then reforming the school in front. They quickly disappeared and I entertained long, deep thoughts about the meaning of life, and my place in the cosmos, and swam back to the boat.

I climbed aboard and pulled off my swim foot. I hopped to the head, dripping water all the way. I pulled a towel off the rack. I wiped down the foot, stripped out of the wet trunks and toweled off. I hung the trunks in the oversized shower stall. I stripped off the sodden bandages and took a quick shower. Out of the shower I spread antiseptic across the shallow wound and taped on a new bandage. I hopped, naked, to the front and shut the bow door. The pier was empty, the overhead lights making a soft electrical buzzing sound. I hopped back to the master stateroom and dressed. Dry trunks, a tee shirt and a utility foot.

In the galley I fixed a drink. Lots of ice, scotch and a splash of water. I held the glass up to the light and admired the color. Just right.

I took the drink to the stern and slid the door closed behind me to conserve the air conditioning. I settled onto a comfortable deck chair. While a little warm, it wasn't bad enough to have to give up the drink on the stern deck. I took a drink and admired the full moon. The mountains were awash in its light.

I thought about Eddie and Billy Bragg. It was obvious Billy was innocent. But there was no empirical proof. Not enough to get Billy out of jail. I began wondering why Atef had not videotaped Mooney.

I could understand a guy like Atef being radicalized, but I didn't get Dwyer. A homegrown redneck with a penchant for rebellion, that was probably more suited to white supremacy than radical Islam. But despite my not understanding, they were obviously together. And I'm willing to bet, one of the two, and probably Dwyer, had planted Billy's bloody knife. Which, I still thought, was too circumstantial to put the guy in jail. But hey, I'm not the county attorney. And it's a small town and a small county, and it's better for the county attorney to quickly solve such a gruesome case than have to answer questions every time he goes to the store. Or gets a haircut. Or plays golf at the country club.

And where is Atef now? By now they have figured out

that Dwyer was tailed to S&K Rigging, so their little Avondale mosque is blown. The truck is blown.

I took another drink and the ice clinked against my teeth.

Hell, they could be anywhere. I went to bed.

39

The sound of a gong entered my dream. When it sounded again I was awake, and it was the alarm next to the bed. Someone had stepped on board. As I swung my legs over the edge I pulled the Ruger free of the magnet. By feel, I attached my foot. I managed my feet into the trunks and pulled them up one-handed. Outside it was just at the beginnings of sunrise. I pushed the stem of my watch to illuminate the dial and it told me it was four forty-seven in the morning.

I moved silently through the hall and the galley, and through the lounge. I had not pulled the blinds when I had gone to bed, so there was enough light outside to make out my surroundings. I could see someone sitting on the bow. Someone sitting on the same locker that Eddie and his six-pack had occupied a few days ago.

It was Boyce.

She was staring off into the near distance, then she must have sensed that I was there. She turned and looked in. We stared at each other through the glass sliding door. The pier light gave her dark hair an iridescent gleam. Like the wing of a crow. She was smoking. I tossed the Ruger onto the couch, then unlocked and opened the door.

"I thought you quit."

"You're the only thing I quit," she said.

So that was how it was going to be. I studied her, but she gave me nothing. "Can I get you something to drink?"

She sat quietly. She took a long drag on the cigarette. She sat looking at me for a long time.

Finally, "Bottle of water would be nice."

I turned back to the galley, opened the oversized refrigerator and grabbed a bottle of water. I loosened the cap as I came back out. I handed it to her. She took a long swallow, then another one. I leaned against the bulwark and crossed my arms over my chest. She took a last drag and flipped the cigarette overboard.

"I do wish you wouldn't do that," I said.

"Smoke?"

"Throw your butts overboard. Me and a half million fish swim there."

She looked at me again, studying me. She shook her head and rubbed her hand across her face.

"I'm tired," she said, "I'm dirty and I stink. So let's just get to it. Tell me about what happened tonight."

"I took a nice swim."

She looked at my bandage. "So, what is that, a fish bite? Let's quit the games. Tell me what happened tonight."

I shrugged. "I got a lead on a Shiite mosque in Avondale, and I went to check it out. It seems Atef is Shiite, at least the Mullah Ghazi doesn't know him, and he knows most of the

Sunnis. That's where I saw Buddy Dwyer and I followed him to S&K Rigging."

"Ghazi gave you the tip?"

That didn't require an answer.

She nodded, "Yeah, one of the guys said he saw you there. You pissed him off because you didn't wait outside for him when he told you to."

I just looked at her. That didn't require an answer.

"What did you do when you got to S&K Rigging?" she said.

"Parked and waited."

"Alone?"

"As far as you or anyone else is concerned, I was alone."

"Then what?"

"Well, Officer, then I heard shooting, and saw Atef and Dwyer exit the premises at a high rate of speed."

"You being a smartass?"

"Just the facts, ma'am."

And again she looked at me for a long time. She shook her head in resignation.

"We found two men dead, and one unconscious. All three of them are on the Homeland Security list of potential threats."

"If you check DNA samples in their little bathroom, you will find that Atef was there."

"It's being checked. But we know he was there. How do you know he was in the bathroom?"

"Just a guess."

"We found a barrel bomb with a partially welded top.

There was a bullet hole in the upper lip. If the round had hit three inches lower, the whole place, and maybe the whole block would have gone up."

I thought about me taking refuge behind the barrel when the shooting started. Dang.

"So if I suggested," she continued, "we get a search warrant and confiscated your pistols and check them against evidence we found, what do you think the conclusion would be?"

I shrugged.

"And if we tested for powder residue, what would we find?"

Again, I shrugged.

"And if I asked you to strip off your bandage would I find a fish bite or a bullet wound?"

She stood up and stepped off the boat. She finished the bottle of water, screwed the cap back on and tossed the empty onto the bow.

"One of these days, you are going to step over the wrong line."

I started to say something, but she had already turned and was walking away.

I picked up the empty water bottle and watched her until she was out of sight.

40

I was applying a coat of white, glossy paint to the outside of the topside cockpit. I had discovered some dry rot in a corner where moisture had accumulated over the years. I had replaced it with a hand-sanded piece of tempered wood and was hoping the color would match once it dried.

I was wearing an old, worn chambray shirt I had yanked the sleeves off of, and an old pair of trunks. It had gotten hot and the sweat was running into my eyes so badly I had wrapped a bandana around my forehead to stem the tide. All I needed was an eye patch and a sword. Arrrrgh.

"Hey Jackson!"

The voice came from behind and below me. I turned and looked over the edge and Dahlia and Megan stood on the pier, each shielding their eyes with one hand.

I smiled. "Hey, guys."

"We are on our way into town and thought we'd look you up. Megan wanted to see your boat. Billy's uncle was at the store and let us onto your dock."

"Come on aboard," I said. "Just watch your step. This

old scow is floating, but as stable as she is, she might still move. I'll be down."

I put the lid on the paint can and set it in the cockpit in the shade. I took the brush with me. I could wash it out in the sink if I was done, or wrap it with plastic wrap if I was going to keep painting later.

The interior of the boat was pleasantly cool, and I slid the doors open and the two girls stepped in. Dahlia had on a short-sleeved brocaded blouse and a pair of cream-colored capris. Megan had a sleeveless white blouse and a pair of shorts. She wore flip flops.

"I hope you don't mind," Dahlia said. "We started talking about you, and your boat, as we came down the hill and when we saw the sign to the lake, we decided to take a chance."

"My good fortune," I said. I looked at Megan. "Would you like a tour?"

She smiled and nodded.

"It will be a short one," I said. "This isn't a very big boat."

I indicated the area we were standing in, "This is the main salon, or you could call it the lounge."

"You don't just call it the front room?"

"Boats have a special name for everything," Dahlia said.

Megan was looking around, taking everything in.

"For instance," I said. "What you would call the kitchen is called the galley."

I moved into the galley.

"The bedrooms are called staterooms. The beds are called berths and the bathroom is called a head."

"Head? Why would they call it a head?"

I laughed. "Because back in the good old days of wind-powered sailboats they always put the bathroom at the front, or at the head of the ship, so as the wind filled the sails from behind it blew the smell away from the boat."

"Yew."

"And I called it a bathroom, but usually it was just a hole over the water."

"Double yew!"

"You asked a question, and you got an answer," Dahlia said, smiling.

"Let me show you the rest," I said.

They followed me down the hall. I was glad I had made the bed. "This boat has an unusually large bath and bed in the master stateroom."

I moved through the stateroom and out onto the stern. They followed. There was a light breeze. I looked at Megan, "See, I told you it wasn't much of a tour. The back of a boat is the stern and the front is the bow. Do you know what the left side and right side of the boat is called?"

Dahlia looked expectantly at her daughter. She turned to me. "The reason we're here is that Megan had some issues with her grades and I promised to bring her on a shopping trip if she resolved the issue, which she did. "So I'll bet she's smart enough to know that answer."

Megan gave her mom that teenaged look. "Mom. They don't teach boats in high school."

"Your mom just thinks you are smart. Any guess?" I said.

"Is it starboard or something?"

"Bingo, you win the prize. Port and starboard. Do you know which is which?"

She shrugged.

"Here's a trick to remember which is which. Port is the left side. Port and left have the same number of letters."

"Four."

"Exactimudo." I smiled. "Let's go topside."

I led the way up the ladder. When we were all on top, Megan was looking at my foot. Or, rather, my prosthetic.

"How did you lose your foot?" she said.

"Megan!"

"It's okay." I waved my hand, "This is the upper deck. It is a very pleasant place to watch a sunset. As you see, it has a cockpit so I can steer the boat from up here."

"Can we go on a boat ride?" Megan asked.

"Megan!" Dahlia turned to me, "I'm so sorry."

I waved a dismissive hand.

She turned back to Megan. "Honey, we didn't stop here to get Mr. Jackson to give us a boat ride. We are interrupting his day already."

"Well, it is a pleasant interruption." I pointed across the marina to the small boat pier. "You see that runabout over there? The fifth one from the end, with the green canvas cover?"

Megan said, "Yeah, I see it." She looked at her mother who was obviously not finding it.

"Next to the red one, Mom."

"Oh, yeah."

"That's also mine, and if you decide you have the time, I'd be happy to take you out on it."

"Oh, that's way too much...." Dahlia said.

"Could we, Mom?" Megan begged. "Please, could we?"

Dahlia looked at me. "Really, Jackson. We couldn't possibly put you out like that."

"I'll make you a deal," I said. "If we go on a boat ride, I'll tell you how I lost my foot."

Dahlia shook her head, looking at me. "If you put it that way, how could we refuse?"

41

We were in the lounge.

"Why don't you girls relax a second? I haven't cleaned up today, so let me take a quick shower, then we'll walk over."

"You're okay," Dahlia said.

I got two bottles of water from the refrigerator. I handed each one.

"My mama said I was to keep myself tidy in body and mind."

"Where's your mother?" Megan asked.

"She's gone."

"Gone where?"

Dahlia turned to her daughter, "Mr. Jackson is saying his mother is deceased."

"Oh, sorry."

"Nothing to be sorry about," I said.

"How about your dad," Megan asked.

"Megan, don't be so nosy." Dahlia shook her head, "I'm sorry, Jackson."

"It really is okay." I looked at Megan, "My father is deceased also. Let me get a shower and we'll take a ride."

I was quick. Fifteen minutes later, I was pulling the canvas cover off of Swoop. I helped the girls on board. Swoop was a nineteen-foot Grumman Sport Deck with a V hull and an eight-foot beam. It was very stable. I pumped the gas bulb, then started the 120-horsepower Johnson motor, and let it idle. I pulled lifejackets from the floor locker and handed one each to the girls.

"I can swim," Megan said.

"My boat, my rules, please put it on."

She didn't argue.

I took it easy through the no-wake zone. Once past the buoy, I slowly brought her up on plane. I headed across the water, putting her nose on Scorpion Bay in the distance.

The day was heating up, so I kept a strong enough pace to keep a breeze on us. It would be hot enough on the trip back when the wind would be with us. I cruised Scorpion Bay and headed up to Castle Creek. When I glanced behind me, Megan was taking it all in, but Dahlia was watching me. She smiled quickly, then turned her head.

In no chop, Swoop could go forty miles per hour, but I kept it steady at about twenty-five. A little over an hour later I pulled Swoop back into her mooring.

Megan hopped out on the pier, then helped her mom out.

"Thank you so much, Mr. Jackson," Megan said.

"Just Jackson," I said. "It was my pleasure. Can I interest you ladies in some lunch?"

"Only if you let me buy," Dahlia said.

"Done. Let me batten this down and I'll meet you at the restaurant."

Megan had moved down the pier looking at the other boats, Dahlia took my arm, pulling me into her. She looked at me for a long moment.

"You have been very nice, thank you," she said, and leaned up and kissed me on the cheek.

"That made it more than worthwhile," I said.

I could have sworn she blushed as she turned away.

The restaurant bar was very large with huge windows on the north side. The windows were garage-door styled, and they had them rolled open. With the swamp cooler running, and a breeze, it was pleasant. I guided us to a window seat so they could watch the boats.

The waitress was a sturdy blonde named Dawn. She'd been working there since spring. She brought menus and a bottle of Dos Equis without being asked. She set the beer in front of me. She handed the menus to the girls.

"Can I get you girls something to drink?"

Dahlia said she'd have a Dos Equis also, and Megan ordered a Coke. Dawn went to get the drinks.

Dahlia studied the menu, but Megan said, "You promised to tell us about your foot."

"It's really not much of a story," I said.

"You promised," Megan said. Dahlia just shook her head.

I took a drink of the beer and studied the label. "I was stationed overseas and I made the mistake of stepping on an IED."

"You were in the Army?" Dahlia said.

"What's an IED?" Megan said.

"Marines," I said. I smiled at Megan. "An IED is an improvised explosive device. A homemade bomb. The bad guys hid them in places hoping we would step on them and I obliged."

"Did it hurt?"

"It hurt a lot worse later."

"So now you have a fake foot."

"It's called a prosthetic, and I have several of them. I have one just for swimming."

Dawn brought the drinks and set them in front of the girls.

"Are we ready to order?" she said brightly.

We all ordered hamburgers. She wrote it on her order pad and turned to the kitchen.

Out the window and across the pier, a lone sailor in a small expensive sailboat was trying to tie off on the dock. He didn't have bumpers out and the wind kept banging him against the dock as he struggled. Every time the wind banged the beautiful little boat into the dock, I winced.

Dahlia followed my eyes. "Someone should help him," she said.

"He doesn't want help," I said.

She looked at me, "He doesn't?"

I took a drink of the beer, "That boat is not designed for a crowd. He's new at it, but he bought that for solo sailing. He knows he has to learn and I'll bet he wants to learn on his own."

"Really?"

"People that sail are a special breed."

"That's your new neighbor," Eddie's voice said from behind me.

I turned and looked at him, "You off work?"

"Damn kid finally showed up."

"Join us," Dahlia said.

He hooked a chair and pulled it around.

"Jackson says that guy doesn't want any help," Megan said.

Eddie watched the man finally get his bow tied off but now the stern had drifted out to where he couldn't reach the dock.

"Jackson's right," he said. "Man's gotta learn."

"Man that has trouble docking his own boat will have a bad time of it out in a squall," I said. "My new neighbor?"

"Bought the Moneypenny," Eddie said.

"I saw the name change."

Dawn brought the food. "PBR?" she asked Eddie. He nodded and she hustled back to the bar.

"Hired me to take him out on her, show him the ropes."

"Local?" I asked.

"From L.A.," he said. "He's a writer. Wrote for some TV show."

"Hence the name," I said.

Megan perked up, "Which show?"

He shook his head, "Don't know. I don't watch TV."

Megan gave him a look of disbelief. "You don't watch TV? None?"

"Doesn't make him strange," I laughed.

"Did you see a television on Jackson's boat?" Eddie asked.

Megan and Dahlia looked at each other, then both looked at me.

"No. No we didn't," Dahlia said.

"You don't have a television?" Megan said.

I started to reply when we heard Dawn cry out, "Stop it!"

We all turned to look.

Dawn was trying to wrest her arm away from a tall, rangy young man. He was a good head taller than her. He had a thick mop of blond hair, a ragged tee shirt torn off at the arms and short enough to show his stomach. His arms were muscled and veined.

She tried to jerk away but he was much stronger and was jerking her like a rag doll. In an instant, Eddie was out of his chair and across the room. I followed.

42

"That's enough!" Eddie bellowed as he crossed the room.

The man didn't even glance at him.

Dawn was hitting at the guy, screaming, "Stop it, Jerry! Stop it! Stop it!"

Eddie reached to grab the guy's arm and the guy dodged his grasp, and released Dawn by shoving her. She fell against the bar stools. Eddie stepped between the guy and Dawn. The guy glared at him, his eyes narrowed, with pinprick pupils. He was several inches taller than Eddie and had thirty pounds on him. Eddie didn't flinch.

"I think the lady wants you to leave," I said.

He stood very still, then slowly turned to look at me. He leaned forward until his face was barely an inch from mine. He was a good inch taller than me.

"Why don't you fuck off," he said, moving in real close. I guess this was his intimidation move.

I sneezed and blew spit all over him.

"Jesus Christ!" he exploded, jumping back. "What the fuck's wrong with you?" He was madly wiping his face with his bare arm.

"Sorry," I said. "I guess I'm allergic to assholes."

Dahlia and Megan had moved up behind us. Megan laughed out loud.

"You looking for a fight," Jerry said, recovering.

"Jerry, get out of here," Dawn said, straightening the stools. "You know you are permanently 86'd." She pointed out the window. "Your picture's out on the board, you're not even supposed to be on this lake. I'm gonna call security."

"Jackson doesn't look for fights," Eddie said.

"Well, he fucking found one," Jerry said and swung a wide, looping right-handed roundhouse at me.

For all the muscles, he was pretty slow. I guess he was big enough he didn't have to be fast. I moved just enough to let his fist move the air as it whipped pass my face. I stepped back, my hands at my side.

"Son, better listen to the girl," Eddie said. "You're biting off more that you can chew."

Jerry swung at me again, lunging forward. I backed up again. He starting swinging right and left, and I kept moving, just enough for him to miss every time. Finally, he stopped; by now he was breathing heavily. I just looked at him, waiting. I thought I knew what was coming next, and I was right. He lunged forward, trying to wrap me up in his long, muscled arms. I kicked him in the meat of his upper thigh. Kicked him hard. I had shifted so my prosthetic was behind me, my left foot forward in the classic T-stance. When I kicked, I whipped the prosthetic with great velocity and except for the large muscles of his leg, I would have broken it.

He howled and went over sideways.

"Shit," he cried. "Shit, shit, shit," his face all crunched up in pain.

"Oh my God!" Dawn screamed and knelt down beside him. "Are you okay? Are you okay?"

She looked up at me with anguish. "You didn't have to hurt him!"

"What is wrong with you girl," Dahlia said.

Eddie smiled at me. "No good deed goes unpunished." He picked up his PBR from where Dawn had set it on the bar. We all followed him back to our table. Jerry continued to writhe and moan.

Our hamburgers were cold, but we began to eat them anyway. The French fries were soggy. We watched as Dawn struggled to get Jerry to his feet, and help him out the door. As they went out the door, she turned and gave me a very dirty look. I couldn't help but shake my head. As they went out, the sailor, who had struggled with his boat, came in.

"I don't get that girl," Megan said. "Jackson and Mr. Bragg tried to help her, and she acts mad at Jackson."

Eddie chuckled. "I had many years on the force in Chicago, honey. The situation every patrolman hated was a domestic call. A man and wife fighting. Or for that matter, lovers of any kind."

"Those two are lovers," Megan said, looking out the door. "Eew."

The sailor had turned to watch Dawn help Jerry, then turned back and looked around. He seemed undecided as to what to do. Eddie waved at him.

"Hey, Pete!" Eddie called. "Come meet a neighbor."

The man smiled and made his way across the wide floor. He was probably twenty years older than me but infinitely younger than Eddie. Eddie pushed his chair back and stood. They shook hands.

Eddie indicated me. "This is Jackson. He lives on the Tiger Lily at the end of the dock. Jackson, meet Pete Dunn."

"So you are the Tiger Lily," Pete grinned.

I stood and shook hands.

"Yes I am. One and the same. Pleased to meet you." I indicated Dahlia and Megan. "These are the Martin girls. Dahlia and her daughter Megan."

"My pleasure," he said.

"You are welcome to join us," I said.

"Thanks, maybe next time, I was just picking up a couple of things from the store."

"What TV show?" Megan said.

"Beg pardon?"

"Megan, mind your manners," Dahlia said.

"I told them you wrote for a TV show, but I guess I never asked you which one," Eddie said.

Pete shook his head. "You probably never watched it."

"That's safe to say," I said. "Eddie doesn't watch TV."

"Good for him," Pete said. He looked at Megan, "It was called Survival of the Fittest."

"I've seen that," Megan laughed. She turned to her mom. "You remember that. Those people out in the middle of the woods, some kinda commune or something, but they're always fighting and doing stuff to each other. Some of them were kinda mean."

"Which is why I'm here instead of there," Pete said.

"What's that mean?" Dahlia asked.

"Well, I wrote it, intending for it to be a serious study on how a small community can survive without modern materials. Supermarkets, electricity, etc., but the powers that be saw they could get better ratings if they pitted these poor souls against each other. So now, they think up ways to get these folks to stab each other in the back. The nastier the better."

"Do you still write it?" I asked.

He shook his head, "No. My ideas didn't fit the direction they wanted to go. I owned the concept so they bought me out. And I bought a boat, and here I am."

Eddie looked at Megan. "Now you see why I don't watch television."

"I thought it was funny," Megan said.

"You and a couple of million viewers," Pete said.

"Are you here full time?" I asked.

"For the time being, I thought I would try my hand at a novel."

"I want to read it," Megan said.

"Wonderful, my first sale. But I have to write it first."

"What's it going to be about?" Dahlia asked.

"Damned if I know," Pete said. He turned to Eddie, "You know, while you are here I'm wondering if you could look at my little boat. It doesn't always want to respond to the rudder."

Eddie stood up again. "Sure."

"What's the name of your sailboat?" I asked.

"The Mosquito," he said. "When I'm out there all alone, that's about as significant as I feel."

"That's why you bought it," I said.

He smiled at me, "Yes, yes it is."

Dahlia stood. "We have to get going also," she said. "We're meeting Aunt Betty at Norterra and Megan has stuff to buy."

"Lucky Megan," I said.

Eddie followed Pete out.

"Thanks for the boat ride, Jackson," Megan said.

Dahlia stood for a moment looking at me, "Me too," she said. She touched my arm, "Thanks a lot."

I watched them as they left, and as they went through the door I heard Megan say, "I didn't think boys were supposed to kick."

43

I called Blackhawk. He told me Elena had decided she wanted him to take her to Prescott shopping, so Diaz and his problem were on hold. She loves her aunty but shopping is shopping.

I dug the paint brush out and, in a couple of hours, I finished the job topside. I was cleaning the brush when my phone beeped at me. I can't even describe the sound it makes when I have an incoming call. Whatever the default tone is. Some genius at the phone factory decided this was the one. It made me wonder what kind of drugs they do at the phone factory.

It was Dahlia.

"Hey," I said.

"I know we just saw you, but I was wondering if you don't have a policewoman to take care of, if you were busy tonight?"

"She's just a friend," I said. "Honestly, just a friend. Let's see. Tonight I was going to shine my prosthetics."

There was silence.

"Oh," she said. "You're kidding me."

"I have no plans. In fact, the thing I thought I was going to do got canceled. What do you have in mind?"

"Well, Megan is in a rush to get back home. I think she's got a boyfriend. So she's going to ride back with Aunt Betty, which leaves me on my own. So I thought maybe we could meet for dinner?"

"You don't know if Megan has a boyfriend?"

"We are at the age where we don't talk about such things. Give her a couple of years and she'll be spilling her guts. It was just an idea. If you can't make it, that's okay."

"I think it's a great idea. How about this? I've got two prime filets in the freezer. Why don't I cook here? Medium rare, baked, asparagus? I even have some Ben and Jerry's for desert."

"Are you sure? I don't want to put you out."

"Really, it would be great. I think Danny's running the shuttle, just have him bring you out. We could watch TV after we eat."

Again, the silence.

"One thing you need to know," she said. "I don't kiss on the first date."

"I can respect that," I said. "How about we hold hands and watch the moonlight?"

"How can a girl resist moonlight?"

44

There was little conversation as we attacked the meal. As promised, we both polished off a cup of Ben and Jerry's. She scraped the last of it onto her spoon, licked it off, then dropped the spoon into the bowl with a satisfied clatter. She leaned back with a smile and released a small belch.

"Oh my, excuse me."

"In some cultures, a belch at the end of the meal is a sign to the host that the meal was satisfactory."

She looked at me and smiled, "How do you know this? From the Travel Channel? Oh, that's right, you don't have a TV."

"Experience firsthand," I said. I slid out of the booth and collected her bowl. As I put them in the sink, she moved up behind me and reached across to start the water running.

"I can get this," I said.

"In my house," she said, "the cook doesn't clean."

"Does Megan cook?"

"Megan orders pizza."

"So Megan does the majority of dishes?"

"Pretty much."

I moved out of the way. I opened a drawer and extracted a dish towel. Or, what passed as a dish towel on my boat. As she washed the dishes, I dried them and put them away.

As we finished, she turned and said, "That was a wonderful meal."

"I don't know about wonderful, but it was filling."

"More than that," she smiled.

I looked out the starboard portal.

"The sun is down," I said. "We have some pretty spectacular sunsets out here. How about we go topside and enjoy it?"

"Sounds good."

"More wine?"

She picked up her wine glass and drank the small amount that remained, then handed it to me.

"Just a taste," she said. "I still have a drive tonight."

"That's disappointing to hear."

"I told you about me and first dates."

"Yes, ma'am."

I poured an inch of wine in the glass and handed it to her. I drained the bottle in my glass. I wasn't driving. I led the way through the master stateroom to the stern. The air had cooled and it was quite pleasant.

The ladder to topside was slightly canted but still steep.

"Let me go first," I said. "If I follow you up, with you wearing that little dress, I might get a glimpse of paradise."

She laughed. "You boys are so easy."

Up top, I pulled two chaise cushions from the locker I

keep them in. I pulled the chaise lounges into a position for optimum sunset viewing. We sat side by side and the sunset, while almost finished, was living up to my expectations. We settled into a comfortable silence. The only sound was the gentle lap of small waves against the neighboring boats and dock.

After a while I looked at her. She was staring out across the water. The slight breeze was gently moving her hair. Occasionally, she would reach up and move it back behind her ear. Without looking, she reached over and took my hand.

"Can I ask a personal question?" I said.

She looked at me.

"You can ask."

"Megan's father. I notice you both use the name Martin but I understand that is your maiden name."

"It's my only name."

She hitched around to look at me.

"Megan's daddy was a sweet young boy I had met and was dating when he decided it was his patriotic duty to join up and go over to the Middle East and protect America."

She looked back out over the water for a moment.

Without looking back, she said, "In a moment of passion we decided to consummate our love for each other before he left. It was one time. It was all it took. He was killed the first month he was there, and I was pregnant."

"I'm sorry. I didn't mean to pry."

"No, no, it's okay. To be honest, I didn't really know him that well."

She looked back at me. "Now it's my turn. Earlier you

told me the story about your parents having to go to your school. How old were you when they died?"

"About a year older. Car crash. A policeman came and took me out of my school and drove me to the hospital. He wouldn't tell me why. Or maybe he couldn't, maybe he didn't know. They were both gone by the time I got there."

"I'm sorry," she said.

I shrugged, "Stuff happens."

She nodded. "Shit happens to everyone."

That made me smile.

"No relatives? Aunts, uncles, brothers, sisters?" she said.

"None," I said. "I never knew any grandparents."

"How sad."

Again, I shrugged. I sipped the wine.

"So, what happened then?"

The sun was well down and it was beginning to get dark. The first stars of the night were becoming visible. I thought about what I would tell her.

"I went into the system. Bounced around a lot. I wasn't, what you would call, real cooperative. When I was old enough, a judge told me I could go into the service or into the prison system. I didn't have the patriotic fervor Megan's daddy had, but in my own way, I decided I wanted to save America. And I think, without realizing it, I wanted to save myself."

"Then you lost your foot."

"Yeah, after a while."

She was quiet.

"Did you save yourself?"

I shrugged. "Time will tell."

"Do you have any friends? Anybody in your life?"

"You mean women?"

"I mean anybody. No man is an island."

"John Donne," I said.

"That's right."

"I told you I read a lot."

"Do you?"

"Read a lot?"

"No, do you have anyone in your life?"

"You've met Boyce," I said.

"The policewoman that is only a friend. Anyone else?"

"Well, there's Eddie."

"That's it?"

I was silent.

"There's Blackhawk. He takes up a lot of space in my life."

"Blackhawk?"

"Yeah."

"There is someone named Blackhawk?"

"Yeah."

"Are you punking me?"

"No, ma'am."

"What is Blackhawk's real name?"

I was silent for a moment. "I don't know. He was introduced to me as Blackhawk and that's all I've ever known."

"Who introduced you?"

"The Colonel."

"Colonel who?"

"Just the Colonel. He was our group leader."

"Are you trying to piss me off?"

I laughed, "No, no, not at all. All is true, so help me God."

"Tell me about it."

"Not much to tell. I went into the service and I decided I wanted to be a SEAL, so I did that."

"I thought you said you were a Marine. You are a Navy SEAL?"

"Not anymore. Even though some say, once a SEAL always a SEAL."

I looked out across the water. The far mountains were now just a dark jagged line across the horizon.

She punched me on the arm.

"You're not leaving me with just that. I want to know about you being a SEAL."

I looked at her. The moon was up and the moonlight trailed across her face and I don't know if it was just the romance of the moment, but she was lovely.

"I made it through the SEALs and the next thing I knew they flew me across the country and that's where I met the Colonel and then they trained me some more and hooked me up with Blackhawk and the rest of the team."

"What did the team do?"

I set forward.

"Okay, you'll just have to believe me on this, but I can't tell you. Most of what we were involved in was top secret."

"You're a spy?" she said, incredulously.

"Oh, no. Nothing like that. Nothing romantic at all. We just did work that bolstered the security of the United States. Most of it was completely boring. But we signed a pledge, under penalty of imprisonment, to never divulge any of the activity we were involved with."

"And you can't tell me, or you'll have to kill me."

I laughed, "You watch too many movies. No, I ain't no James Bond. I was just a soldier doing what my country ordered me to do."

"So if this Colonel introduced you to this Blackhawk person, how did he introduce you to Blackhawk?"

I looked at her. She was grinning at me.

"He said, "Blackhawk, this is Jackson. Jackson, this is Blackhawk.""

She cocked her head and looked at me for a long moment.

"So, what is your real name?"

"Jackson."

"So that's the name you were born with?"

"Depends on your definition of *born*."

45

She hit me on the arm again.

"Now you are playing games with me."

The sun was down but the moon had replaced it. It wasn't full, but close. Between the moonlight and the dock lights, it wasn't just a romantic notion: she really was lovely.

"No, not really. I've seriously always considered my life to have begun when I went into the service. Anything before that was pretty much wasted."

"That sounds sad."

"Not really. When did you really wake up and look around and realize your life had some purpose?"

She nodded. "When Megan was born." She looked back across the moonlit lake.

We sat in silence for a while. We could hear voices from across the water. Not clear enough to make them out, but loud enough to make you wonder, again, about how far sound carries across water.

"So this is all true? About you, I mean."

"I'm afraid so."

"So that story Eddie told us up in Sedona, about the Ambassador's granddaughter, that's true too."

"All true. Except I'm not the hero he tried to make me out to be. I had a lot of help."

"Like who?"

"Well, Blackhawk for one. Boyce, for another. The resources of the Columbian Consulate. The Phoenix Police Department."

She was looking at me hard. "Eddie thinks you are a hero, and you're going to save Billy."

"He asked me to help. I'm not sure what I can do. I am no hero."

"Here's something that Megan and I have talked about, are these bombings connected to Billy?"

"That scenario makes sense, but I can't prove it. I'm just trying to help Eddie."

"And if you can't?"

"I told him I would do what I could. I could fail."

"I like Billy, and it's impossible not to like Eddie. I hope you can help them. I hope you don't fail."

"Me too."

She stood up. "Unfortunately, failure is always an option. In everything. I have to go. This has been a beautiful night. Thank you so much."

As I started to protest, I heard two people coming down the dock. I stood and looked. It was Eddie and his new friend Pete. They were coming to the Tiger Lily.

"Looks like I have company," I said.

She took my arm.

"I said I don't kiss on the first date," she said. She leaned in against me, putting her arms around my neck. My hands automatically went to her waist.

"I lied," she said, and kissed me on the mouth. Then she did it again, then again. She pulled away, keeping her arms around my neck. From five inches away she stared at me, her mouth slightly open, and her eyes so dark they disappeared. A lock of hair had fallen across her forehead. Now I kissed her. And again.

After an age, and very slowly, we untangled.

"Hey Jackson, you home?" Eddie yelled from below.

"Come up and see me some time," Dahlia said, doing her best Mae West. She leaned forward and kissed me again.

I started to say something along the line of, 'if we're quiet maybe they'll go away,' when she walked to the edge and looked down. "Hey, Eddie," she said.

46

We were in the lounge, all standing. Eddie was looking uncomfortable. "I'm sorry, Miss Dahlia," he said. "I sure didn't mean to interrupt."

She smiled at him. "Nothing to be sorry for. Honestly, I was just leaving. I still have a teenager at home and it's a long drive."

Eddie looked at me.

"Sadly, it's true," I said.

"The teenager, or the drive," Pete said.

Dahlia laughed. "Both." She reached out and touched my arm. "Thanks a lot. Give me a call."

She looked at Pete. "Nice to see you again."

"Likewise," he said.

She hugged Eddie. "Billy didn't do anything wrong, and they'll find that out."

Eddie nodded.

With a small wave of the hand, she went out the sliding doors and stepped onto the dock. We followed. We watched her walk to the gate where Danny had the shuttle waiting.

Pete said, "Wow."

After we heard the gate clang shut, Eddie turned to me.

"What's a guy got to do to get a beer around this joint?"

I smiled. "Come on in and sit a spell. I'll see what I can do."

I dug a bottle of Dos Equis from the refrigerator. I waved one at Pete.

"No thanks," he said, settling on the couch. "Not much of a beer drinker. Not this late, anyway."

"First bad thing I've learned about him," Eddie said, accepting the beer I handed him.

"Something from the bar?"

"Now, that I can do. Do you have gin?"

"Plymouth okay?"

"Indeed. Maybe with a splash of lime and a dash of bitters."

"Man after my own heart." I made two.

I could tell Eddie had something on his mind, but I knew it wouldn't come out until he was ready. I channeled the music from up top to the lounge. I settled in the highback chair and sipped my drink.

"This is a nice boat," Pete said.

"It's no Moneypenny," I said.

"Beg pardon?"

"Oh, sorry. You've changed the name."

He took a drink, "Oh, yeah, *13 Episodes*. That's what bought it." He looked at his drink. "Just right," he said.

"Tell Jackson what you were telling me, earlier," Eddie said. Pete set his drink aside.

"Eddie was telling me about his nephew, and you helping to look into it. What I was telling him was that before my current incarnation as a writer, I was an attorney."

"I won't hold it against you," I said.

He laughed. "Thanks. Just do me a favor and don't spread the word. I want to fit in here."

"Secret's safe with me."

"I had worked at a firm that is licensed in most of the western states," he continued. "I didn't really do criminal law, but listening to Eddie, I said that in my opinion, the only thing keeping his nephew in jail was bad representation."

"Attorney Taggart."

He shrugged. "Eddie says he's local. One of the good ol' boys."

"You think another attorney can get Billy out?"

"I'm not trying to spread false hope. But it sounds like a case could be made to, at least, get him from behind bars."

"What do you think?" Eddie said, looking at me.

I looked at Pete. My bullshit meter didn't move. He seemed to be sincere.

"You willing to do more than talk about it? You willing to go up with Eddie and see what you can do?"

Pete nodded. "Yeah, I can do that, I'm not doing anything else. But as a consultant. It's probably smart to leave the local attorney as the attorney of record."

"You wanna come up with us?" Eddie asked.

I thought about Blackhawk and Diaz.

"Later, maybe. Blackhawk's got a small problem he wants me to help with."

Eddie smiled. "I don't see Blackhawk needing much help on anything."

"I brush his suits and shine his shoes."

"There *is* somebody named Blackhawk?" Pete said.

I smiled. "Nobody seems to believe it," I said.

"Hell," Eddie said. "They got rappers call themselves Pump Diddle and such. Blackhawk don't seem much of a stretch."

47

The next evening I was sitting, with the very real Blackhawk, at El Patron. I was nursing a beer. I was sitting at my favorite stool, on the corner. Nacho was across from me, reading the paper. Blackhawk was next to me, sipping a club soda.

"I'm going to start calling you Joe, or something," I said.

He looked at me.

"Why?"

"Every time I tell people your name is Blackhawk, they don't believe me."

He was silent a moment.

"Well, that's okay with me. My name was Joe."

"Really?"

Nacho looked up.

"No," Blackhawk laughed.

Nacho shook his head in disgust, and looked back to his paper.

I heard someone come in behind me and Blackhawk looked past me. I swiveled. It was Diaz. He was bleeding and one eye was almost shut. He stood in the middle of the floor looking at us.

"You are bleeding on my dance floor," Blackhawk said. He turned and signaled Jimmy. "Bring a bar towel." Jimmy came around the bar with a towel. Blackhawk took it and walked over to Diaz. He tossed Diaz the towel while he was still five feet away. Diaz caught it and started to wipe his face.

"Clean my floor," Blackhawk said.

Diaz looked at him. Expecting sympathy, maybe. Blackhawk was impassive. Diaz finally leaned down and mopped the floor, then straightened and pressed the towel against his face. Blackhawk turned and went back to the bar.

"Get the first aid kit," he told Jimmy.

Jimmy retrieved it and set it in front of me. I motioned Diaz over. He was bleeding from his nose and lip. Blackhawk and I, both, had extensive medic training. Diaz's wounds were mostly superficial. His lip was split and a blow to his eye had burst blood vessels, making the eye ugly and red. The lid was swelling. His eyebrow was split and bleeding.

I motioned him to sit beside me. I opened the kit and selected a couple of butterfly bandages and a tube of antibiotic. I swabbed him with the towel and he whined like a kitten. Every time I tried to apply antibiotic, he flinched and pulled away.

"Sit still, or I'm going to knock you off the stool," I said.

He forced himself to sit still while I finished. I snapped the kit shut and Jimmy took it and put it under the bar. Blackhawk sat a stool down from Diaz so he could swivel and look at him.

"You fall out of bed in that motel," he said.

"They snatched me off the street."

"Who they?" I said.

"Rojo and that other guy, Omar. The guy that let me out of the bathroom when I was hijacked."

"What were you doing on the street?" Blackhawk said.

"Hey, man. I was just taking a walk. Man, I was sick of sitting in that motel."

"That the whore's name?" Nacho said. "Walk? She got a sister, Don't Walk?"

I studied the man for a long moment. I knew he was lying, and I knew Blackhawk knew he was lying. What for?

"Why would they try to snatch you? Garza would be happy if they just put a round in your head."

"That's what they said they were going to do. They beat on me and told me they were going to kill me. I told them to let me talk to Garza but Rojo said 'Fuck Garza'. That's when I believed them. Man, I was scared shitless. They threw me in the car. They didn't tell me where they were going, but I knew where they were taking me."

"Where?"

"Down to the river bottom. You shoot a man down there, and his bones are picked clean in a week."

"How come you aren't dead in the river bottom."

"Omar was driving, and the dumb fucker was out of gas so they stopped to get some, and while he's pumping, a cop car pulls into the pump across from us. I know they can't do anything, so I just get out and walked away."

"A cop car," Blackhawk said.

"Yeah man, pulled up right next to us. They didn't tie me up or nothing. Just Rojo sitting next to me with a gun."

"They chase you?"

"Hell, yeah they chased me. But Omar had to put the gas nozzle back and get in and start it up, and I went the other way so they had to pull out and turn around. Gave me time to ditch them."

"What does 'fuck Garza' mean?" Blackhawk asked.

"It means they weren't getting rid of him for Garza. They were doing it for themselves," I said. I was tired of the dancing. I reached over and yanked him off the stool and slapped him in the ear. He let out a high-pitched yelp, like a puppy.

"You and Rojo and this other guy stole the money." It wasn't a question.

He covered his ear with his forearm and ducked away from me. Blackhawk grabbed him and shook him.

"Tell me," he said.

"Okay, okay. Cool it, man. It was Rojo and Omar. They took the money, I just drove the truck. I went in the bathroom like Rojo told me, and stayed there until Omar opened the door. I took the truck across the border and acted surprised when the money wasn't there."

"You actually thought Garza was going to let that slide."

"Rojo's in thick with Garza. He was going to vouch for me and we'd lay low for a while, then just disappear, man."

"But he turned you out."

"The fucker ratted me, man. So I came here."

Nacho spoke up. "So you were just feeding me a line of

shit when you acted like you recognized that guy, Omar, but didn't know him."

Diaz didn't say anything.

"You one dumb son of a bitch to believe somebody like Rojo," Nacho said in disgust.

"You the one that believed me, man," Diaz said.

Nacho came off the stool and Diaz backed up, his palm out to ward Nacho off. "Hey, hey, man, I don't mean nothin'."

"Who's got the money?" Blackhawk said.

"Those guys."

"Which one?"

"I don't know."

"Where does Rojo live?"

"I don't know, but Omar has a crib south of Roosevelt."

Blackhawk looked at me.

"Place to start," I said

48

Nacho wanted to come with us, so we took his Jeep Cherokee. He drove and I sat next to him. Blackhawk was behind me and Diaz behind Nacho. Omar's place was a dump south of Roosevelt just west of Interstate 17. I had retrieved the Kahr .45 from the trunk of the Mustang. Blackhawk had slipped a shoulder holster under his impeccable jacket, and slid his 9mm Sig Sauer into it. He pocketed a small Ruger .380. Best way to not get in a war is to be prepared for one.

The place turned out to be ten minutes from the club. Nacho took us up to the freeway then north to McDowell and across, to where we could come down to Roosevelt, then down the side street it was on. It was the kind of neighborhood where people sat on their front porch steps, even in the summer. The houses were a mix, from rundown shacks, to nicely kept small homes with neat yards. Omar's was a wreck.

Nacho cruised past the house and Diaz said, "That's it."

"Keep going," Blackhawk said. "Go around the block."

Nacho turned right at the next street, then right again. When we were back on Omar's street, a block away, Blackhawk said, "Park here."

Nacho pulled to the curb, but didn't turn the motor off. I twisted around and looked at Blackhawk, following his lead.

Blackhawk looked at me, "This guy knows Diaz, but not us. Let's go pay him a visit, see what we can shake out of him."

Nacho turned in the seat. "Me too?"

"Hell yes, you are ugly enough to scare anyone into spilling their guts," I said.

"With such power comes great responsibility," he said, opening the car door.

Blackhawk looked at Diaz. "You stay here." He opened his door and stepped out. He started down the street. Nacho and I followed.

The house was old, made of blocks, with a shingled roof. Some of the shingles were missing. There was a weedy carport on our side of the house. We came up the drive to the small porch. There was just one step up. A rusty metal chair sat by itself next to the door. It was one of those porch chairs with a back that opened out like a fan. The height of fashion in 1950. It was hard to tell what the original color was. The door had a window in it, and there was a bay window behind the chair. Closed, ratty-looking blinds covered both windows.

I signaled Blackhawk to circle back through the carport and check the back door. Nacho and I stood where anyone inside couldn't see us. I was giving Blackhawk plenty of time to get into position when the door opened, and Blackhawk stepped out.

"Back door was unlocked," he said. He nodded toward the interior of the house, "You better see this."

Nacho and I followed him in. The place was a dump. There was a heavily soiled couch with a ripped arm just inside, under the window. A stuffed chair that didn't match anything was against the wall. There was a tin tray table next to it, with an overflowing ashtray. The floors were hardwood, scuffed and worn. There were fast-food wrappers everywhere. Whoever had eaten out of them had finished and left them where they lay. Some had old, moldy food on them. The place stank of decay, cigarettes and marijuana. Over the top of that was another dull and pungent odor. An odor familiar to me.

Blackhawk moved through the house with purpose, so we followed. He led us into the kitchen. On the floor was a body. It was a man. His body had the shrunken look of having been there a while. There was a stain of dried blood under him. He was wearing a Phoenix Suns jersey and a pair of jeans. His arms were covered in tattoos. On his feet was a pair of tennis shoes that were the most improbable color of lime green. They looked brand new, and stood out in the room like a rose in a meat locker.

"Hello, Omar," Nacho said.

Omar was on his back, his glassy eyes filmed over and half closed. He had been shot center mass. The bullet had burst his heart and he was dead before he hit the floor.

Blackhawk picked up a dirty rag and wrapped it around his hand then gingerly rolled the body on its side. He studied the exit wound, then let the body roll back onto its back. The movement loosened some body gas and my stomach lurched. I looked around the room. There was splattered blood on the back of one of the kitchen chairs, and on the small half table that still had dirty dishes on it.

I looked at Nacho, "Go to the front window and watch."

"Watch for what?" he said.

"For anything. Blackhawk and I are going to shake the place down, and we don't want someone walking in on us."

He turned to leave. "And don't touch a thing but your shoe soles on the floor," Blackhawk said.

Using the hand wrapped in the rag, Blackhawk began opening cabinets. He found a stained roll of paper towels and handed them to me. I unwrapped several and wrapped my hands with them. We began to methodically search the house.

Omar seemed to have lived a Spartan existence. What closets there were, were empty. Very few dishes, and nothing but beer and cheese in the refrigerator. The cheese had green mold on it. In the one inch space between the cabinet holding the kitchen sink and the refrigerator, I saw a piece of paper. I fished it out. It was a tri-folded schedule for the local Greyhound Bus service. I showed it to Blackhawk. He looked it over.

"You steal that much money, why you taking the bus?" he said.

I shook my head. We went back through, room by room,

overturning the furniture, tearing out the batting on the bottom. We pulled each drawer out, checking for anything taped underneath. We looked for false bottoms. Blackhawk pulled his pocket knife and unscrewed the light fixtures. We looked in the back of the filthy toilet. The bathroom had a toothbrush, toothpaste, shaving things and a really obnoxious aftershave. We took the medicine cabinet down. Nothing was in the freezer at all. There was a dishwasher, but it was rusted, empty and disconnected. I pulled it out. Nothing behind it. We turned the bed over. Nothing. Blackhawk took the ceiling fan down. Nothing. There was a mirror screwed to the wall. I pulled my pocketknife to unscrew it when Blackhawk stepped over and smashed it with the butt of the Sig Sauer. Nothing was behind it. In the bedroom closet we found a trapdoor in the ceiling that led to a crawlspace. We brought a kitchen chair over and I climbed up and pushed it aside. I used the flashlight function on my phone. There was hardly enough room up top for a man to climb into. The light revealed nothing but insulation.

I climbed back down and leaving the chair there, we went back into the kitchen. Omar was really starting to smell.

"Nothing here," I said.

"I didn't expect to find anything. Omar wouldn't have the money anyway," Blackhawk said. "I'm betting on Rojo."

"Yeah, me too. Let's vamoose."

"That a pure American colloquialism?"

"Sho 'nuff."

Nacho was standing by the window, dutifully watching the driveway and the porch.

"Anything?" I asked.

He shook his head. "Street's clear."

I opened the door, wiping the knob at the same time. We moved out onto the porch.

Nacho said, "Son of a bitch!"

We looked down the street and his Jeep was gone. Diaz was gone with it.

49

Blackhawk was looking at Nacho, but Nacho wouldn't meet his eye.

"How'd he do that?" Blackhawk asked.

"I left the keys under the seat," Nacho said sheepishly.

"You just handed him the keys?"

"No, I didn't hand them to him," he protested. "I left them under the seat. Shit man, what with the club and all, I got too many keys. I always leave them under the seat."

"Always?"

"Everyone knows that if they take my car, I'll kill them."

"Diaz took your car," I said.

"And I'm going to kill him," Nacho said.

I looked at Blackhawk. He was seeing the humor in it but didn't want to show it. He pulled his phone.

A half hour later, and five blocks away, Elena picked us up. Elena is one of the few women that could pick us up without making a skirmish out of it. We piled into her car and she just looked at Blackhawk.

I had her drive to a Food City. Outside the entrance was

one of the world's last remaining payphones. I had to borrow change from Nacho. I thumbed the money in and dialed Boyce's number.

She answered on the third ring. The first two rings were spent with her looking at the phone wondering who the hell was calling her.

"Detective Boyce," she said.

I rattled off Omar's address. Then did it again more slowly.

"Jackson, what the hell are you doing?" she said and I hung up.

We hit the mid-morning traffic and it jammed us up enough that it took longer to get back to the club. Nacho was anxious, then visibly disappointed when his Jeep wasn't in the parking lot. As Elena parked in her reserved spot, Boyce pulled in behind us. Elena stepped out and hit her remote and her car responded with a short honk. You can lock the car without the honk, but Elena didn't feel the car was locked unless she heard the honk.

Boyce stopped her car at a random angle in the middle of the lot. As if she owned the place, and she'll park where she damn well pleases. As she got out, Elena went across to her and they hugged each other. I stood there feeling dumb and helpless. It was like this when these women got together, and Boyce and I were no longer a couple. Elena shot daggers at me as they walked past. I thought Boyce was enjoying herself.

We followed them inside. Elena took Boyce's arm as they went through the door. They led us down the hall. We followed them into the main bar. Blackhawk and Nacho went behind the bar. I angled for my stool but Boyce got there first. Elena leaned over and said something to Boyce in a low voice, then with a glance at me, turned and went upstairs. I sat on the other side of the corner. I didn't like the entrance being behind me, but I liked less having Boyce where I couldn't watch her.

"What was that about?" I said, looking up at Elena as she walked across the balcony that surrounded three sides of the room. She disappeared through the upstairs door that led to Blackhawk's office and apartment.

Boyce looked at me with innocent eyes. "She said to make you beg."

Before I had a witty retort, her cell phone buzzed. She dug it out of the satchel she carried as a purse. Besides the phone, I knew there was a .40 Caliber Glock 27 in there.

"Detective Boyce," she said, curtly. She listened for a long while. "Call Mendoza," she finally said. "Thanks for calling me, Officer." She disconnected and replaced the phone in the bag. She looked at me, showing nothing.

Finally, after we had played that game for a while, she said, "I'll find out eventually, but, hey why wait. Who's the dead guy?"

I looked at Blackhawk, as he was washing beer mugs and lining them up on a dish towel. He shrugged.

"Guy named Omar. He's Valdez," I said.

She sat quietly, watching me. She waited. Finally, she said, "You want to tell me about it?"

I looked again at Blackhawk. Again, he shrugged.

"Better you than Mendoza," I said. So I told her about Elena's cousin and the missing money. I told her about Garza, Rojo and the faked hijacking. When I came to the missing Jeep, she turned and looked at Nacho, but he was busy at the other end of the bar. He turned his face away. I'll be damned if he wasn't blushing.

She turned back to me.

"Omar is Omar Menotti. He's a low-end soldier. A long record but mostly petty stuff. Rojo is Eduardo Padilla. He's like the lieutenant to Garza. He keeps the soldiers in line. How much money is it?"

"You know a lot," I said.

"Jackson, I've been in gangs for four years. I would hope that I would know a lot."

"I thought you were Homeland now."

"On assignment; when it's done I'm back to gangs," she said. "How much is it?"

I looked at Blackhawk. He turned and looked at Nacho. Nacho was trying to ignore us.

"Nacho?" Blackhawk said.

Nacho reluctantly looked up, "What?"

"Detective Boyce wants to know how much Diaz hijacked."

"He said north of half a mil."

She looked at Blackhawk. "Your cousin is in deep shit."

"Elena's cousin," he said.

She shook her head. "Same, same." She turned to me. "What now?"

"We figure Diaz is headed to the money. We figure it's

Rojo. Diaz knows Nacho won't report his car stolen, so he's got a free ride for a while."

"So you find Rojo, you find the stolen drug money?"

"That's the plan," I said.

"Where's Rojo?" she said.

I shrugged, "We don't know."

"I do," she said.

Now Blackhawk and Nacho both turned to look at her.

"You do?" I said.

"Sure."

"You want to tell us?" I said.

"Then what will you do?"

I looked at Blackhawk. He shrugged. He had a lot of that going on.

"We go get Nacho's car back."

"And maybe the money?"

This time it was my turn to shrug.

She slid off the stool. "I'll go with you," she said. "You ride with me."

"Where we going?" Blackhawk said.

She looked at him, "You follow me."

50

I rode in her big Crown Vic. Blackhawk and Nacho followed in Blackhawk's Jag. She led across to Nineteenth Avenue and north to Bethany Home Road. We turned east.

"Where are we headed?" I asked.

"Try some patience," she said, without looking at me.

We continued on in silence. We went through Central. At Ninth Street, she indicated an apartment complex on the north side. The sign on the corner called it *The Armitage*. She turned south on Tenth, drove a half a block, then pulled to the curb. Blackhawk came in behind us. She dropped all four windows and cut the engine. In a moment, Blackhawk and Nacho slid into the backseat.

She half-turned, left arm on the wheel, right arm on the back of the seat, so she could look at all of us.

"That place is a Valdez place. Everyone living there is connected to Valdez. This is where Rojo lives."

"Just round them all up." Nacho said.

"Arrest them for what? Living in a crappy apartment? They are smart enough to not crap in the nest. They keep the place tight and clean. Not that they don't bring drugs and women in there, but they have the whole place buttoned up. As soon as a cop shows, it all just disappears."

"Small fish," I said.

She nodded. She looked at me. "What now?"

I looked at Blackhawk. He didn't shrug this time.

"I want my Jeep back," Nacho said.

"We'll get your Jeep," Blackhawk said.

"Do you know which apartment Rojo is in?" I asked.

Boyce shook her head.

"Nacho can find out," Blackhawk said.

Nacho looked at him, surprised, "I can? How?"

"You have a message from Garza to deliver to him personally," Blackhawk said.

"What message?"

Boyce leaned across me and opened the glove box. She rummaged for a moment, then pulled out an envelope. It had a State of Arizona logo on it. It looked like Department of Motor Vehicle stuff. She pulled the contents out, selected one piece at random and put it back in the envelope. The rest she placed back into the glove box. She handed the envelope to Nacho.

"This message," she said.

"The guard is going to want to take it," I said. "Tell him Garza insists you deliver it personally. In fact, you are not supposed to disturb Rojo. You are supposed to slip it under his door. He was up all night and is sleeping. He'll be meaner than a junk yard dog if he gets woke up. You get the apartment number and text it to Blackhawk."

"Then what?" Boyce said.

"You cause a diversion with your big badge, and Jackson and I will go in behind Nacho and take the little shit out," Blackhawk said

"Take him out?" Boyce said, cocking her head.

"Out of the building," I said. I opened the door and slid out. The others followed.

We stood in someone's driveway, and looked back at the complex. There were no sidewalks. Our street traveled past Bethany Home with the apartment building on its west side. Along Bethany Home the complex was essentially a long wall with windows. There was a sidewalk along the street. Bushes against the wall. All of the windows looked covered. The building was two stories high.

"Nacho I can see, but I don't see how you two are going to get in. There are only two ways in, off of Ninth Street and Tenth. But they keep Tenth blocked, so really the only way into the parking is off of Ninth."

"Valdez guards?"

"At the guard gate there are two lanes in, one lane out. All gated. The entrance has one lane for residents, who have a code they have to punch in on the pad, for the gate to lift. The other lane is next to the guard gate. There is one security guy; he has to approve you before he lets you in. There are usually two or three Valdez guys just hanging close by. They have rakes and stuff sitting close so they can look like landscapers if they have to. We are guessing they are armed."

"You know the code?"

She shook her head. "They change it every week."

I stood looking at the building.

"What's the call, boss?" Blackhawk said.

"Boss?" Boyce smiled at me.

"He lets me be the boss when he thinks things are likely to turn to shit," I said.

They stood quietly while I thought. Boyce kept a bemused smile on.

Finally, I said, "Nacho goes in." I looked at Blackhawk. "We wait till Nacho texts Rojo's apartment number, then Boyce follows close on the next car that goes in. We are on her tail so the gate arm doesn't come back down. She pulls up just far enough for us to get by her. She jumps out, one hand on her gun, waving the badge and yelling at the landscaper guards. Yelling they are illegal and she wants to see their identification."

"They'll think she's crazy," Nacho said.

"Exactly. Nacho, you get to the right building, you stand out front for us to see. We pull up, park, and go in to get Rojo."

"How do we get out?" Nacho said.

"I'll make sure the guard obliges us," Boyce said.

"When do I get my Jeep?" Nacho said.

Blackhawk shook his head, exasperated. "When we find Diaz, you'll get your damn Jeep."

"He better not have done nothing to it," he said.

"You are going to kill him anyway, remember?" I said

51

We did a drive by. Normal speed. I was in the backseat of Boyce's car with Nacho in the front passenger seat. A half block back, Blackhawk followed. We didn't gawk and stare. Boyce and Nacho kept their faces forward. I slumped against the back door behind Boyce and studied the main entrance through the back passenger window. The guard appeared to be reading. I couldn't see the other guards. There was a wall with landscaping that connected the guard gate to the two-story apartments on either side. Through the gate, I could see across the inside parking to an interior compound with grass and trees, and more apartments far across.

"Those other guards are always on the job?" I said.

"Best to think so," Boyce said.

"Go on around," I said.

I twisted around and looked out the back. Blackhawk hung far enough back that is was unlikely anyone would put us together. Boyce drove to the end of the block and turned right. The Armitage was really several buildings with maybe a fifteen-foot space between them. The best I could tell, each building housed two apartments for each floor. They all faced inward. Between the buildings there were connecting walls one story high that hid the interior. There was wrought-iron fencing with pikes at the top. She turned right again and we passed the entrance on Tenth Street. There was a wrought-iron gate across it. It was chained and padlocked. Again, I could see parking, then grass and trees, then the parking on the other side. Another right and we ended up about where we had started.

"Pull to the curb," I said. She did.

I opened the back door and stepped out. Nacho followed. A moment later Blackhawk pulled up behind us. He got out. I leaned down, and Boyce lowered the passenger window.

"Give Nacho time to get through the gate. Maybe park on the wrong side of the street so you can watch him. When he leaves the guard shack, follow the next car that goes in. We'll be right behind you."

"What if another car doesn't come along right away?"

"Try a little patience," I smiled. Her right hand was on the wheel; she raised her middle finger. Keeping her finger extended, she pulled away from the curb.

I turned to Nacho. "You're up," I said, handing him the envelope.

"What if he gives me trouble?"

"Just ask him if he wants you to call Garza and have him come down."

He turned and started toward the corner. I looked at Blackhawk. He pulled the Sig Sauer from under his arm and slid a round in, then replaced it.

We slid back into the Jag. There was no parking allowed on the street so there was nothing to keep Blackhawk from picking a spot on the curb. He pulled forward until we could see Boyce parked around the corner. As I had suggested, she was parked on the left side of the street. We watched Nacho disappear into the guard shack. It seemed longer, but it was probably only a couple of minutes, when Blackhawk's phone dinged. He had laid it on the dash. He picked it up.

"1102," He said.

"Bottom floor. Good."

"Bigshot drug capos don't climb stairs," Blackhawk said, watching Boyce's car.

And we sat there for a long time with no traffic.

Finally, Blackhawk turned, and just looked at me.

"It's a big complex," I said. "Surely someone is going to visit eventually."

My phone rang. It was Boyce.

Before I could speak, she said, "I'm going in. I'm going in the resident gate and the stupid dumb blonde won't be able to work the keypad gizmo so I'll draw the guard out, then I'll show him my great big badge and my great big gun. In no particular order. And he'll open the gate. You be ready to follow me in."

"You're not blonde," I said, but she'd hung up.

Her car was moving. Blackhawk pulled around the corner and got on her tail. She pulled into the resident gate and pretended to punch a code into the keypad. Nothing happened and she kept trying. The guard put down his magazine and stood up.

Blackhawk had pulled up within a foot of her bumper.

"Honk at her," I said. He leaned on the horn, and the guard came out of the shack. He waved a hand at us, trying to quiet us down. To Boyce's right, three men stood up from where they had been sitting in the shade of the wall. The guard moved importantly to Boyce. He leaned down scowling, then took a sudden step back. Boyce brought both hands out of the window. One with the badge and one with her pistol. The guard was staring at her, swallowing hard. Boyce waved the gun at him and he turned and punched a code into the keypad. The gate went up. She said something to him and he turned and walked ahead of her. She cleared the gate and we had room to follow.

"Let's find Nacho," I said.

Blackhawk maneuvered around Boyce's Crown Vic, and accelerated into the parking area. I turned to look out the back. Boyce was out of her car, and waving her badge in one hand, her pistol in the other. I could hear her barking orders but couldn't make out the exact words. The guard and the three men, reluctantly, lined up against the wall. Boyce could be a badass when she wanted to.

"There he is," Blackhawk said. I turned and scanned the fronts of the apartments. I didn't see him.

"Where?"

"Over by his fucking Jeep," Blackhawk said. Sure enough, instead of in front of 1102 where he was supposed to be, he was in the middle of the lot staring at his Jeep. He looked disgusted.

We pulled up next to him.

"Where the hell is Rojo's place?" Blackhawk said out the window.

Nacho didn't look at him. He was looking at a bad scratch that went all the way across the quarter panel. He looked like he might cry. He waved an absent hand toward a building behind him and three down.

"That bastard," he said, almost shaking. "I'm going to kill him."

"You already said that," I said, coming out of the Jag. I went around and looked into the Jeep. The key was in the ignition, attached to a ring with a wad of other keys. There were enough to weight a body down in a deep lake.

I looked at Nacho, "You wait here for us, okay?"

He nodded. Blackhawk was out of the Jag, leaving it running, and was already moving toward the building. "You coming?" he said over his shoulder.

I pulled the Kahr clear, checked the round, and went after him.

52

All of the buildings were alike. They were like giant boxes surrounded by a ten-foot-wide strip of decorative granite with sporadic islands of cactus. Each one had a walkway leading to a centered, recessed, space that went back about twelve feet. Like an open-ended box. At the back, two doors were separated by about six feet. Rojo's building had the door on the left marked 1101, the other 1102. On the outside, at the right, were stairs that went up to a landing, then on up to the second floor. There were cigarette butts all over the place. There were windows from each apartment facing front, but they were covered on the inside with tin foil. Overgrown bushes covered the bottom half of each first-floor window.

We went in quick. Each hugging a wall. As we reached the doors, Blackhawk, standing to the side against the far wall, reached out and banged on the door with the butt of his gun. We waited. No one answered the door. He did it again. He looked across at me.

"Kick it open?" I said.

"Wait," he said. He reached over and turned the knob. It was unlocked. The door swung slowly open. He pushed it open all the way. We waited. There was no sound. I went in low with Blackhawk high, covering me.

No one home.

We went through the apartment. Rojo had the same crappy taste that Omar had.

"Let's check the neighbors," I said.

We went back out.

"If they're home they've already heard us," Blackhawk said.

I nodded, but knocked on the door anyway. Again, nothing. This time the door was locked. I pulled my knife, snapped it open and had the door open in moments.

Again, no one home.

I walked through while Blackhawk stayed outside. Boyce was right, crappy apartments. I came back out.

"I'm going to try upstairs," I said. Blackhawk shrugged. He moved over to where he could watch the parking lot. I went up the stairs two at a time. The landing had a chair sitting out facing the parking lot. Again, there were cigarette butts everywhere. I knocked on the door.

This time, I could sense someone was inside. I put my thumb on the peep hole. After a moment, the knob turned and the door opened. A young woman stood there. She looked like she had just woken up. Her skin was very light brown and she was showing a lot of it. Her hair was large and wild like she had been sleeping on it. She was naked except for small blue, sheer panties with a symbol of a smiling sun on the front. Her breasts were heavy and large with wide, round areolas.

"Whaa' you want?"

"I'm looking for Rojo," I said, maintaining eye contact. It wasn't easy.

"Downstairs," she said and started to shut the door.

"I've been there. He's not there. You know when he will be back?"

"What the fuck do I look like, his secretary?" she said, shutting the door forcefully.

No, she didn't.

Behind me, and across the parking lot, I heard Nacho roar something unintelligible. I turned and he was pointing across the lot into the middle part of the complex. Two men were walking toward us, weaving around the parked cars. It was Diaz and Rojo and they were having an intense conversation.

When they heard Nacho yell, they stopped and stared at him. It took Diaz a moment to figure out who he was looking at. He said something, then they turned and ran. Below me, Blackhawk sprinted after them. I came down the stairs too fast and caught my prosthetic on the last step and tumbled into the quarter minus granite. I rolled into a staghorn cactus. I came up feeling the cactus spines sticking me.

Now, if I had the time to put on one of those blade runner prosthetics, I could run like the wind. But without it, I wasn't going to win any races. Blackhawk, on the other hand was quick like rabbit. He would probably say quick like cheetah. Nevertheless, he was racing across the parking lot, flying across the hoods of cars, and gaining on them. He was closing fast.

Diaz looked over his shoulder, and realized Blackhawk was going to catch them. He angled close to Rojo, and suddenly shoved him in the back. Rojo tumbled hard, flat out, arms outstretched, skidding on the asphalt.

Diaz skidded to a halt, stretched out his hand with a gun in it and shot the man in the back.

As Blackhawk reached him, Diaz turned with a large grin. He raised both hands, keeping the gun. "Hey! I got him!"

"You stupid shit!" Blackhawk said, brushing him aside. He went to one knee and rolled Rojo over. He felt Rojo's neck for a pulse.

"Goddam it, you dumb shit." He started compressions on Rojo. "They aren't going to let you run far enough now."

Diaz stepped back, behind Blackhawk. He pointed his gun at the back of Blackhawk's head.

I was running full out. I skidded to a stop, desperately trying to get my front sights on Diaz, and then, there was a gunshot and Diaz pitched sideways. I hadn't pulled the trigger. At the shot, Blackhawk jerked around, the Sig in his hand.

Boyce came up from my right, gun in hand, arms extended, her front sight still on Diaz.

"So much for family," Boyce said.

Blackhawk looked at Diaz, then up at Boyce. He looked at me as I walked up. "Elena is going to be pissed," he said.

"Imagine how Diaz feels," I said.

Nacho had come up behind me. "Diaz don't feel nothing, dude."

I could hear the sirens, and turned to see the flashing lights coming through the front gate. I looked at Boyce. She smiled.

53

We were all in an interrogation room when Mendoza and Boyce came in. Mendoza was crisp and immaculate as always. He wore a gray suit straight off the rack, with a mauve tie, the tie buttoned up and straight. His dark hair was cropped so short his scalp gleamed underneath. His shoes shined like patent leather, but weren't. His eyes grazed Blackhawk and Nacho, then came to light on me. He hooked a straight backed wooden chair with a toe and dragged it out from the wall. He turned it and sat on it backwards, his elbows on the back. He was chewing a toothpick he had nestled in the corner of his mouth.

He sat quietly, studying me. Boyce moved to the back of the room, and leaned against the wall, her arms crossed. I met Mendoza's gaze with my best choir-boy look.

Finally he shook his head, "Why is it, Jackson? Why is it, that wherever you go a shit storm follows?"

I sensed that this wasn't the time for a smartass answer. I was silent. It was hard. I glanced at Boyce. She had a bemused smile on her face. She was watching me also.

"All due respect, Captain," she said, still smiling, "the last time Jackson was here, everyone thought he was a hero. Everyone but me, of course."

He shook his head impatiently. "I've got three dead Valdez," he said."One shot by you, Detective Boyce. Which puts you out of the field because of shooting protocols. Which will really piss off the Feds, and they are going to want to know why you are chasing low-end drug thugs instead of concentrating on finding a terrorist who is blowing people up."

"It was just an accident," Blackhawk said.

Mendoza looked at him. "Pray tell."

"Her being involved, I mean. Sir, I don't know if you know it or not, but while Boyce was convalescing, my girl, Elena, and Boyce became good friends. You know I own El Patron and Elena performs there."

Mendoza gave an imperceptible nod.

"Boyce just stopped in to say hi at the same time Nacho's Jeep had been taken by Elena's cousin, Luis. Just coincidence."

"Diaz."

"Right."

He looked around the room.

"Okay, tell me about the missing drug money and Eduardo Padilla."

Boyce stared innocently at the floor. Nacho's eyebrows went up and Blackhawk looked at me. I shrugged. He had the floor.

Blackhawk looked back at the Captain.

"Luis was a driver for Valdez. Padilla was his boss. On

283

one of his trips the money he was carrying somehow disappeared. He claimed not to know anything about it. Of course, the Valdez people didn't believe him and worse yet, didn't care. They were going to kill him. He came to Elena for help."

"He came to you to hide?" Mendoza said.

"Yeah, he came to me. I didn't believe him, but I didn't want him dead. For Elena's sake."

"So you hid him?"

"Put him up at a motel. I didn't want him at El Patron. Valdez people coming in, shooting the place up." He shook his head. "Bad for business."

"Tell me about Omar Menotti."

Now Nacho was looking at the floor. Again, Blackhawk looked at me. I nodded.

Blackhawk looked back at Mendoza and thought about it. "Only time we saw Menotti, he was already dead. Jackson and I figured the money thing had to be an inside job. We talked to some people that knew how it worked and it had to be Rojo. That's what everyone called Padilla. Had to be Rojo, Luis, and the other guy. The Omar guy." Blackhawk paused.

"Keep going," Mendoza said curtly.

"Not much else, sir. Luis took us to Omar's, and he was dead."

"Looking for the money?"

"Be fools not to," I said.

"I could arrest you for leaving." Mendoza said.

"I called Boyce and reported it," I said.

Mendoza looked at her.

"He did," she said. "It's in the report."

"You still left," he said looking at me. "Then what?"

I shrugged. "Diaz said he didn't know where Rojo lived, so we went back to El Patron. We had a beer, Nacho put his keys on the bar. Diaz said he had to go to the men's room. That's when Boyce came in." I looked at her. "To see Elena. It was a while before we missed Diaz and Nacho missed his keys."

Mendoza looked at Boyce, "You told them Rojo lived at the Armitage?"

She nodded.

"And you took them there."

"To get the Jeep," I said.

"And maybe the money," he said.

"There was no money," I said. "Rojo's place was empty."

"You searched it?"

"The door was open."

He looked at Boyce.

"There was no money," she said.

"So there is no money. And these guys ended up getting shot, just how?"

"The three of us drove over. Boyce followed us. But we didn't know that right away. We went to Rojo's apartment. He wasn't there. We searched it. There was no money. Nothing. Then we see Diaz and Rojo out on the grounds, and they see us and start running."

"Why did they run?"

"Because Diaz knew that Nacho was going to beat the shit out him for taking the car."

"Man, he put a big fucking scratch in it," Nacho said. He looked at Boyce, "Excuse my French."

Boyce said, "I saw it. Big fucking scratch."

Mendoza ignored her. He looked at Nacho, "That right, Ignacio? He ran because of you?"

"I was going to kill him," Nacho said.

"I've known you a while, Ignacio. I'll take that as a figure of speech," Mendoza said. He looked back to me. "So why the shooting?"

"When Diaz saw that Blackhawk was going to catch them, they were running full-out. He shoved Rojo. Rojo fell and Diaz pulled and shot him in the back. Then he turned around all proud, like he had done Blackhawk a favor."

"And you shot him, why?" he said, looking at Boyce.

"When Blackhawk went to Rojo's aid," I said. "Diaz pointed his gun at Blackhawk, and Boyce shot him. Saved his life."

He glanced at me, irritated that I had answered. "You saw it?"

I nodded.

"That right?" he said to Boyce.

"Yes, sir," she said.

"Justified," he said.

"You're damned right," Blackhawk said. He looked at Boyce. "Thank you."

She smiled at him, "My pleasure."

Mendoza sat for a long while, looking at me. Finally, he stood and hooked the back of the chair with a finger and placed it against the wall.

He tilted his head at Boyce and turned and left the room. Boyce followed, glancing at me on the way out. The three of us looked at each other.

After a long moment, Nacho said, "Is that it?"

Blackhawk raised his eyebrows at me, and I shrugged.

"We'll sit here for a while," I said.

By the big, round, white industrial clock on the wall it was twenty-eight minutes later when Boyce came back into the room.

She looked at me. "Get the hell out of here before he changes his mind."

54

Elena got really pissed. Just not the way we thought she would. But that was typical Elena.

"He pointed a gun at you?" she said to Blackhawk.

Blackhawk nodded.

"The little bastard. I'm glad he got shot!"

I looked at Blackhawk.

He just looked back, trying hard not to smile.

We were at El Patron, sitting at the bar. Elena had been rehearsing, and had come over to sit beside Blackhawk. She had a faint glow of perspiration on her upper lip. She wore a beige, scooped neck, short-sleeve blouse with fringes across the bottom. Her jeans were so tight they were almost inside out.

There were a handful of customers. Mostly friends or family of the band. One of them was Anita. She kept staring at me. I tried to appear as if I didn't notice.

The band was putting their stuff away. Jimmy had set a Dos Equis in front of Nacho and me, a club soda with lime in front of Blackhawk. He sat one of those nasty power drinks in front of Elena. He poured tequila in a shot glass and set it beside the power drink.

"I thought you'd be upset," Blackhawk said.

"He shot this other guy in the back, and pointed the gun at you?"

Blackhawk nodded.

"He got what he deserved. Aunty will be upset, but not too much. He always was a pissant."

She picked up the shot glass and tossed it back. She chased it with a large gulp of the power drink. She set both on the bar.

"He stole that money, didn't he?"

Blackhawk nodded.

She looked at me, then back to him. "You get the money?"

He shook his head.

"Too bad," she said, sliding off the stool. "I could use some new shoes." She pushed the power drink to the edge of the bar, toward Jimmy, indicating she was finished with it. "I'm going up to rest." She turned and started away, then turned back. "You guys be careful. Those bad people might start thinking you have that money, even if you don't." She looked at me, hard. "You don't, right?"

"No, ma'am, we don't. We'll be careful," I said.

She stood looking at me. Then at Blackhawk. "My friend Boyce has saved both of your lives. What have you done for her?"

Then she zeroed in on me again. She looked across the room, then back to me. "Anita is a very nice girl. You have not treated her very well."

I took a drink as a delaying tactic. She turned abruptly and walked away. We both watched her walk away, and up the steps. Poetry in motion.

Jimmy came down when it was safe. "You want another one?" he asked me.

Before I could answer, Anita was beside me. Her eyes were large and dark and fierce.

"You said you would call," she said.

"I'm sorry," I said. "I really am. I was very drunk that night."

"There are things a man says to a woman that he remembers, even if he is drunk. You said those things to me."

I looked at Blackhawk for help. He was laughing. She couldn't see him. Nacho stood up and moved to the other end of the bar.

"Anita, I am truly sorry. I can't remember a thing I said."

She looked at me coolly.

"Men are pigs," she said and turned and walked away.

If Elena was poetry, Anita was a shorter, plumper verse.

Jimmy watched her, then looked at me with a smile. "Another one?"

I shook my head, "No thanks. I think I'll head home."

"I thought maybe we'd take a drive," Blackhawk said.

I looked at him, "A drive?"

He reached into his breast pocket and took something out and laid it in front of me. It was a key.

"That looks like a locker key," I said.

"Bus station locker," he said. "Has the number right on it."

"Where'd it come from?"

"Found it on a chain around Rojo's neck," he smiled.

55

The main bus terminal was at 21st Street and Baseline. There was a Target store close by on 21st. We took the Mustang to the Target store. We bought matching hoodies, and the largest, cheapest sunglasses we could find. We also purchased a large duffel bag. We paid cash. Outside, I discarded the sales tags on the bag and popped the trunk of the Mustang. We put in our wallets, watches and Blackhawk's ring. I don't wear rings, but Blackhawk had a gaudy thing of gold and diamonds that Elena had given him. If his hand were captured on a surveillance camera, anyone that knew him would know who it was. I pulled two pair of rubber gloves from a box and handed one pair to Blackhawk. I wore jeans and plain white tennis shoes. Blackhawk had changed from his usual dressy clothes to look more like me. He didn't say a word, but I know it pained him.

We hiked from the store to the bus terminal. Before we got within range of the surveillance cameras, we slipped on the hoodies and glasses. I lounged around outside while he went in. I waited five minutes, then went in. It wasn't crowded. I casually walked through, identifying where the cameras were. This may seem like paranoia, but we never leave anything to chance.

There were a handful of people throughout the station. There was a young man asleep on a bench with his arm thrown across his eyes. Against the wall, under the *No Smoking* sign, sat a young girl with spiked red and black hair, sleeves of tattoos, a stud in her lip, a ring in her nose, one in her eyebrow and a series of rings up her left ear. She was smoking a cigarette. Nobody seemed to care.

Blackhawk was sitting on a bench at the far end. Just beyond him was a wall of lockers. As I started across the open space, he stood and walked to a specific locker. He stood facing it. I came up behind. Shielding our movements from the cameras, we slipped the rubber gloves on. He unlocked it. Inside was a package wrapped in plastic. There were also two more keys. He palmed the keys and without turning, he slipped the package into the duffel while I held it.

I followed as he stepped sideways to the next locker. Using the new key, he opened it, and there was a similar package. We slipped it into the duffel with its brother. He slid sideways to the next locker. Again, there was a package. Now the damn duffel was heavy. No more keys.

I zipped it up and slung it over my shoulder. He went left, I went right. I kept my head down and away from the cameras. I went by the adorned girl, and she didn't even glance at me.

A block down the street, Blackhawk relieved me of the bag. I gladly let him have it. He carried it to the car. We loaded it into the trunk, retrieved our stuff and climbed into the front. We sat there in silence for a moment. Finally, I started the car.

"Where to?" I said.

"Let's head to the boat and talk over our new dilemma," he smiled.

It was full-on dark when I pulled the Mustang into its parking slot. We lay the duffel out on the ground as Blackhawk helped me cover the Mustang with its custom canvas cover. Danny gave us a ride down to the dock gate.

Once inside Tiger Lily, I pulled all the blackout curtains and cranked the air. Even while the temperature was low, the air was stuffy. I opened the stern door and left the curtains back. The low lights of the marina twinkled across the ebony black of the water. I could feel the soft, cool, evening breeze.

Blackhawk was in the lounge unwrapping the packages. Each one was the size of two shoeboxes. They were wrapped and taped bricks of $100 bills. Each brick had an attached adding machine tape.

"You hungry?" I asked.

"You betcha," he said. "Counting money always makes me hungry."

"You count, I'll cook," I said.

I pulled two steaks from the locker and put them in the microwave to thaw. I was low on supplies but I found a head of cauliflower I could trim the brown spots off of. I found some frozen peas and a frozen loaf of bread I had wrapped in clear wrap.

While the meat was thawing, I made two Old Fashions. I always overfill them and had to sip mine to keep from slopping it. I slopped Blackhawk's. I took it into the lounge and set it in front of him. He had a pencil and a slip of paper, and was into tallying numbers. His concentration can be laser-like. Without looking up, he took the glass and took a deep drink.

I went to the galley, and started the vegetables to steaming. The microwave dinged and I took the mostly thawed meat out. I rubbed them with salt and pepper and let them rest while I fired the grill on the stern. When I came back in, Blackhawk was in the galley, fixing another drink. I put the bread in the microwave to thaw it out.

"Look at this," he said, holding up his hand, palm out.

He had a fine dusting of some kind of powder on his fingers.

"Is that what I think it is?"

He nodded. "Cocaine. The money is coated with it."

I shook my head, smiling. "You have a tally?"

"Yeah. Little Diaz was optimistic. Unless there is more somewhere else, which I doubt. Or they spent some, which I also doubt."

"How much?"

"Three hundred eighty thousand dollars. Even."

"Jesus," I said. "That's one shipment?"

Blackhawk smiled. "Americans like their dope."

I picked up the steaks and took them out and put them on the grill. They sizzled when they hit. The vegetables were beginning to steam.

I came back in. He was leaning back against the stainless refrigerator, sipping his drink. His dark eyes looked amused. I took plates and cutlery to the counter. I grabbed a couple of paper towels. I came back into the galley. He was watching me. I took the bread out and began slicing it.

"You need money for anything?" I said.

He shrugged, shaking his head, "Not really."

"New shoes for Elena?"

"Elena has more shoes that Nordstrom's," he said. "How about you?"

"I was going to paint the boat sometime this winter."

"How much does that cost?"

"I don't know. If Eddie helps, maybe two – three hundred."

"What do you want to do with this? Give it to Boyce?"

"I just can't see this sitting in an evidence locker."

"Yeah, somebody might steal it," he said. "How about your Father Correa and his home for girls?"

"He's still good," I said. "If we gave him more money, he would begin to worry where it came from. We'll think of something," I said.

I went out to check the steaks. They were just right.

56

We were meeting Emil at Einstein Brothers, across from his office building. The sun was shining in from the big plate glass window, and the sky was cloudless. Driving in, the radio had said there was a ten percent chance of rain. In my time here, I have learned that this means one hundred percent chance of no rain.

I was sitting at a table in the back, facing the door. Blackhawk was leaning against the wall across the room from me. We had the door in a crossfire. Wasn't sure we needed to, but seeing as Emil was bringing Emilio Garza with him, it seemed like a good idea. Blackhawk was wearing one of his million dollar suits. His shoes gleamed with polish. An adolescent boy could have used them to look up a girl's dress. He was so relaxed, leaning against the wall, someone else might have thought he was asleep.

Emil was late. It was mid-morning. There were a couple of college-aged kids in the corner. They were busy with their bagels and smart phones. It looked like they were, maybe, texting each other. A middle-aged man, with a dog lying beside him, was reading the paper. The dog was large and blond. He had his head on his paws and his big eyes were watching me. Whenever the man turned a page of the paper the dog looked hopefully for a falling morsel.

I sat quietly, waiting. The kid behind the counter kept working without wondering why we didn't buy anything. It was twenty minutes past the agreed upon time when the doorway was blocked by Emil's immense figure. He came in, nodding at Blackhawk. He walked straight over to me. Following him in, and trying hard not to look nervous, was Garza. He was working on cocky and tried hard to swagger, but it didn't seem convincing. Blackhawk stepped up behind them. Garza didn't like that.

I almost felt sorry for Garza. He had spent his entire life building up this tough, gang-banger image. The biggest element of his job was to be so badass and intimidating that all the minions that worked for him would stay in line. And then, you're standing next to Emil and Blackhawk. Two genuine articles. Nobody tougher. Makes you feel a little small.

"Fucker made me wait on him," Emil said. Garza shifted uncomfortably.

I stood, shrugging. "Not a problem."

"What'cha got," Emil said.

"Outside," Blackhawk said. Without waiting for a response, he turned toward the door. We followed him. I was the last one out. I glanced across the street. Nacho was sitting on the stoop of an office building. He ran a forefinger down his nose. *All clear.*

"Down this way," Blackhawk said, leading the way down the sidewalk. We had parked the Mustang in a commercial lot, a half block down.

"What the fuck is going on?" Garza said. Emil raised a hand to silence him and followed Blackhawk. Garza reluctantly followed. When we got to the Mustang, I thumbed the remote and popped the trunk. Blackhawk leaned in and pulled the duffel bag out. He did it effortlessly. He laid it on the ground.

"What's that?" Garza said.

"Open it," I said.

He looked from me and Blackhawk to Emil, then leaned down and unzipped it. He pulled the sides apart to reveal the bricks of money. He straightened up and looked at me. He was perplexed.

"We said we would get your money back to you."

He looked suspicious. He twisted his head around, looking for the surprise. He looked back to me. "The little shit Diaz is dead. You said you would get the money back if we didn't kill Diaz."

"You didn't kill Diaz," Blackhawk said. "The cops killed Diaz."

"And Diaz killed your guy, Rojo. And Rojo and Diaz and another guy, name of Omar, were the ones that hijacked the money in the first place," I said.

"Rojo?"

"Yes, Rojo. And now, all are dead," Blackhawk said. "And you have your money back."

Garza stood looking from one to the other of us.

"Pick up your money and get," Emil said.

Garza looked around again. He leaned down, zipped the duffel and struggled it to his shoulder. He walked away, listing a little from the weight.

We all watched him.

"Did you give it all back?" Emil said.

"Yep," I said.

"Didn't keep a finder's fee?"

"Nope."

He looked from Blackhawk to me.

"You are two strange motherfuckers."

57

It was late afternoon before I came west off the Interstate and angled the few miles to the marina road. I parked in my slot. I buttoned up the Mustang, covering her with the custom canvas. Danny ran me down the hill.

Eddie and Pete Dunn were sitting on the bow of the *13 Episodes*. They were in a couple of captain chairs, drinking beer from cans. Eddie looked normal: work shirt, work pants and the world's nastiest, stained ball cap. Even the stains were stained. Pete wore a pale blue Polo shirt, linen slacks and loafers with tassels and no socks. They watched me walk down the pier toward them. As I drew abreast of them I could tell something was up. Eddie looked like the cat with the catnip.

"How are you gentlemen?" I said. They were smiling. I wondered how many beers they'd had.

"Waiting on you," Eddie grinned. Pete stood up.

"Got something to show you," he said. "Come on aboard."

I stepped aboard. The sliding glass door that led to the

lounge was wide open. Pete went in. Eddie waved me in ahead of him. Pete had remodeled. The last time I was aboard this boat it was called the *Moneypenny*. It had been owned by a cartel boss named Frank Bavaro. Now deceased. He had suffered at the hands of a fatal disease called double cross. The boat had been occupied by a beautiful woman. She had been the disease carrier. Cherchez la femme.

Pete had put in all new furniture, including a wraparound leather couch. He was going to hate it in the summer. A flat-screen television was attached to the wall across from the couch. It was fed from a dish he had installed up top. He had new lamps, and new stools at the galley counter. The only thing I remembered from the old boat was the glass top coffee table. There was a rock glass on it with a quarter inch of liquid in the bottom. Left from last night. Pete sat on the couch, and Eddie waved me to a spot beside Pete. Next to the glass was a remote. Pete picked it up.

"This was on the news last night. I recorded it." He pointed the remote at the television, and the television made a clicking, humming sound. In a moment, the television came up. There was a soap opera on. The sound was down. The beautiful people mouthed words at each other. One pretty girl was crying. Another one looked defiant.

He pushed some more buttons and a list of recordings came on. He selected one. He pushed the button to play. When he pushed the button his hand made a small movement toward the television. Like he was helping the signal along.

My old friend Ronnie Hawkins showed. Pete raised the

volume. Ronnie was speaking in his careful modulated way. His hair was perfect, his teeth bright. A guy not hard to hate.

".......*in the newsroom just about one hour ago. We have to warn our viewers, the content of the video is disturbing and may not be suitable for younger children.*"

"How about old men," Eddie said.

The next image was a shaky blur, then settled to focus on a man in camo clothes with his face wrapped in a black cloth. Only his eyes were showing. He was holding a large knife in his right hand. His left hand held the collar of an orange jumpsuit. Inside the jumpsuit, kneeling, was Boyce's old adversary, Calvin. Calvin was crying. Despite the cover-up, I was certain the man with the knife was Ali Ibrahim Atef. Atef was speaking. His voice carried a slight accent.

"America hear my voice! You are soft. You believe you can sit in your soft lives and have your military push buttons and rain bombs on our innocent people. Kill our women. Kill our children. You think you can sit in your fat houses and believe you are safe. You are not safe. We are here. We placed the bomb in Sedona. Beware America, you do not know where we will strike next. There will be no more warnings like in Sedona. Praise Allah, we will have our revenge!"

He jerked Calvin's collar and you could hear Calvin sobbing. *"This man is a traitor, and he will be dealt with as a traitor."* He turned the knife toward Calvin and the screen went black.

Now Ronnie Hawkins was leaning forward, looking off-camera, apparently watching the video. He turned back to the camera.

"It is important for our viewers to know that this station did not end this video at this moment. You have seen the video we received in its entirety. We did catch up with a member of the Homeland Security team that is investigating the bombing in Sedona."

The screen showed a close-up of a startled Boyce. She put her hand out to fend off the camera. You could barely hear her say, *"Get that damn thing out of my face."*

"There was no comment," Ronnie beamed. *"And there you have it."*

Pete paused the video. I looked at Eddie and he was looking at me, a half-smile on his face.

I tilted my head toward the television. "That make you happy?"

He pushed me on the shoulder. "You recognize that boy?"

"I recognized them both," I said.

"You know what this means," Pete said.

I leaned back on the couch, "It means you can, at least, probably get Billy out of jail."

"We can make a strong case," Pete said.

"Show it to me again."

I watched it again and this time I paid attention to the background. Behind them was desert. They were up high and there was a broad vista of cactus and scrub brush behind. There was something that made me itch. I made him show it to me three more times. I was looking for something. I couldn't figure out what.

58

We waited until the next morning. Pete had a red Honda Pilot, and Eddie rode with him. I threw a small bag in the trunk, and followed in the Mustang. We drove up the Interstate as the sun crested the eastern mountains. We pulled into town an hour and a half later. It was too early for Attorney Taggart, so we went to our favorite Mom and Dad diner for coffee. We joined a half dozen people quietly sipping their coffee, waking up.

The diner and parking lot sat elevated on a knoll above the main drag. We selected a booth next to the windows and watched the morning traffic slide by as we sipped our coffee.

Eddie looked over his cup at Pete, "I'd still just as soon let you take over for that gasbag Taggart."

"Not that easy," Pete said. "First of all, I've haven't practiced law in a while, and definitely not in Arizona, so I'd have to make sure my license was up to date. Secondly, and more importantly, this is a small town and Taggart is a local guy. If I came barging in, who knows who he's buddies with, and what kind of obstacles they could throw at us."

"We are on Taggart's turf," I said. Eddie shook his head, not liking it. "We can handle Taggart," I said. He shrugged.

The waitress came by and warmed our coffee without being asked. We lapsed into silence. Everything had been said the night before. We sat like that until Eddie couldn't stand it anymore. Pete left a twenty on the table and we left.

We drove to Taggart's but he wasn't in yet. There was an old Chevy and a SUV in the lot in front of the barber shop. Through the plate glass window I could see the barber and the guy in his chair. I wondered if the barber was Dwyer's dad. We parked on the other side of the SUV. I climbed into the back of the Pilot and we waited. It was after ten before Taggart pulled in.

"Wait till he gets settled," I said.

We sat a few more minutes, then Eddie said, "Fuck this," opened his door and stepped out. We followed. As we reached the front door Pete said, "Let me do the talking."

Pete led the way in. As before, the outer room was dusty and empty. Taggart heard us and stuck his head out. He smiled as he looked at Pete, then it faded when he saw Eddie and me.

"Mr. Bragg, Mr. Jackson," he said. He stuck his hand out to Pete. "I don't believe I've had the pleasure."

"Peter Dunn," Pete said, shaking his hand.

"Please come in, Mr. Dunn," he said, waving us into the office. "I don't have an appointment for a few minutes." As we crowded into the small office he said, "Please, have a chair." We arranged ourselves.

"How can I help you gentlemen?" he said.

We looked at Pete.

"I am a friend of Eddie's," Pete said. "I am also an attorney."

Taggart made a small noise. He leaned back. "I see. Where did you study?"

"Stanford."

"I see. Excellent."

"I'm not here as an attorney. Just a friend. I'm just telling you this so you know."

"I'll say it again, how can I help?"

"Have you seen the news?"

"If you mean the terrorist beheading that unfortunate man, everyone has seen it. It is the only thing this town is talking about."

I leaned forward. "Has there been more video released? The video we saw didn't actually show a beheading."

Taggart looked at me. "No, no, Mr. Jackson, you are correct. I don't believe anyone has seen video of the actual beheading, unless it was the authorities."

"You have seen the video?" I said.

He nodded, "Yes, Mr. Jackson. As I said, I think the whole town has seen it."

"Do you know the two men that were on it?"

He shook his head. "Why would I know them?"

"I don't know about the one that was covered up, but I met the other guy right here in Cottonwood."

"He's from here?" Taggart was surprised.

"Not just that," I said. "But he's Dick Mooney's cousin."

Taggart's eyebrows went up.

"Do you realize the implications of this to the case against Mr. Bragg's nephew?" Pete said.

Taggart picked up a pen and tapped it on the desktop.

Taggart looked thoughtful. "Mr. Dunn, just because I practice in a small town, doesn't make me some kind of backward yokel. Of course I understand. In fact, I have an appointment in front of Judge Brown at two-thirty this afternoon on another matter."

He looked hard at me. "You are sure about this?"

"His name is Calvin. Not sure about the last name, maybe Mooney, but the bartender at the Sunset Corral would know. Shouldn't be hard for someone local to identify him."

He nodded. "Okay, I'm going to have to verify that. I'll get a deposition from the bartender before I meet with Judge Brown."

"I'll go with you," Pete said.

Taggart looked at him, "As you wish. If this comes together I'm going to request that, due to the new circumstances, Billy be released on his own recognizance."

"We can get Billy out?" Eddie said.

"That's up to Judge Brown, but I think we have a good chance."

Pete looked at me. "That was easy."

Taggart looked reprovingly at me. "Mr. Jackson, did you think I would be an obstacle?"

"Never crossed my mind," I said, standing.

Outside in the parking lot the air was crisp, bright and cold.

"It may be a day or two for the wheels to turn," Pete said.

"Before Billy can get out?" Eddie said.

Pete nodded.

Eddie looked at me. "You gonna stick around?"

I nodded. "Sure."

Eddie looked at Pete. "I'll stick with you. I want to make sure Taggart will do this."

"He'll do it. He could lose his license if he doesn't." He turned to me. "What are you going to do?"

"I think I'll go to the library," I said.

59

The parking lot at the library was filled. Half of it had been roped off and there were a dozen tables set up, piled high with books. The sign in front had declared the *Cottonwood Book Fair*. It was a success; there were a lot of people milling about.

I couldn't find a spot, so I pulled across the street to the police station and parked in that lot. I thought about Billy Bragg in his cell inside. I thought about him not knowing that there was a possibility he would be out soon. The thought cheered me.

I crossed the street mid-block. What a rebel. Blatantly jaywalking right in front of the police station. It took a couple of minutes to find Dahlia. I finally spotted her manning a pay point at the far corner of the lot. She had a half dozen people in line. I stood and watched her. She wore a brilliantly white Angora sweater that glowed in the sunlight. The sweater hugged her breasts and came down over her hips. Her jeans, below the sweater, looked as if they had been painted on. She kept pulling her hair back behind her ears. Sometimes she used a pencil to do it. She gave a bright smile to each customer, and had something to say about their purchase with each one.

I browsed around, waiting for her line to diminish. I found a paperback of John D. MacDonald's that I hadn't read. All the paperbacks were fifty cents. I felt like a kid in a candy store. I picked up an Elmore Leonard western and a Donald Westlake, writing as Richard Stark. Finally, when her line was down to three, I carried my plunder over. She didn't notice me until I was in front of her.

"Thank you so much," she said to the lady in front of me. She turned her eyes to me, and her smile got even larger.

"Well, there you are," she said.

I lay the books on the table, "Here to do my part, ma'am."

"Glad to see it," she said. She had a ten key with a roll of paper and a cash register drawer sitting open next to her. She ran the three books up on the ten key. "That is one dollar fifty cents," she said. She looked at each of the books. "Interesting choice."

"I try to stick with the classics," I said. I dug in my pocket and extracted the exact change.

"There you go. Any chance of you getting a break anytime soon?"

She looked at the silver watch on her slender arm, "Half an hour, I get a lunch break."

"Can I buy you lunch?"

She tilted her head. A lock of dark hair fell across her forehead. Her eyes were mischievous. "You can buy me lunch and dinner," she said.

I suddenly felt like the fifteen year-old boy who had been asked to dance by the prom queen. "Excellent," I managed.

She kept smiling at me. When I didn't move, she looked past me to the person behind me, "All set?" she said.

I gathered my books and stepped away, slightly flustered. I wandered around picking up random books, trying not to look at my watch. I was deep into a hard-back copy of Shel Silverstein's book of nonsensical poems *A Light in the Attic* when suddenly, Dahlia was standing next to me. She took the book from my hands and looked at it. She handed it back.

"I used to read these to Megan when she was little," she said.

"I discovered it in the barrack's library when I was in boot camp," I said.

She smiled at me, shaking her head. "That sounds about right, for you." She took my arm and I set the book back on the table. "Not going to buy it?" she said.

"Already have it," I said.

She pulled on me. "Come on, you can take me to Mimi's."

Mimi's was down the road a bit. Unlike the breakfast place that was elevated, Mimi's was lower than the road. We had jaywalked back to the Mustang, and I drove us to the restaurant. I pulled down the decline to the parking area, and parked in the first parking spot.

This was a true small town lunch place. The breakfast and lunch specials were listed on a chalkboard next to the door. Dahlia led the way to the back where she chose a booth. The booth was red, and the vinyl on the seat was cracked and repaired with red tape. All the help were young girls, not much older than Megan. One of them came over with menus, and took our drink order. I had water, Dahlia ordered iced tea.

I looked at the menu. No kiwi fruit or spinach greens to be found. Good. Heavy on mac and cheese, meatloaf with mashed potatoes and thick brown gravy, chicken fried chicken and today's ham loaf special.

I looked up at Dahlia and she was watching me.

"Ham loaf?" I said.

She laughed. "The hamburgers are good."

"When in doubt," I said.

The waitress came and Dahlia ordered a dinner salad with French on the side. I went with the burger and fries, and made it the all American lunch by asking for my very own Coke.

We sat in silence as the waitress gathered the menus, and took our order toward the kitchen.

Dahlia had her chin on her hand, "What brings you up here?"

"Would you believe me if I said, you?"

She shook her head with a laugh, "No."

"Really?"

"Let's try to keep this an honest relationship."

"Well, let's say you are the cherry on top, but I came up with Eddie and Pete Dunn to see if we can get Billy out of jail."

"Because of that video on the news?"

"Yeah, pretty much. Pete's an attorney and he thinks we can make a case to get Billy out."

"I thought Pete was a TV writer."

"That too."

"I hope you get him out. Billy didn't do anything to Dick Mooney except threaten him. And there was a long line of guys doing that."

"We went to see Billy's attorney this morning and he's supposed to meet with a judge this afternoon. Keep your fingers crossed."

The waitress brought our drinks. I peeled the straw and poked it down into the Coke and took a sip.

"How's Megan?"

"Megan's great. Grades are good. Happy, happy."

"Great time of life for most."

"Most?"

"Yeah, most. It would go against our honest relationship if I said all teenagers are happy, happy."

She nodded, drinking from her straw.

"What's Megan's biggest problem?" I said to make conversation.

"Why do you think she has a problem?"

"All teens have problems. Usually, they are mundane, but to the teenager the problems are gigantic. To us they are just a part of growing up."

She looked out across the room for a moment.

"Boys," she said.

"I'm shocked."

"Thought you would be. She's got this football player

that likes her, and he's popular around the school, so all her friends want her to go with him."

"But?"

"But there is this boy in her art class that paints funny little abstracts, and she likes him. Says he has a poetic soul, and she says she is drawn to that."

I smiled, shaking my head. "The poet will go on to be a powerful writer whose books will change the world, and the jock will end up selling insurance and growing a pot belly."

"God, you are awful."

I looked across the room, and the waitress was bringing our food. Right behind her was Joe Whitney. In uniform. The waitress carefully arranged our food in front of us.

"Can I get you anything else?" she asked.

I looked at Dahlia. "No, thanks," she said.

The waitress looked at Joe. "Hey, Joe. Can I get you anything?"

"No thanks, Brenda," he said and the girl moved away.

Dahlia scooted over and Joe slid into the booth next to her.

"Saw your car out front," he said.

"Glad you stopped," I said.

"What brings you up?"

I repeated what I had told Dahlia.

He nodded. "The chief and I were talking about that this morning. I think he'll be glad."

"Glad?"

"Sure. He likes Billy. I don't think he believes Billy did this thing, but once someone's in the jail it's not up to him anymore. Once an arrest warrant is executed it's up to the courts and lawyers."

"Has anyone seen more of that video, other than what's been showing on the news?"

He shook his head, "We haven't. As yet, no one has confirmed that Calvin is dead or alive."

"Why did they pick on poor Calvin?" Dahlia said.

Joe shook his head again, "We don't know. Calvin was a dipshit. He is Dick Mooney's cousin and I don't know, by association I guess, he was involved with the militia."

"Which is really a terrorist cell."

"Don't have a comment on that. Not while I'm in uniform, anyway."

"Homeland Security people have witnesses that put Atef and Dwyer at a bomb making factory in Phoenix," I said. "And it was Atef on that video."

"Atef?" Dahlia said.

"He was known here as Ramirez."

Joe nodded. "Yeah, you're right. Now that you say it. That was Ramirez."

"I watched the video several times," I said. "Something about the location that makes me itch."

"Desert," Joe said. "Lots of desert in Arizona."

I nodded.

He stood. "Just wanted to say hi." He looked at Dahlia. "See you later."

"Good to see you," I said. We both watched him walk away.

After a moment, I looked back at Dahlia. "So where are we going to dinner?"

She smiled, shaking her head. "I'm not going to hold you to that."

"Yes, you are."

60

We made arrangements for me to pick her up at 6. I got a room at the same motel Eddie and I had used before. I sent a text to Pete telling him the room number, and asking if there were any developments. I took a long walk to kill time, and then took a shower. No reply from Pete.

I was at Dahlia's door at 6 on the dot, and Lucy answered the door.

"Oh, great," she said with a big smile. "This is perfect."

"Hard to achieve," I said, a little bewildered. Dahlia came into the room behind Lucy.

"Hi," I said to Dahlia.

"Billy's out," she said.

"Good," I said.

Lucy pulled me inside, and Dahlia came over and gave me a small hug.

"Lucy has talked to Billy and they want us all to get together at the Sunset. Kind of a celebration." She was turned away from Lucy and mouthed the word *sorry*.

"Wonderful," I said.

"I want to go," Megan's voice floated in from the back.

"There, it's unanimous," Lucy said.

"You're supposed to go to your Aunt Betty's to spend the night," Dahlia said.

Megan came out from the back. "I can still go. I want to see Billy, you can take me after."

Dahlia shook her head, smiling. She took my arm. "Come in and sit down, while we get ready. Can I get you a drink?"

"No thanks, I'll get one when we get to the bar," I said.

They all went to the back to get ready. They looked ready to me, but a woman isn't ready until she says she's ready. After fifteen minutes I went to the kitchen and fixed a drink. A little scotch and a lot of ice.

Two drinks and an hour later they were ready.

Megan insisted on riding with me. The sisters led the way with Lucy's ten-year old sedan. Megan insisted I put the top down.

"It's too cold," I said.

"Don't be an old fud," she said with a challenging look.

I put the top down, raised the windows and put the heater on high. The sun was down and so was the temperature. Megan begged me to take the long way around. Her eyes were bright as she scanned the street hoping to see someone she knew. Hard to be the coolest girl in school if no one knew it. It was cold. There was no one out.

The parking lot at the Sunset Corral was full, and I had to park on the outer edge of the lot. I put the top up and slid out, locking the car. Megan was waiting for me. She took my arm and we walked to the door. I held the door and she went in.

It was a wall of noise. A hundred conversations at once, each raising the decibel over the one next to them. I saw Billy and Eddie seated at a table at the back. It was actually four tables all pushed together to make one big one. Just about everyone I had met in Cottonwood was there. After the dark outside, the lights in the large bar were warm and yellow, giving everyone a golden cast.

Dahlia and Lucy were sitting across from Billy and Eddie. Joe Whitney, out of uniform, was sitting at the end next to Pete Dunn. There were two other couples next to Joe. I had not seen them before. The men had that same young, crew-cut, cop look that Joe had. There were two large pitchers of beer on the table. Actually, mostly empty pitchers. Janine, the waitress, was carrying two more pitchers from the bar to the table. She carefully set them down. Dahlia and Lucy slid over, making room for Megan. I snagged an empty chair across the room and carried it over. Eddie slid over and made room for me. Billy was beaming. He appeared to have been celebrating a while. He thrust his hand out to me, and I shook it.

"Congratulations," I shouted.

He grinned at me, and said something in return, but it was lost in the din. I could watch Dahlia and Lucy talk but they were far enough away that I couldn't hear them. Dahlia listened to Lucy but was looking at me. I winked at her, and she grinned.

Janine brought a chilled glass, and set it in front of me.

Eddie filled it with beer. I took a small drink and leaned back and watched Billy celebrate. Janine had a Coke for Megan. Pete was engaged in a deep conversation with one of the young cops. Lucy was talking to Dahlia, but kept looking at Billy. Billy kept emptying his glass and Eddie, happily, kept filling it.

I sipped the beer.

About an hour had passed when Dahlia leaned over and said something to Megan. They stood up. Dahlia looked over at me. I stood and moved around the table.

I leaned into Dahlia. "Leaving?"

"I have to take Megan to Aunt Betty's."

"Sedona?"

"I'll be about forty minutes."

"You stay here with your sister. I'll take her."

"You don't have to do that."

I looked at Megan. "My pleasure. I'll be right back. Maybe we can make that dinner date after all."

Megan was listening.

"You guys have a date?"

"You are too nosy," Dahlia said.

"Come on, kid," I said. "Let's go see Aunt Betty."

I took Megan's arm and tugged on it. "Come on, kid."

Megan was grinning at her mom. She followed me out, grinning at me.

"You guys have a date?"

61

"You guys have a date?" she repeated as we reached the Mustang.

I laughed. "You are just too nosy."

I held her door for her and she slid in.

"Put your seatbelt on," I said.

The highway to Sedona was on the opposite side of town. I drove carefully through the sleepy town. There was no traffic. There was a stoplight at the intersection with the highway. There was no traffic there either. The stoplight cast a glow inside the car. I glanced at Megan. She was grinning at me.

"What?"

"You guys have a date. I can't remember the last time my mom had a date."

"Hard to believe," I said, turning onto the highway as the light changed. "Your mom is a very attractive woman."

She was hooked around, looking at me.

"Do you like her?"

"That's a silly question. Would I take her on a date if I didn't?"

"No, I mean really like her?

"You mean the way you like the football player, or the artist?"

She frowned at me. "How do you know about them?" Then, "My mom. My mom told you."

"I asked your mom a question and she answered it. But to answer your question, yes, I do like your mom."

"Do you love her?"

I laughed. I felt like I was in high school study hall again.

"Do you?" She repeated.

"If you mean love, as in *in love*, no I don't."

"Why not?"

I glanced at her. She was watching me, her face illuminated by the dashboard lights. The night was black dark, the headlights the only source of light. It was as if the moving splash of illuminated asphalt in front was the only thing in the universe.

"I don't know your mom," I said. "We barely know each other. Tonight was to be our first date. It's much too early get to the *love* thing."

She was silent for a while. "Tommy Ball is the football player," she said. "He's lettered in every sport."

"Do you love him?" I asked, teasing.

"Oh, gosh no."

"How about the other one?"

"I'm too young for that stuff."

I nodded, "Smart girl."

"I'm glad Billy's out."

"Me too." The heater was blasting us so I turned it down.

I set the cruise control on sixty. Precious cargo.

"I never did believe he did that thing."

I was glad to get on another subject, "Me too."

She was looking at me again, "Who do you think did it?"

I took my time answering. Finally, I said, "I think it was very bad men who are trying to frighten us."

"Why?"

Again, I took my time.

"Some people need to have someone to hate. I think these guys need to hate us. Us Americans."

"What have we done to them?"

"We are successful. America is the biggest success in the history of the world. As a country and as a society. They come from countries where there is poverty and disease. Their society is one where a small number of men have all the power. They govern by fear. If their people had the freedoms that Americans have they couldn't keep the power. And there has been a thousand years of hatred. Hating anyone that isn't like them. If you don't believe and don't behave the same as them, you are the enemy and must be destroyed. They look at us and see our riches and they believe because we are a rich country, we have to be a decadent country. They call us the Great Satan."

"I don't get it," she said. "How can someone just kill another person? Mom says you were in the Army and were all over the world. Why do you think one person can just kill another? Even in America?"

"Well," I said watching the road and thinking about my words. "Lots of reasons. A lot of times it's passion of the moment. Greed or jealousy or during a crime that goes wrong. Sometimes it's territory. One gang protecting their turf from another gang. And sometimes you have armies of soldiers killing each other for political or power reasons. That's when everyone thinks their side is right, so that seems to be okay. They believe God is on their side so that makes it okay. In the Civil War, hundreds of thousands of Americans killed each other, both sides firmly believing they were in the right, and believing God was on their side."

"We studied that in the eighth grade."

"But usually, when one person murders another person for whatever reason, most people don't think that is okay."

"How can they do that? Just kill someone?"

"Some people aren't as human as others."

"What does that mean?"

"It's hard to explain. It's like some people aren't completely formed. That is, when they are born something is left out. Something essential to be fully human. But for every one of those people, those evil ones I've seen, I've seen thousands of good people."

"You've seen evil people?"

"Unfortunately, I have."

"How do you recognize them?"

"Unfortunately, we usually don't. Until it's too late. All the mass shootings you hear about. Most of those shooters were living among us. People went to school with them, worked with them, lived next door to them. Then one day this seemingly normal person does crazy things and innocent people die."

Again, she was silent. I started to think that maybe I should have stayed with the love topic.

"So I could know an evil person, and not even know it."

"Or not. The odds are in your favor. It's highly possible no one you know is evil."

"It's kinda creepy to think about."

"It is. Let's change the subject. Do you visit your Aunt Betty often?"

"I help her with the shop on weekends, when there are lots of tourists."

"I can tell you like your Aunt Betty."

"I love her. She was my grandma's sister."

In the darkness, off to my left I saw the flash of a distant light. Then it was gone.

"What happened to Grandma?"

"Cancer," she said. "When I was little."

"Do you remember her?"

"I can remember how she smelled. She always smelled good. It was like when she held me I was safe. It seemed like she always smelled like cookies. I know that's silly, but that's my memory. I have other memories of her at a hospital, but I don't like to think of those."

"Grandmas are good," I said. "What about Grandpa?"

"I never knew him. I've seen pictures."

"Did cancer get him too?"

"I don't know. Probably. I think he was about fifty-six. He was a soldier once."

We rode in silence for a while.

"So your parents died when you were a kid?" she asked.

"Yes, I'm afraid so. I never knew them very well."

She was silent, thinking about that. I glanced at her and she was sitting forward staring across me. "What is he doing?"

I looked left and there was a big black something, barreling at us from out of the night. Then headlights came on, blinding me, and he was coming too fast and I twisted the wheel and hit the brakes but couldn't react fast enough. He hit us with great violence and we spun and Megan was screaming. Air bags slammed us as we tipped and began to roll. All went black.

62

I slowly became aware. I was on something hard, and it was moving. I was bounced into the air, and slammed back down. I couldn't move. Everything was black. I hurt. I hurt badly. I was in the back of a truck and large bump had thrown me into the air. We hit another large bump, and I disappeared again.

I woke up. I wasn't in the truck. I felt like I was on the ground. I tried to move. My body screamed at me, and I blacked out.

I woke up and could hear voices. They were muffled. I couldn't stay awake.

Someone was shaking me. Yelling at me. All I could do was moan. Everything went black again.

A long time later I woke up. This time it was quiet. This time I was awake. It was black. Very black. My right eye was swollen shut. Dried blood had sealed it. I could turn my head but there was nothing. I could feel I was missing two teeth on the right side of my jaw, and, with my tongue, could feel a broken one. I stuck my tongue out and it pressed against cloth. I had a hood on. I tried my hands but they were fastened behind me. My back and legs ached, my ankles were fastened together.

Captured.

I was captured. I had been trained to be captured. For what they told me later was two full weeks, they had beat on me, dunked me upside down in a tank of water, switched me with a willow switch, all to make me reveal the number they had given me before they started. Then it was over, and they debriefed me, and walked me through the mental process of surviving being captured. I don't think any of us believed it would happen to us.

Then I had another thought.

Megan?

I quit moving, and began to listen. It was silent. It must be the middle of the night. I thought about what the Colonel had told us. I could hear his voice. *If you are captured, they don't know who you are. Even if they have you in a cage, you are still the tiger.*

A tiger that feels like it's been beaten with a baseball bat. Grrrr. I closed the eye that worked, and tried not to think of Megan.

I must have slept. When I heard voices, I awoke. They were muffled. There were two or three different voices. Three. They were moving around. I used my hands to feel the ground. It felt like plastic. Like a tarp, no, like the bottom of a tent. The one nostril that wasn't clogged with dried blood could smell coffee. Use your senses. If one is taken, use the others. I breathed silently and listened. I listened for anything and everything. I ignored the pain and listened. I don't know what happened to Megan. I couldn't help Megan. I had to help me first.

It is difficult to be completely silent for a long period of time. I had practiced it. If there was anyone in here with me I will hear them. I waited, not making a sound. No breathing, no nothing. You do that by opening your mouth as wide as possible and breathing very shallowly. The cool air hurt my teeth. It's only pain, I had been taught. After a long while of hearing nothing I decided either they were better trained, or there was no one there. There was no one there. The muffled voices started again. I listened, trying to make out the conversation. I began to assess my body.

I could wiggle my toes. Whoopee. They had left my prosthetic on. Good, I was at enough of a disadvantage. Either they missed it or they didn't care. If they didn't care, it probably meant they didn't expect me to be around for long. My right thigh ached, like a deep bruise. I slowly bent my knees. No bone grinding. My shoulders were cramping and I tried to relax them. My head hurt like a son of a bitch. Especially my jaw on the side of the missing teeth. I moved my jaw. There was no grinding. I couldn't sense any broken bones. Okay assholes, beware the tiger. I've got you right where I want you.

63

I had no idea if I was in the line of sight of any of them. I forced myself not to move. I wanted to listen. I needed to learn more. Use your senses. I only heard three of them. They were talking in a language I didn't know. By the tone there didn't seem to be any excitement, no urgency. They were settled in. My head was throbbing. The noises told me they had a camp set up. The metallic sound of a pan or coffee pot being set on a camp stove. The crackle of a fire. No wild life. No birds, or quail. The occasional buzz of an insect. The air temperature was rising, so it was daytime.

One of them walked a few feet away from where I lay and urinated. I could hear the urine splatter on the hard dirt. Then I heard him walk around me, and then the sound of a flap of the tent being lifted. I lay still, barely breathing. He was looking in; he didn't come in. He lowered the flap, and I took a deep breath. Good. I was inside, out of sight.

Now I started trying to figure out how I was bound. I rolled to my side and bent my legs up behind me. It hurt like hell but I forced my legs up until my heels were touching just below my buttocks. I stretched my hands down. I felt a thin, hard plastic zip tie. I tried forcing my hands apart and this was a zip tie also, biting into the flesh of my wrists. Good. Plastic degrades. All I had to do was wait six months and the zip ties would become brittle, and I'd break them easily.

Now I began to explore the tent. I stretched out slowly, listening all the while. I didn't want to be caught moving around. The tent was about eight feet long and six feet wide. There was absolutely nothing in it. Just me.

I moved back to my original position and waited.

In the movies, the hero slips his butt and legs through his bound arms and then works his hands free with his teeth. They had the zip ties too high on my wrists. I was in the wrong movie.

Things were quiet for a long time. At least three hours went by. I needed something to happen. Then it did. I heard a vehicle. It was in the distance, but coming closer. I heard the men rouse. Then I heard the distinct metallic sound of a round being ratcheted into an automatic weapon.

The vehicle came into the camp and stopped. The men were talking over the top of themselves, excited with their company. I listened as the vehicle motor was killed and the doors slammed. The vehicle had brought more men. One of the newcomers began barking orders in the same language the others had been using. I could hear noises, maybe of unloading the truck if it was a truck. There was a lot of movement. Then the voices were muted. They had moved away.

It was startling when a voice close by said, in English, "Bring him out here."

I went limp. They were going to kick me. I tried to prepare for it. There was the sound of the tent flap pulled back, and there were at least three in with me. One of them kicked me. I groaned involuntarily. They put their hands on me and dragged me out of the tent. I remained limp. They dumped me on the ground and one of them ripped the hood off. My face bounced down onto the dirt. Through my one hooded eye I could see the military boots and camo legs of a man in front of me. He squatted down and grabbed my hair and pulled my head up. Playing dead wasn't going to work.

"Mr. Atef, I presume," I said through bruised lips.

"Ah, yes," he said in his soft accent. "The hero."

He stood and said, "Get him to his knees." He stayed in English.

Two others grabbed my arms and roughly pulled me up to my knees. I tried to stand but they pushed me back down. I used the movement to look around. It was desert with heavy undergrowth. We were in a stand of mesquite, palo verdes and junipers. There were a number of tents scattered around. Each had been erected under a tree, presumably to be hidden from the air. Beyond the trees were creosote and sage and what appeared to be miles of empty desert. My tent backed up to a wide sandy wash and I had seen it before with Eddie and Joe Whitney. I was sure it was the same wash, just a different place. A mountain was in the distance. There were contrails in the sky. All desert looks alike. The truck was an old Chevy Bronco. It was parked a few yards off.

There were eight men surrounding me. None were Dwyer. All were wearing black niqabs. Headscarves draped around their faces with only the eyes showing. They all wore camo hunting attire. All carried automatic rifles except one. He worried me. He carried an older GoPro video camera. Atef wore a black niqab but his face wasn't covered.

"Get the girl," Atef said. My heart leapt but I kept my face impassive. Two of the men went to a small tent on the opposite side of the camp. The tent was backed into thicket of brambles. One held the tent flap and the other went in. A moment later he was back with Megan. Her feet were free but her hands were bound. Her hair was a tangled mess. Her face was smudged and dirty and puffy from crying. I was never so glad to see someone in my life. She didn't seem to be hurt. Thank God for air bags. I looked away from her. Her best protection from these assholes was me not seeming to give a damn if she lived or died. No leverage.

"Put them together," Atef commanded. They brought Megan close to me and forced her to her knees. Her head hung down. She stared at the earth. Atef signaled the man with the camera and pointed to where he wanted the man to stand. The man took his place.

Atef signaled to another one of the men. "Put your weapon at his head. If he moves, kill him."

The man came behind me and with a little too much enthusiasm banged me in the back of the head with the rifle barrel. Megan was starting to keen. Trying to catch her breath. Her head rocked back and forth. I wanted to touch her. To give her comfort, but I didn't move.

Atef came to stand beside Megan. He wrapped his face with his scarf. Only his eyes showed through. He pulled a K-bar knife from his belt and pointed it at the camera. The man began filming.

"Allah is great," Atef said. "I speak now to every man, woman and child that belongs to this great evil, the United States. Your country is the great Satan. You are governed by evil people. You kill our people with no thought of what you do, but you cannot defeat us. We are a great caliphate and we are everywhere. Our numbers of true believers are vast beyond your knowledge and grow every minute, and every hour, and every day."

He brandished the knife above Megan's head. "Do not think that you are safe because you live in America. We are here. This is our fatwa. We are in your cities, and we are in your small towns. Just like these two, not one of you is safe from our revenge."

He pointed the knife at Megan. "This woman could be your daughter. Now she belongs to me. I own her. She is my property. She is no more than a mule or a camp dog." He pointed the knife at me. "This man is supposed to be one of the best of your military. And now he is on his knees. He is mine. His head belongs to me. Your military cannot stand against us." He paused. "Our enemies have confiscated billions of our dollars across the world. Money that belongs to us. I will give you twenty-four hours to release our money back to us or the next time you see me, I will be holding two heads. Death to all infidels." He waved the knife between us.

He flourished the knife at the camera and the man

stopped filming. Atef turned and walked away. Two of the men grabbed me and roughly pulled me to my feet. One of them shoved the hood over my head. I heard Megan yelp, then begin sobbing. They half-walked, half-dragged me to the tent. One kicked me in the small of my back. I flew forward into the tent, landing face down. I landed hard. It hurt. I didn't move until I heard them fasten the tent flap. I took several deep breaths then rolled to the back of the tent. Now was the hard part. The waiting part.

64

I lay for a long time, in the hooded darkness. Listening. If Atef was good at his word I had twenty-four hours. I couldn't count on it, but it gave me something. The first pressing problem I had was a full bladder. Nothing to be done. I let it go. It was of no consequence. I had been trained to not move for hours. This had happened before. I had bigger problems.

They had not tightened the hood. Satisfied they weren't coming back in, I lay on the ground. Rubbing my face against the hard tent bottom, I slowly worked the hood up my face and finally I could see. Small victories. There was a crack of light where the tent flap didn't quite meet the tent wall. I rolled to it and rocked myself up on my knees. I peered out. Two of the men sat within eyesight. One of them was the camera man. He was studying the camera, checking the performance. Atef and the rest were out of eyesight.

Several minutes later I heard another vehicle approaching. I listened as it pulled into camp and the motor was cut. I heard someone shutting the door and footsteps that receded. The two men had swiveled, looking toward the sound. As the footsteps receded, they turned back to what they were doing. In the silence that followed I could hear the muffled sounds from across the camp. Megan was crying.

I needed a lucky break, and I needed it to get dark. Not necessarily in that order. I took deep, silent breaths and made my body relax. I began to wait. And wait. And wait some more. A year and a half later, the sun fell behind the mountains.

The men in camp lit a fire. Dumb. You try to hide your tents from the sky but you light a fire. As the darkness grew, I quit looking out. The fire made me nightblind.

I listened hard as the men talked softly among themselves. And now, the occasional clink of metal on metal. They were cooking. I could smell the food and my stomach rumbled. I tried hard not to keep touching my broken teeth with my tongue. Then suddenly, I heard footsteps coming toward me. I slid across the tent to the far side, and curled up, my back to the tent flap.

The tent flap was thrown back. I didn't move. I relaxed my entire body. He stood silently at the doorway for a long moment. I was afraid he was going to go away. But he did what I needed. He came inside. I heard the flap drop behind him, and he was alone. I was barely breathing. It seemed to take forever but he finally moved over to me. He jabbed me in the back with the toe of his boot. I groaned but didn't move. I waited. He kicked me again. I moved.

Black Mamba.

I swung my entire body around and knocked his feet out

from under him. With a grunt, he slammed to the ground, and I scrambled on top of him. I propelled myself into the air and landed hard with both knees on his chest. The air exploded from his lungs. I did it again. The air was out of him, and he was gasping. He tried to move and I slammed my forehead against his face. I felt the warm gush of blood as his nose broke. He was still game. He rolled to his knees and tried to push himself up. I was still on top. I spun on his back, getting his head between my thighs. I clamped down with all I had and rolled hard. His neck popped like cracking a knuckle. He went limp.

I lay still, my mouth as open as I could get it, breathing silently, listening. At first there was no sound. Then I heard voices. None were excited. I turned my attention to the man. Yowzer, he had a K-bar strapped to his right thigh. I turned my back and pulled it from its sheath. A second later, my hands and feet were free. I frisked the body. He was wearing cargo pants. There was a wallet in the rear pocket. In one of the deep side pockets I found his phone. Hooray. It was an old i-phone. I pressed the button and it lit up. I held it to his face.

Buddy Dwyer.

The phone was one of those that required you to slide your finger to open it. Call Blackhawk, have him bring the cavalry. It required a numbered password.

Damn.

I looked through the wallet hoping he was one of those that wrote his password down. Thirty- two dollars, a credit card, driver's license and a worn picture of a nude woman.

Also, a hunting license and a slip of paper with a phone number on it. The number wasn't the password. Time to move.

I spit in my hand and rubbed the saliva onto my closed eye. Rinse, repeat. Now I could see. I went to the crack of light and looked out, keeping the bad eye shut. One man sitting next to the fire. I moved to the back, squeezing my eyes shut. I waited until the dot of light behind the lid of the one eye receded, and then was gone. I pushed the K-Bar knife through the canvas and silently slit the fabric. I went through the opening and was in my element. In the wild, in the dark.

I moved silently, which meant slowly, through the brambles. Every few seconds I paused and listened. My favorite part of training was in the forest, in the dark. When I was a kid, my long-gone brother and I spent our youth in the forest, and in the dark. When asked if we were afraid, we replied, of what? We were the scariest things out there.

I worked my way around the camp, purposely not looking toward the light. I didn't know how much time I had, so I was caught between stealth and speed. I knew where Megan was, but I didn't know if she was alone. It seemed to take forever to reach the back of her tent, but finally I was there. As I approached I slowed to a snail's pace. I placed each foot with infinite care. I leaned into the back of the tent, placing my ear against it. I didn't breathe. In the silence, I could hear her moaning softly. I listened long enough to conclude she was alone.

No time to waste. I pressed the tip of the K-Bar into the

tent wall until it punctured, then sliced downward. It made the sound of a zipper. I stepped through the opening into the darkness of the tent. As I went in, I went low and sideways, the knife ready.

I could barely make her out. She scrambled away from me with a low, frightened animal sound.

"It's Jackson," I said quietly. "Megan, it's okay, it's Jackson."

She began to cry. I moved to her and took her in my arms. I petted her. "Ssh now," I whispered. "I've got you."

Her hands were free and they came up around my neck and she buried her face in the hollow of my neck and began to sob.

"Shush now," I said, a little more forcefully. "Don't let them hear you. Are you hurt?"

She cut the sobbing off, but her shoulders were still shaking. She shook her head. I got my arm around her and moved her to the slit in the tent. I went out first then, holding her hand, led her out. The brambles were thick, and they tore at us.

I placed my mouth next to her ear, "Stay right up close to me. Don't make any noise."

"Where's my mom?" she said in my ear.

"Your mom's okay," I whispered. "I'll get you to her. Don't talk now."

I took her hand and pulled her gently with me. I slowly started putting some distance between us and the camp. My fear was that Dwyer would be found, and the flashlights would come out.

Good luck, bad luck. The stars were out. Good luck, making it easier for me to work us through the underbrush, and I could see the North Star so I knew which direction we were going. Bad luck, making it easier for us to be seen. We came to the wide wash. I found a place where we could climb down into it. The bottom was sandy. Deep sand. Every step caused a sandy impression. I kept us moving, close to the bank. The ground was harder there. Megan held the belt loop on the back of my jeans. I kept us moving as fast as I could. We had been working the wash about fifteen minutes, when I heard the shout. I stopped and looked back. A quarter mile back I could see lights moving. I started moving again. Now I wasn't so cautious. In a couple of minutes, we came to a cattle crossing. The herd had left a trail across the wide wash in the soft sand. Just what I needed. Our tracks would blend with theirs.

A minute later we were across the wash and scrambling up the other side. I followed the cattle trail until it disappeared into the desert. I could hear distant shouts. Megan's breath was ragged. We needed a hiding spot. We needed to go to ground.

"My mom's going to be really worried," she said softly.

I stopped and put my arms around her. She was shivering.

"I can't help that right now," I said. "I'll get you safe."

Pulling her behind, I began angling southeast, trying to keep Megan out of the barbed cholla. We came to a smaller wash. Not nearly as wide. Only about twelve feet across. I stood on the bank and studied it. To the right, there was a wall of brambles that filled the wash. I led Megan there.

"Wait right here," I said softly. I moved down into the wash, in front of the wall of brush. A moment later I was back with Megan.

"Follow me," I said. I went down into the wash, then turned and held my hand up. She took it, and I helped her down.

I put my back to the brambles and turned her so she was backed up into me. I pulled her close.

I spoke into her ear, "We are going to get a little scratched up but we'll be safe. They won't find us here." The air was turning cold and she shivered. I pulled her even closer and began to back into the brambles. I tried to shield her from the thorns. What did John Wayne say? Everything out here will bite you, stab you or stick you.

The thorns scratched at my arms and back. I shielded Megan as much as possible. I kept pushing, deeper and deeper. Every once in a while, Megan emitted a soft cry as a thorn dug into her. As bad as they were, the thorns were what would keep others from finding us. I got us as low as I could and pushed back into the brambles, pulling Megan with me. The brambles closed in around us.

"There are snakes in here," she said, her body stiffening.

"No honey, no snakes."

"How do you know?"

"The sand is too cold. They like rocks, and things that stay warm."

"You sure?"

"Yes honey, I'm sure."

I sat, pulling Megan down on my lap. The sand was cold against my rear, and legs. I held her, trying to share my body warmth. We were as far as we could go.

I held her. She lay her head back on me.

After a few long moments, she whispered, "Jackson?"

"Yes, honey," I whispered.

"You smell bad."

I laughed.

"Sorry, can't be helped."

Another moment and she said, "I'm scared. I thought you were dead. We wrecked your car."

"I know, honey."

"They put me in their front seat. I could see you when they pulled you out. You were all blood and stuff. I thought you were dead. I started to scream and one of them slapped me.'

"We're okay now, sweetie. Try to sleep."

After a long moment, she said, "I hate those guys."

"So do I."

"What do we do now?"

"Ssh, baby. We need to stop talking. We need to sleep. Now we wait."

"What are we waiting for?"

I thought about that.

"Blackhawk," I said.

"How is he going to find us?"

I had no idea.

65

The voices never came close. After a while Megan's breathing slowed and deepened, and she slept. Eventually I dozed.

I awoke, and it was still dark. My legs and butt were numb. Megan's breathing was deep and regular. I cleared my mind, and slept some more.

When I opened my eyes again, I could see faint eastern light through the brambles. I hugged Megan to wake her. She moaned, then started.

"It's okay," I whispered. "We have to move before it gets too light. Try to slide forward. Protect your face with your arms."

She struggled forward. I tried to help as well as I could. Getting out was easier than getting in. Finally, we were out. She started to climb out of the wash but I grabbed her arm and held her back.

"Stay here," I whispered. "I need to look around."

I silently climbed up the bank. I stood for a long time, listening. My jaw and my thigh throbbed. I put it out of my mind. There were no sounds. No birds, no insects. Suddenly, there was a rustling behind me. I spun around. The small, dark form of an animal scuttled into the brush. I smiled. That's a good sign. The little guy wouldn't be here if humans were. But to be sure, I moved away from the wash and worked around our hiding spot in a circle. I stopped every few feet and listened. By the time I was back to Megan, I was convinced there were no bad guys close.

I helped Megan up and out of the wash. I started east, toward where the sun would rise. If they were behind us, which they probably were, the sun would be in their eyes.

I moved as quickly as I could, but it was tough for Megan. She was a city girl. We made our way through, around and sometimes in the creosote, mesquite and sage. I wasn't sure where I was headed. I remembered my trip with Eddie and Joe Whitney and knew there was a hundred miles of desert, and it all looked the same.

As the sun rose slowly in front of us, the wildlife came out. We startled a jackrabbit as big as a small dog. It went bounding away from us. After a while I realized that we were moving up a gradual knoll. I didn't want to do that. If we were above Atef, our movements would be easy to spot. I changed direction and began working around the knoll.

The sun was now fully up and the warmth felt good. Megan was game but eventually she begged to stop.

"My foot is hurting," she said. "I think I'm getting a blister."

"Let me see," I said.

She plopped down on the ground and pulled her shoe off

without untying it. She rubbed her foot and held it up for me to see. She was right. Her little toe was taking a beating. I took the knife and forced a slit in the side of the shoe.

"Hey! What are you doing?"

"Trying to make it easier for you to walk."

"Mom just bought those. She's going to kill me."

I started to laugh. I couldn't help it. Then she started to laugh and we laughed together. It was good.

I handed her the shoe. She slid it on and stood. She tested it.

"Better?"

She nodded.

"Let's keep moving," I said.

As we moved, I kept checking our back trail. I didn't see anyone, but I had no doubt they were there. Atef didn't strike me as the type that gave up easily. We circled the knoll and kept moving east. My hope was I would cross a ranch road eventually. The cattle track had told me that this was grazing land. I had read that it took several acres of desert to sustain a single cow. There were lots of acres to spare out here, but where there are cattle, there is water. And where there is water, there are ranchers.

We came to another knoll. This one higher. It would give me a really good point of view. Off to our right was a small grove of palo verdes. I led Megan to it.

"I want you to get in under these trees," I said. "I'm going up to the top here, and scout around."

"You are going to leave me?"

"No, I'm not leaving, but I need to see where those guys are."

She looked frightened, but she didn't protest. I moved away and began working my way up to the top of the knoll. As I neared the top I became more cautious. I kept behind any cover there was. I finally dropped to the ground and began crawling until I reached the top. I could see for miles. I had been trained to gauge distance. The trainers would point something out, then ask how far it was. We would guess, then we were handed a range finder. We did this over and over until we became pretty good at knowing the distance. At least a mile away and down below, I could see the wide wash. Back as far as I could see, I could see a man-made color. Something there that wasn't desert. Something red. Like a truck.

I started to back away from the crest when something caught my eye. I looked to my left. There were saguaros dotting the slope. The one at the top had caught my eye. I worked my way around it, and there he was. My old friend. The large saguaro, bowing from the waist with one arm sweeping in front. And now I knew where I was.

I worked my way back to Megan. She had been a good girl, and had stayed where I had left her.

"Did you see them?"

"I saw something, but it was a long way away. I saw nothing close."

I pulled Dwyer's phone from my pocket. I pushed the button and it lit up. I slid my finger and got the keyboard.

"Where'd you get that?" Megan asked.

"Took off a guy in camp. I wish I knew the password."

"Can I see it?" she asked.

I handed it to her. She typed four numbers in. It buzzed at her, rejecting her effort. She did it again, again it rejected. She did it a third time. This time it didn't buzz. She grinned and handed it to me. It was open.

"How'd you do that?"

She was pleased with herself.

"People are idiots with their passcodes. The most common passcode is 1234. This one was 2222."

"This have a camera on it?"

She moved up beside me and touched the screen. The camera app activated.

"I'll be right back," I said.

I made my way to the top and took a picture of the saguaro. I attached it to a text and sent it to Blackhawk. It failed. I tried again. Same result. Discouraged, I went back down.

"What's the matter," Megan said.

I handed her the phone. "It won't send a message."

"It's an iPhone," she said by way of explanation.

"Aren't they all?"

"iPhones work through the internet." She continued, fiddling with the phone. "We don't have service here, so it won't send."

I looked around. Where the hell was service?

She fiddled some more, then, "You want to send a message to this number you just tried?"

"Yeah, but we have no service."

"Not all phones need broadband. What do you want to say?"

"Attach the picture of the cactus, and say show this to Eddie. Put my name on it."

She fiddled some more, then handed me the phone.

"There you go."

"It went?"

"Seems so."

I was looking at the blank screen. "So I could have called someone?"

"Sure."

"Why didn't you tell me that?"

"You said you wanted to send a text. Lots of people don't call now. They just text."

I pushed the button on the phone. Nothing happened. I tried again.

"The battery's dead," she said.

"Did the text go?"

She shrugged. "Don't know. I think so.

66

"What do we do now?"

"We wait."

"For Blackhawk?"

"Yeah."

"How does he know where we are?"

"If the text went through he'll see the cactus in the picture. Eddie and Joe Whitney and I were here before. This is where they found Frankie Wambaugh. Eddie and I noticed the cactus because it looked funny. Let's get under cover."

She didn't move. She was embarrassed.

I looked at her. "What's the matter?"

"I have to go to the bathroom."

I smiled. I waved a hand, "Go. Find a bush."

She hesitated.

"What?"

"I don't have any toilet paper," she said.

I laughed. I couldn't help it. I took the knife and cut off a piece of my shirt. I handed it to her.

"Here."

She took it, but wouldn't look at me. I turned my back and went into the palo verde. I sat, my back to her. I heard her moving away. A few minutes later she was back. She came and sat next to me. We sat silently for a long time.

The day moved slowly. I calculated how long it would take Blackhawk to get from the El Patron to us. A half hour to prep. At least two hours to drive to Cottonwood. Another hour to our area. Call it four hours. I pushed a stick into the earth and we watched the shadow creep around it.

After a while, Megan leaned against me and went to sleep. When I calculated enough time had passed, I roused her.

"I'm going to look around," I said. She mumbled something, stretched out on the ground and lay her head on her arm. I moved silently out of the cover. I worked my way up the knoll.

Again, I crawled to the top. The red truck was gone. The air had warmed and was clear. I could see a long way. Suddenly, there was crashing movement in the brush by the big wash. A huge bull came hustling out of the brambles and scrambled down into the wash, then across toward me. Behind him came five cows and two calves, the calves skittish and spooked. They crashed through the brush without thought of staying in the cattle track. I watched. A minute later six men came out of the brush and stood on the bank of the wash. They wore black niqabs. They carried automatic rifles. They stood for a long time, then they started across. They disappeared in the brush on this side. I watched for a long moment, then turned and looked all around. The desert stretched out toward the distant mountains. There was a hawk gliding in circles, so far off he was but a dot.

In the far distance behind me, I saw dust. Could be a vehicle. Could be a dust devil. I watched that area for a long moment. If it wasn't Blackhawk, I hoped it was a dust devil.

I went back down. Megan was sitting up.

"We have to move," I said.

"Why?"

"We are going to have company." I took her hand and pulled her up.

Her face was pale and pinched with fear. Her hair was matted and her face was smudged. Her hands were filthy.

"Is it those guys?"

I put an arm around her. "Yes, it is." I wasn't going to lie to her. "We have to move. I have to find you a safe place to hide."

"What are you going to do?"

"The best I can. Let's get you safe."

Pulling her along, I moved us quickly across the desert floor. At the bottom of the slope the brush and the cactus were thicker. Fed by runoff. We had gone about two hundred yards when we came upon a very small wash. More of a depression than a wash. Caused by the occasional heavy rains running downhill. It was shallow and had brush on its sides. I had her lie down in it. From ten yards away she couldn't be seen. She didn't like it. She sat up.

"I want to stay with you."

"It will be more dangerous if you do. I'll be back soon."

"What if you're not?"

"If I'm not here in two hours, start walking east." I pointed. "That way. You will eventually hit a road. But I'll be back."

She looked like she would cry. "How will I know when two hours is up?"

"You'll know." I squatted down and looked at her. "You are doing fine. You've been great. You've been tough. Just hang tough and I'll be back."

"I'm scared," she said.

"I know, honey. Lie down. I'll be back."

She reluctantly lay down and I moved away quickly before anything changed.

I angled back to the crazy cactus. If Eddie and Blackhawk got the message, this is where they would come.

I got back to the palo verdes, and worked my way behind a thicket of creosote. I squatted low and tried to blend in. I was like that a long time. My mouth and jaw were throbbing. My thigh had stiffened and I could feel the hurt with every beat of my pulse. I was a little dizzy.

I tried the meditation techniques I had been taught. I thought of my capture instructions, how to keep the mind on the right things. After a while, I decided I was losing the mental exercise when I heard a man pushing through a thicket of thorns and brush. He was thirty yards off, and to my left. He was cursing under his breath. I pulled the K-Bar out of my belt. I didn't move. I wanted him close enough I could take him out quickly. He pushed through the brambles a few feet away, and stepped into the open.

It was Eddie. He was carrying a backpack and a rifle. I stepped out. He started, bringing the rifle up. He broke into a big wide grin. Mine matched his. I sensed movement behind me and I whirled, and Blackhawk stepped out of the brush a few feet away.

"What the hell took you?" I said.

"We stopped for a couple of beers. I figured you had this under control." He stepped to me and wrapped his arms around me and gave me a bear hug. He looked into my face.

"Jesus, you look like hell."

"I've told you not to call me Jesus."

67

I led them to the girl. When I called her name, she came up out of the brush with a squeal and ran to Eddie. She threw her arms around him. We didn't have time for celebration. We hurried her back to the vehicles. A truck and Nacho's Jeep. The truck was Billy's. I figured we had less than a half hour before the men I had seen came over the knoll. Nacho stood beside his Jeep with a sawed- off shotgun. He was trying to rub the Arizona pinstriping off the Jeep. That's what happens when you run a vehicle through the desert with the creosote and desert thorn digging at its sides.

Nacho grinned at me. He studied my face, cocking his head one way then the other.

"At least it wasn't your foot, this time," he said.

"Just good luck," I said. I looked at Eddie. "Get the girl back to her mama." I turned to Nacho. "You have a phone, let the girl call her mama. You go with them, in case there's trouble."

Megan came to me and wrapped her arms around me. She buried her face into my chest and hugged me tight. It didn't affect me at all. Tough guy.

She looked up at me. "What are you going to do?"

"I'm not sure, honey. Blackhawk and I are going to talk that over."

"Let's get going, honey," Eddie said. He opened the Jeep door.

Megan moved her arms to around my neck and squeezed her face against mine. I winced.

She pulled back. "Does that hurt?" she said, concerned.

"Naw," I lied.

She climbed in the back and ran the window down. "What are you really going to do?"

I smiled. "We thought maybe we'd go talk with those guys. Get 'em to surrender."

Nacho and Eddie climbed into the front. Nacho started the engine.

Megan was still looking at me. As they started moving, she had Nacho's phone and was staring at it. She held it out the window at me. "Signal," she shouted.

Blackhawk and I watched the Jeep move out of sight.

Blackhawk said, "So much for stealth."

"Tough girl," I said.

He was looking at my face.

"That hurt?"

"Like a son-of-a-bitch."

I looked into the back of the pickup. There was a large, army-issued duffle bag. It appeared to be full. "Whatcha got?"

He opened the tailgate, and pulled the bag onto it. He unzipped it. He handed me some camo clothes. I stripped down and put them on while he pulled more out of the bag. In the daylight, my thigh was a mixture of saffron, yellow and purple. I pulled the trousers up and resolved not to think about it anymore.

He had a Spikes Tactical SBR 300 automatic rifle and three clips, a Remington 870 with the adjustable stock and an ammo belt filled with 10 gauge shells. He handed me my Kahr .45 and a shoulder holster.

"How's my Mustang?" I said.

He didn't look at me. "You don't have a Mustang."

He had filled canteens. I strapped the ammo belt around me, and hooked on the canteen.

He looked down. "Your feet okay? I didn't take time to stop at the boat for the hiking foot."

I shrugged. "Been okay so far."

He pulled a first aid kit out of the bag. He opened a pack of ibuprofen and I swallowed all of them.

"You going to make it?" he asked.

I nodded.

"Sure you just don't want to wait for the cavalry?"

"I'm sure," I said. "They'll be gone." I thumbed shells into the shotgun. It was a pump with a seven-shell extension tube on it.

He snapped a clip into the Spikes, and slung on a small backpack.

"You know where they are?"

With a nod, I indicated the knoll I had spotted them from. "On the other side of that hill."

"How much time do we have?"

"If they are coming straight over, not much."

"What's the plan?"

I looked around. "I figure they're following the same cattle track I was. The ground was soft so they'll see our tracks. Let's move the truck into some brush, then double time up the hill. Get the high ground.

68

He backed the truck into a thicket of eight-foot high brush. You'd have to be right in front of it to see it. I turned for the hill, and he followed. It was possible that they could beat us to the top, and if they did we would be in for it.

We hustled up, thinking more about speed than quiet. We reached the crest without incident, and I dropped to the ground with Blackhawk beside me. We crawled until we could see the wash below. There was no one in sight. No one. I was so sure I would see them, I shut my eyes, then opened them, expecting a change. No one.

Blackhawk slid back so he couldn't be seen, then went up on his knees. He dropped the backpack strap off one shoulder and slung it around. He opened the flap and pulled out a pair of ten power Nikon binoculars. He crawled back up beside me. He methodically scanned the area.

He was looking to our left when he said, "There."

I looked to where he was looking. I didn't see anything. He handed me the binoculars.

"Along the wash where it begins to split out."

Then I saw them. Or at least, two of them. They were moving away from us and they were moving quickly. I handed him the binoculars and he slid them into the backpack.

"Let's go," I said.

We slid back out of sight, then began moving quickly to the south. I had no idea where they were going, but I knew we had to catch them. If they disappeared into this desert, and had transportation, they could quickly disappear into the world. Once in the world, they could raise all kinds of hell.

We skittered along the side of the rise for several hundred yards, then the ground began to dip and rise into a series of rocky hills. These were the foothills that would eventually lead up into the mountains. The ground was littered with basalt volcanic rock. A million years ago, volcanoes had ripped and formed this land. It made the footing treacherous. We kept pushing. Every few minutes Blackhawk would slow down to let me catch up.

Since I wasn't sure where they were headed, I wanted to get our eyes on them again. When we came to a steep rise I moved us straight up till we reached a very steep outcropping. We kept very low, and edged up to the top. We peered around a very large basalt boulder. You could see a long way. Down below us, a hundred yards away, there were buildings. And corrals. The corral gates were open. In one of the corrals was a large stilted water tank. On the ground below it was a four-feet high, oval metal cattle tank. It had water in it. The ground in the corrals was covered with cattle dung. There were no cows in sight. The buildings were old and rickety and looked more like ruined barns than houses. Boards were busted out and you could see the light from the other side. On the back side of the buildings the land was steep and covered with brush and cactus. This place wasn't for living. It was what the rancher used at round up.

Inside one of the buildings there was shadowy movement. Then one of them showed us why they were there. He pushed an ATV out into the sunshine.

"They take off on those and they are gone," I said.

"Then we have to hit them now. Let's go at them from the back side," Blackhawk said softly.

He pushed himself up and began to move quickly down and around. I followed. We kept higher ground between us and them, and began to move as fast as we could. When we calculated we were behind the buildings, we began scrambling up the basalt hill. We were in the right place. The buildings were just below us. We went over the top and came down the other side. We were shielded by mesquite and heavy brush. The corrals were strung with barbed wire. Keeping the buildings between us and where the men would be, Blackhawk held the wire as I slipped through. Then his turn. We carefully slid up to the side of the building and listened. There were cracks between some of the wall boards and I peered in. It was empty, but I could see the men, now out into the corral. We could hear one of the ATVs start.

I looked at Blackhawk and he shrugged. He jacked the first round into the Spikes. I pumped a shell in. He winked at me, then went around his corner. I went around mine.

Two angles of fire, and surprise evened the odds.

All six men were gathered by the metal tank next to three ATVs. I didn't look to my left at Blackhawk. I knew he was there. Two of the men were on ATVs. One was Atef. The man standing to the left was tall with a scraggly beard that barely covered a prominent Adam's apple. To his left stood a short stocky man. His beard was as scraggly as the first guy. The other two were rinsing their faces in the water tank. At least they had decent beards.

Adam's apple caught sight of Blackhawk from the corner of his eye, and began to turn.

"Which one of you guys is Ike Clanton?" I said.

Adam's apple raised his weapon, and Blackhawk shot him. He crumpled. Just melted to the ground. I was at a park once watching nine, ten-year old boys playing army with toy guns. They had divided into two groups and were waging war. It wasn't about winning the shoot-out, it was about who could get shot the most dramatically. Flopping and tumbling, like the movies. Real life wasn't like that.

The guy just crumpled, and then Blackhawk shot the stocky guy. Down he went.

Atef was quick. He took off so fast the ATV did a wheelie. I fired from the hip and the right rear tire blew. The machine dumped on its side. He hit the ground rolling and rolled behind the water tank. I pumped another shell in and shot one of the bathers. This was like the movies. The buckshot hit him hard and he went into the tank with a big splash. I pumped another round in.

The last one standing charged me. He was digging his

pistol out of the holster, and screaming at the top of his lungs. I shot him in the chest and the force of his momentum spun him and he crumpled at my feet. I pumped a round in. Now there was just Atef.

His hands were in the air as he climbed to his feet.

"I surrender," he shouted. "Don't shoot, I surrender."

Blackhawk and I walked forward. We stopped with the cattle tank, with the body in it, between us and him.

"How about that U.S. military training?" I said.

Atef was silent, but he didn't look scared.

Blackhawk said to me, "What now?"

"I don't know," I said. "I hadn't thought about it." I moved farther to my right. "We take him in and then there's a big trial and he gets to run his mouth all over the media, and the whole world sees it. They'll drag Megan through their media shit."

"He'll be a big time hero. A big time martyr," Blackhawk said. "He'll be the ISIS poster boy."

"Yeah, their A number-one recruiter. Incite hundreds more just like him."

"I have surrendered," Atef said. "You have to take me in."

I looked at him. His eyes were black, expressionless like a snake. I didn't see one glint of humanity.

"Why did you cut Dick Mooney's head off?"

He was silent, then he shrugged, "He had a loud mouth. He was a cretin. He was worthless to me. He made good practice."

Blackhawk made a noise, deep in his throat.

"How about the other guy? You took his hand off."

"He was a thief. It is the law."

"What did you do to the girl?"

"I did nothing to her," he said.

I shook my head, "I don't know. It looked like you were going to cut her head off. You remember that? I remember that. What were you going to do? Have a little fun with her before you killed her?"

Atef frowned. "You Americans are soft. Allah gave us women to use. They cook our food. They have our babies. They wash our clothes. They are inferior to men. That is all. She is cattle. We didn't expect her to be with you. But she was. Then the girl belonged to me. She was mine, to do with as I wish."

"You speak of Allah, but you are a Godless fuck."

He put his hands down and looked at me with scorn. "What do you know of God?" He shook his head. "You know nothing. You are infidels, born of whores, and raised like rats."

I looked at Blackhawk. He stood, in his quiet way, looking at Atef.

"I was taught that God made all of us," I said. "Including rats and whores. And, unfortunately, men like you."

He spit on the ground.

"But, my Dad taught me that even though God loved all his creatures it was our moral duty to fight and stop evil when we can. I asked how he knew this and he said God talks to all good men. All you have to do is listen hard enough. Maybe you should have a few more discussions with God."

"I'll arrange the meeting," Blackhawk said, and shot him.

The bullet sliced through him and Atef looked completely shocked. His hand went to the entry wound. He looked at Blackhawk, his eyes wide with surprise. Then he collapsed. He was dead before he hit the ground.

We watched him bleed.

"No sense delaying the inevitable," I said.

69

It was May and the days were getting warmer. There truly was not a cloud in the sky. Perfect chamber of commerce weather. I was sitting topside drinking beer with Eddie. We had concluded a long and tough negotiation. It had taken several beers. He insisted he owed me money for helping get Billy cleared. I had insisted that nothing I did directly led to getting Billy cleared. The amount he offered was ridiculously large. I countered with the idea that maybe he could help me dry dock the Tiger Lily and scrape and paint her hull.

"Done," he said, tapping my beer can with his.

We both heard the metal gate at the end of the dock clang. Eddie leaned forward and peered down its length.

"You have company," he said. He struggled up out of his comfortable chair.

I pushed myself up out of the chaise lounge and went to the bow. Coming toward me was a huge bald head atop a massive body. Behind Emil was Emilio Garza. They both wore sunglasses, shorts and Hawaiian styled shirts. Emil wore flip flops while Garza wore brown shoes and black socks. His legs were uncommonly white for a Mexican. He also carried a bag that looked familiar.

Eddy moved up beside me.

"You want I should stick around?"

I shook my head, "It's okay. They're friendlies."

Eddie grinned at me and shook his head. "Strange bedfellows."

He set his empty beer can down, and moved to the ladder. "Let me know when you want to take her out of the water." He went down to the stern. He had come over in his skiff, which was tied off the stern. He stepped over the railing and into the boat. The motor started on one pull. He had spent the morning tinkering with it.

"Purrs like a tomcat in the dairy," he grinned up at me. I waved. I walked back to the bow, and the two men were below me.

"If you are trying to blend in, it's not working," I said.

Emil indicated the beer in my hand. "You got another one of those?"

"Come on aboard."

I came down to the lounge, and opened the sliding door. Emil came in and made himself comfortable, sitting on the oversized couch. Garza stood by the door looking uncomfortable. I went to the galley and extracted two beers from the locker. I handed one to Emil, and offered the other to Garza. He held his hand up to decline.

Emil popped the beer and drank half of it in one motion. He looked at Garza. "Mr. Garza asked me to bring him out here."

I looked at Garza. Garza held the bag out. "We began thinking that maybe we had not expressed our appreciation for the return of our money. This is that appreciation."

I looked at the bag. "This is not necessary."

"It is a matter of honor," Garza said. "I would appreciate it if you would accept it."

"If you don't take it," Emil said, standing, "Mr. Garza will have trouble at home."

"In that case," I smiled, "I accept."

"Thought you would," Emil said, tipping the can and swallowing the rest of the beer. "I swear, you are the luckiest bastard I know. Seems people give you money all the time." He emitted a low belch and set the beer can on the end table. "We are off. Thanks for the beer."

"My pleasure," I said, setting the bag on the couch.

They moved outside and without looking back, they moved down the dock. I stood watching them, and Dahlia came through the gate and started toward me. The two men stood aside for her, with Garza turning to watch her with appreciation. Emil said something and Garza said something and they both grinned. Dahlia was in a bright blouse, shorts and stylish boat shoes. She carried a small bag. It had been a while since I had seen her.

When she reached me, I said, "This is truly my lucky day."

She grinned at me. "I thought I'd come see you."

"Wonderful. I was just drinking beers with Eddie. Would you care for one?"

"Love it," she said as I helped her on board. She followed me into the lounge.

"Just happen to be in the neighborhood?"

"No," she said. "I came to see you."

"Great, where's Megan?"

"She's spending the weekend with Aunt Betty."

She handed me the bag she was carrying.

"What's this?"

"A present."

"What is it?"

"My overnight bag," she said, then smiled a smile of infinite promise.

Following is an excerpt from
the next exciting Jackson Blackhawk novel.

THE BAG LADY, THE BARFLY
AND THE WEST SIDE KING

by Sam Lee Jackson
Available at samleejackson.com

The, dirty, emaciated, bad smelling, bag lady winked at me.

I was sitting on my favorite barstool at El Patron. It was mid-afternoon and there were no customers. Nacho sat across from me reading a newspaper. Jimmy was behind the bar. Blackhawk and Elena were upstairs. She had a show tonight.

The bag lady had slipped through the door into the main saloon. El Patron had three saloons, two of which spun off either side of the wide, long hallway that led from the main entrance to the big double doors of the third saloon. Each had its own dance floor, but this one was by far the largest. This was where Elena performed. Packing them in. Jimmy saw the bag lady and moved toward me to intercept her.

"Ma'am," he said. "If you go back outside, and go around to the back I'll bring you some food."

That's when she winked at me.

With a jolt, I realized it was Detective First Grade Boyce.

Boyce was a mess. Just a mess. Clothes all raggedy, smudges under her eyes. Hair all greasy and uncombed. On top of that hair was a ragged cloth stocking hat. For an instant I thought my eyes were playing tricks. Fastidious Boyce. Looking rode hard, and put away wet. There was even a slight, disturbing odor.

I could do nothing but stare. She moved up to me and slipped up on the next barstool. She slid the arms of her dirty jacket up to her elbows and leaned on them. She cocked her head and looked at me. With that damned knowing smile of hers. Her arms had angry little tracks on them. The tracks of an addict.

I guess I was speechless, so she said, "Looking for a good time, sailor?"

I reached a finger and rubbed one of the spots on her arm. It rubbed off.

"Early for Halloween," I said.

Jimmy was confused.

"Ma'am," he said. "If you'll go back outside, I'll get you something to eat."

"I'm not hungry, Jimmy," Boyce said.

Jimmy frowned, then leaned closer, "Oh my God."

Boyce laughed. She looked at Nacho, "How you doin', Nacho?"

He was smiling, "Just fine Ma'am. I like your outfit."

She grinned at him, "Why thanks Nacho. That's the nicest thing you ever said to me."

"Yes Ma'am," he said. "But, not the nicest thing I've ever said about you."

Her face lit up, "Always the sweet talker, Nacho. Always the sweet talker."

"Can I get you something?" Jimmy asked, not sure what was going on. Me too.

"No thanks." She looked at me, "I want you to come outside with me." She slid off her stool. She started away, not looking back. I looked at Nacho. He grinned, shook his head and shrugged. I slid off my stool and followed.

Like I wouldn't.

The sun was dropping in the west. The big parking lot was mostly empty. It wouldn't be for long. This part of the world knew Elena and her big Salsa band were playing tonight, and soon the place would be jammed. Across the lot, by the street, was something I recognized. An unmarked police vehicle. I followed Boyce toward it. There were men inside. I recognized one. Captain Mendoza, Phoenix PD. Mendoza was the head of the city of Phoenix's gang division. Or, he had been the last time I saw him. Maybe, he was the police king by now.

Mendoza was in the front passenger seat. I didn't recognize the other man, but he had cop written all over him. Boyce moved around to the other side, signaling me to follow. I did. She opened the back door and waved me in. I slid in. She shut the door and moved back around and stood at the curb. Mendoza slid his back against the door and put his left arm up on the seatback, so he could look at me.

"Detective Armstead, why don't you join Detective Boyce outside?"

Armstead looked at him, then turned his head to look back at me. "You sure, Sir?"

Mendoza just looked at him.

Armstead looked hard at me, then slid out and shut the door a little too forcefully.

"Temper, temper," I said.

Mendoza studied me.

"Boyce knows why we're here. Armstead doesn't."

That didn't require a response.

He looked out the window, like he needed something to look at. "How's the foot?" he said.

"Still gone," I said.

He almost smiled, but didn't.

He studied me some more. Making up his mind, I guess. I waited. I knew he would get to it. He did.

"Ever heard of guy name of Cicero Paz?"

That took me aback. "Can't say I have."

"Runs the drug trade out of Maryvale. Controls all the meth, heroin, whatever sales throughout most of west and south metro area. Ruthless son of a bitch. Destroys a lot of lives."

"If not him, someone else. He doesn't make them buy it. Why would I know who he is?"

Now he did smile, "No reason. But, yes, you're right, he's the guy now, and I want to take him down."

I looked out the window. Boyce had started smoking again. I shook my head. "You have the full resource of law enforcement."

"And, the key word is law. Something we have to observe."

I laughed out loud. "You need someone to break the law?"

He shook his head, like he was tired. "Let's not play games. We both know who you are, and what you are capable of doing, and, I might add, have taken matters into your own hands more than once."

"Boyce is undercover. You tellin' me that undercover cops never bend or even break the laws?"

"Not something I would choose," he said. "But, it's more than that."

I didn't say anything.

"I've got Boyce deep under, and Cicero is a psychopath. She's there alone and these are some very bad guys. I can put someone else under, but I don't think I have anyone that could go to the lengths that might be necessary to protect her."

"And, I would?"

"Wouldn't you?"

I looked at him. The son of a bitch.

"You playing that card?"

He didn't say anything.

"You think because she took a bullet for me. You think because we had a relationship. That I'll do this thing for you?"

He didn't say anything.

I studied him. Like looking at a wall.

I leaned back in the seat. "You think your guy will get himself killed. And, if I get myself killed, nobody knows who I am. Just a dead body in an alley."

"I think you are better trained than my guys," he said.

I looked at him for a long time. He didn't waiver.

"She in danger?"

He glanced outside at Boyce. "Oh, yeah. If Paz found her out, she'd be raven bait in the river bottom."

I looked back out at Boyce. She was standing next to Armstead, her back to me. She flipped her cigarette butt into the parking lot. This irritated the shit out of me. Blackhawk would have to have the cleaners come out and pick it up. Yes, he is that fastidious.

"If there is anyone that can take care of themselves, it's Boyce."

He nodded, "Yes, but I still want someone to watch her back. I won't say, you owe her."

"I do owe her," I said.

In this very parking lot, Boyce had shoved me out of the way of an oncoming bullet, and had taken one herself for her efforts.

"Okay," I said. "Tell me specifics?"

He looked at me then ran his window down. "Boyce," he said. She turned to look at us, came around, and opened the back door. She slid in beside me.

"He in?" Boyce asked Mendoza.

Mendoza looked at me, "You in?"

"Tell me about it."

"Cicero Paz operates out of the neighborhood he grew up in. He's like a good old fashion Mafia Don. He controls everything on the west side. Nobody spits that he doesn't get a piece of it. He controls everyone. And, that's because he does a lot of favors. You own a small business and you're having trouble with a vendor. The trouble goes away. You got gangs chasing away your customers, suddenly the gangs go away. You get in a bind and can't pay the mortgage on your shop. He gives you the money, and he doesn't screw you on the vig."

"Sounds like a regular Robin Hood."

"Yeah, it does, doesn't it?"

"But?"

"But, if he's done you a favor, then you can bet the time will come when you will do him a favor. And, there is no choice in the matter. You are going to do it. No matter what it is. You accept his help, and he owns you."

I looked at Boyce, "What's your role?"

"I've established as a homeless bag lady on the block by the bar he operates out of. I watch the activity and report it back to Mendoza."

"But not inside?"

"That would be you."

I looked back to Mendoza, "How are we going to do that?"

Mendoza almost smiled, "Boyce says you have a tactical side to you. You'll figure a way."

I looked at Boyce.

"Jesus, Boyce. You stink to high heaven."

She grinned and pulled a baggie out of her pocket. I looked at it. It looked nasty.

"Old, raw, chicken skin," she said. "Keeps the bad guys away better than a suit of armor."

This time Mendoza did smile.

Did you enjoy The Librarian, Her Daughter and The Man Who Lost His Head?

The most important reward for an author is to have his or her books reviewed. If you enjoyed the book, go to the Amazon address below and let us know what you think. After you get there, just click on the book you read, then click on the reviews.

Go to this address to leave a review or for more Jackson Blackhawk reading adventures

Amazon.com/author/samleejackson

Or

www.samleejackson.com

Made in United States
Orlando, FL
04 September 2024

51123216R00232